"You're Josie Pigeon, aren't you?" the other woman said, tugging on the red bandanna that was holding her hair out of her eyes. Now that they were close together, Josie realized that it was really only the hair, their coloring, and their clothing that caused people to think they looked alike.

"Yes." Josie didn't know what else to say.

"Are we alone?" She looked up at the windows on the large house nearby. A family of six was walking over the dunes on the path from the beach. They looked tired, hungry, and slightly sunburned. Josie's double waited for them to pass before speaking.

"I've been thinking," she began abruptly. "Someone is trying to kill me. But there's no reason for anyone to hate me that much. So I've been thinking," she repeated, her hair flying around as Josie's did, as if it had a life of its own. "It could be a mistake."

"A mistake?"

"They might want to kill you. . . ."

By Valerie Wolzien
Published by Fawcett Books:

Josie Pigeon mysteries:
SHORE TO DIE
PERMIT FOR MURDER

Susan Henshaw mysteries:
MURDER AT THE PTA LUNCHEON
THE FORTIETH BIRTHDAY BODY
WE WISH YOU A MERRY MURDER
ALL HALLOWS' EVIL
AN OLD FAITHFUL MURDER
A STAR-SPANGLED MURDER
A GOOD YEAR FOR A CORPSE
'TIS THE SEASON TO BE MURDERED
REMODELED TO DEATH
ELECTED FOR DEATH

PERMIT FOR MURDER

Valerie Wolzien

FAWCETT GOLD MEDAL • NEW YORK

A Fawcett Gold Medal Book
Published by Ballantine Books
 Published in the United States by Ballantine Books, a division of Random House, Inc., New York, and simultaneously in Canada by Random House of Canada Limited, Toronto.

http://www.randomhouse.com

Library of Congress Catalog Card Number: 96-91029

ISBN 0-449-14960-9

Manufactured in the United States of America

First Edition: May 1997

10 9 8 7 6 5 4 3 2 1

For Evelyn Hill,
an old friend rediscovered through a new technology.

ONE

"I WOULDN'T HAVE mentioned it if I'd known you were going to get this upset."

Josie took three deep breaths the way the lady therapist on the radio suggested for coping with unmanageable stress and then answered. "Betty, if the man wants to hire my workers, he's trying to destroy Island Contracting!"

"No way!" Betty opened her blue eyes wide. "It has nothing to do with Island Contracting. He just wants to go to bed with me."

Life, Josie Pigeon reflected, pushing her unruly red hair over her shoulder, was easy for Betty. She assumed every man she met wanted to go to bed with her—and most of them did. "You said he offered you a job," she reminded her employee. "And you're a skilled carpenter—at least that's why I sign your paycheck."

"And at Island Contracting everyone knows that's *why* you sign my paycheck. If I worked for a man, they might make other assumptions." Betty self-consciously tucked her tight Bud Light T-shirt into the waistband of equally snug cutoff jeans. She looked a lot more like an hourglass than your average carpenter. "And to tell you the truth, I like it better this way."

Josie nodded. She liked it this way, too. The employees of Island Contracting were all women. The company's former owner, Noel Roberts, had made a practice of hiring people who needed a break, a chance to change their lives. All the carpenters, plumbers, and electricians were female when Josie had inherited the company over a year earlier and she had maintained the tradition. But a murder investigation, and other changes, had resulted in a major turnover of staff and Betty Patrick was the only carpenter who remained from the original group. Josie frowned, remembering recent tragedies and losses.

"Don't you think it's spectacular?" Betty asked, mistaking the cause of Josie's distress.

The two women were sitting in Josie's cherry-red pickup, which was parked next to the curb in front of a dramatically modern house. A sign by the truck announced that the home, as yet uncompleted, was for sale. Another sign explained that construction was being done by INNOVATIONS AND RENOVATIONS, INC: A COMPANY DEDICATED TO CREATING ORIGINAL ENVIRONMENTS FOR INTERESTING PEOPLE.

"The house?"

"No, I mean the sign," Betty responded sarcastically. "Of course I mean the house." She paused to adjust her long blond hair. "Although I do like the sign. It's good advertising. Island Contracting's signs are sort of dull."

"We do great work—that's the best advertising any contractor can have," Josie said as she reread the sign. It *was* a good slogan. . . .

"Yeah, you're right. Besides, 'we take the jobs no one else wants' probably wouldn't be good advertising."

"Definitely not," Josie agreed. "And it's not true."

"Are you forgetting the Frank house? And what about the Nissenbaum job? No one else even bid on that job," Betty reminded her boss. "Not that we didn't do good work on both projects," she added, possibly remembering with whom she was arguing.

"The Van Embergh job is a real plum."

"But there's no guarantee we'll get it."

"It's between us and these guys," Josie said. "Everyone else is booked solid. And I think if the Van Emberghs look at this house, they'll choose us . . . if the bids are competitive," she added, biting her lip.

"I don't get it," Betty confessed. "Why should seeing

this project make anyone choose us? This is good work. Just because you like older houses—oh, that's the point, isn't it?"

"Exactly. And I think we can assume that the Van Emberghs prefer old homes, too."

Betty laughed. "I certainly hope so. Why else would they buy the oldest house on the island?"

"And one that needs so much work," Josie agreed. "When I gave Mr. Van Embergh the list of homes Island Contracting had worked on, I put the Victorians right at the top."

"Good thinking."

"And we're free to start work immediately. . . ."

"If not sooner," Betty agreed.

"So . . ."

"So you hope to get back to the office and find out that the Van Emberghs have signed the contract and insisted on an immediate start-up date."

"Stranger things have happened," Josie said cheerfully, starting the truck's engine.

"But what if there's no contract?" Betty asked, becoming serious. "Are we going to be laid off until there is one? There's no way you can keep finding busywork for us to do. Everything that Island Contracting owns has been sorted, cleaned, oiled, labeled, and—oh, no!"

"Everything except this truck—which needs a new clutch and possibly a new radiator," Josie said, pulling her vehicle back to the side of the road as steam billowed from its shiny hood.

"How long do we have to wait before it cools down?"

Before Josie could answer, Betty was pointing at a little sports car slowing down and parking behind them. "Look, there's Sam," she exclaimed. "Your knight in shining armor!"

"That's not exactly the way I see him," Josie muttered, wondering if she risked damaging her engine by starting the truck again.

"You two aren't still arguing!"

"Who says we're arguing?"

"Everyone! Kristen and Fern were talking about it. And just the other day, Basil came into the office and said that Sam was feeling lousy over your breakup."

"I'm not paying Kristen and Fern to discuss my private life," Josie said, feeling her face flush. "And Basil has no business getting all of you worried about Sam. Just why does everyone think this affair is any of their business?"

"Because we care about you," Betty answered simply. "And we talk about your life the same way we talk about Fern's health or—hey, you called it an affair. Did you just admit that you and Sam were sleeping together?"

"I did not," Josie hissed, lowering her voice as Sam Richardson walked up to the car window. "When I called our relationship an affair, I didn't mean it had anything to do with sex."

"What has nothing to do with sex?" Sam asked, a grin on his handsome face. "The truck overheating?"

"Yeah, we passed this huge Mack truck and Josie's little pickup just steamed up," Betty answered, looking up at Sam with a provocative smile on her face.

Josie knew Betty couldn't help herself; if there was a man around, she flirted. But did Sam have to return the look? she wondered.

"So can I give you two a ride somewhere?"

"We were on the way to the office," Josie answered, staring intently at the steering wheel in front of her.

"Wouldn't we be squashed in your car?" Betty said, glancing at the small MGB parked behind them.

"I think we know each other well enough to squeeze in," Sam answered. "And it's not a very long drive. Of course, maybe you're not in a hurry to return to the office—"

"We are," Josie interrupted. "So maybe we shouldn't stand around chatting and get going." She opened the door to the truck and hopped down to the ground. "We can call the garage from the office."

"I'd be happy to look at it for you," Sam offered.

"I'm sure I can handle it," Josie said, walking over to

his sports car and holding the door open for Betty to precede her into the bucket seats.

"You want me to sit on the stick shift?" Betty said.

"I don't think even your skinny little self would fit in the space behind the seats," Sam answered. "You could, of course, sit on Josie's lap."

Josie, perfectly aware of the size difference between herself and her carpenter, scowled as she got in the car. "I don't have a lot of time to fool around today," she announced.

A loyal employee, Betty refrained from mentioning the fact that they had just been discussing Island Contracting's lack of work.

And Sam's next words changed everything anyway. "I guess getting the Van Embergh job will keep Island Contracting hopping until Labor Day."

"What did you say?" Josie asked.

"Not many people know you got the contract yet, do they?" he added, starting his car. "I stopped in at your office to see if you had time to go to lunch and Fern was dancing around the desks with the signed contracts in her hands."

"You're kidding!" Betty said, starting to bounce around herself.

"I guess Fern just heard the good news," Josie said quickly.

Sam glanced over at her suspiciously, but said nothing as he drove them the couple of miles to Island Contracting's tiny office. Josie and Betty were out of the car almost before it had stopped. "Thanks for the ride," Betty said, remembering her manners.

"If you're too busy for lunch, how about a late dinner?" Sam asked. "I really think we need to talk."

Both women knew to whom the question was addressed. As Betty hurried into the charming remodeled fishing shack that served as the headquarters for Island Contracting, Josie paused by planters filled with blazing nasturtiums. "Not yet," she answered quietly, staring at the flowers as though they were a fascinating sight. "With this new contract, I'm so busy that I won't even be able to go to parents' weekend at Tyler's camp. Not that he's expecting me—he's known ever since he sent in his application for the camp scholarship that I might be too busy."

"I'd really like to see Tyler again," Sam said. "When he was home on spring break, he promised to go night blue fishing with me and I heard down at the Fish Wish that the blues are running early this year."

"What were you doing hanging around the bait shop?" It was such an unlikely event that Josie momentarily forgot her goal.

"I've been doing a little fishing in my spare time—with Basil Tilby," he added, apparently thinking that he needed a reference.

"You're kidding!" Sam owned the liquor store that most of the summer people patronized. Not only did he have little free time between Memorial Day and Labor Day, but he was more likely to spend his leisure moments reading, walking the beach, or doing almost anything other than fishing. "When did you get so interested in fishing?"

"I guess I listened to you talking about it for so long that I just became intrigued," Sam answered.

Josie was skeptical, but before she could say more, Betty, Fern, and Kristen came dancing out the forest-green door of the office, glasses of bubbling liquid in their hands. "I think I'd better get going. My crew seems to have started celebrating without me."

"Josie, we can settle everything if we just sit down and talk. I just need to understand what's going on," Sam insisted. "Look, the offer for dinner is always open," he continued when she didn't answer. "Just give me a call."

Josie steeled herself to ignore the way his graying blond hair fell across his tanned forehead and into eyes the color of the sea on a warm summer's day. As he approached his mid-fifties Sam Richardson's crinkles and wrinkles had only increased his appeal. But she had to ignore that and stick to her decisions. "I won't," she said flatly. "And I have to go now. Thanks for the ride."

Without looking back, Josie Pigeon joined her workers, accepting from Betty a copy of the Van Emberghs' contract and a glass of liquid from Kristen Duffy. "Champagne?"

"Diet ginger ale," Kristen answered. "There probably are contracting companies that keep a bottle or two of champagne in the office refrigerator—"

"But Island Contracting isn't one of them," Josie finished for her.

"I'll bet Sam would keep us supplied if you just dropped a few hints at the right times." Kristen glanced over Josie's shoulder at the MGB roaring down the street.

"Sam has other things to worry about," Josie said abruptly. "Now I think I'd better spend some time reading through this contract," she added seriously.

"But Sam always helps you with the legal stuff—" Betty began, stopping when she saw the expression on Josie's face. "Not that you probably can't do it yourself."

"Exactly," Josie declared, entering the office's cool interior. She wasn't as sure as she claimed to be. Sam Richardson, after spending a quarter century as an urban prosecuting attorney, had retired to the island, bought a liquor store that specialized in fine wines, and began dating Josie and helping with her company's paperwork only a few months after she inherited the business. She had, she knew, come to depend on his expertise. But knowing her workers' eyes were on her, she sat down at the large desk in the center of the room, spread the contact before her, and began to read.

The contract, a boilerplate that Island Contracting had always used, contained wonderful news. The Van Emberghs had accepted Josie's offer, and had done so so quickly that Josie wondered if perhaps she had made a mistake in her figuring. She frowned. She had reviewed everything at least a dozen times. She was sure they could bring the job in on time and with a generous profit for the company, even if they had to hire another carpenter.

And there was no question about that: they would have to take on at least one extra person. The Van Emberghs had added an addendum to the contract: they wanted the entire project finished by Labor Day. Upon a timely completion, a ten-percent bonus would be paid. Josie's freckles shifted as a large grin appeared on her face. It was a huge, expensive job and the ten-percent bonus would guarantee the future of Island Contracting. Once the contract was signed and the building permits issued, they'd be on their way. She decided to call in all her employees to witness her signature. This was going to be a day to remember.

TWO

"You buy the seeds already mixed and plant them, then you wait a few weeks, and just pick the tiny leaves as they come up. It's called mesclun and it's really good," Fern was telling her coworkers, gathered on the small deck behind their office. A couple of six-packs of Coors Light had replaced the ginger ale and Josie had emptied her full crab trap into a pot of boiling water. Three large bags of potato chips completed their celebratory dinner.

"So in less than a month we'll have tomato-and-basil salad," Kristen said, glancing over at the four aluminum tubs planted with tiny herbs and healthy tomato plants covered with small green tomatoes.

"I'm looking forward to it," Josie said enthusiastically. "I didn't know we were gaining a resident gardener when you started with Island Contracting," she said to the young woman perched on the wooden rail.

Fern Gast smiled. "I hope they grow. I'm pretty new to this type of thing. I've always wanted to garden, but never thought I had the time until . . . well, until I realized that I either took the time now or I might never have it."

"We—"

"I—"

"That's—"

Josie, Betty, and Kristen all spoke at once.

Fern waved her arms to get their attention. "Hey! I thought we weren't going to pretend that I don't have cancer."

"Yes, but—"

"We don't—"

"I—"

They did it again.

"And that meant I could talk about it without everyone breaking out in a sweat."

"The problem is"—Josie raised her voice and took the initiative—"that I, at least, am always afraid I'll say something that will hurt your feelings or—or make you uncomfortable."

"So instead I get to make all of you uncomfortable. I don't want to do that either." Fern ran her fingers through her very short dark hair. "A lot of companies wouldn't hire someone with cancer—even in remission. I need this job and I appreciate that you took a chance on me—and I don't want to pay you all back by making anyone miserable." There was a gentle smile on her face.

"You've added a lot to all our lives," Josie said, knowing that she was speaking the truth.

"And not just with your herbs and baby vegetables," Kristen added.

The group smiled silently at each other.

"I know this is a touching moment, but I think the crabs are done," Betty spoke up. She was leaning over the steaming pot with a large pair of tongs in one hand.

The women, hard workers and always hungry, grabbed plates and napkins, and as quickly as Betty could pass out the food, they got to work cracking the bright red shells, pulling out the meat, and after dipping it in a shared cup of melted margarine, popping it, dripping, in their mouths.

Kristen, new to this particular island delicacy, was the slowest of the group. "Are these little pointy things edible?" she asked, looking doubtfully into a crab's chest cavity.

"No," Josie answered. "I think those are lungs."

"Yuck! I wish I'd never asked," Kristen said, returning to the little hard legs in her search for succulent white meat.

Betty laughed. "You look just like Sam used to when he first came to the island and ate blue crab. Remember, Josie? And now, of course . . ." She glanced over at her boss and shut her mouth, biting her lips as though that would prevent her from continuing.

There was another awkward silence.

"Well," Kristen began, looking around at her companions, "we can't talk about Fern's cancer and we can't talk about Josie and Sam's breakup, so what are we going to talk about?"

"We're celebrating getting the Van Embergh job, remember?" Josie asked. "That should give us a lot to talk about."

"It's going to be a huge project, isn't it?" Betty asked, sounding relieved by the change of topic.

"Didn't you say something about hiring another carpenter?" Kristen added, giving up on the shellfish and reaching for a bag of sour-cream-and-chive chips.

"Definitely," Josie answered, remembering the bonus clause in the contract. She had decided not to mention it to her crew and to share the wealth with them when—and if—they got the job finished on schedule. "In fact, I need to get on that right away. Anyone know anyone who's looking for work? Someone who'll fit in with Island Contracting? And who'd be available immediately?"

There was silence until Fern spoke up, quietly as usual. "Actually," she began slowly, "I may know someone . . . a woman that I met while I was having a checkup last week. She doesn't have cancer," she added quickly. "She was there waiting for her aunt who was having a bone scan."

"And she's an out-of-work carpenter?" Josie asked, relieved not to be asked to hire another person with cancer—and immediately guilty about such feelings.

"Yes. She said that she had moved to the area to take care of her aunt, but her aunt is doing pretty well and could probably be left alone with some sort of day help. But she needed to work to support it."

"I need someone more than part-time. . . ." Josie mused.

"Well, all we can do is ask. I have her phone number. I was going to call with information on my cancer-patient support group."

"If you called right away, maybe I could sound her out about a job," Josie suggested. "We have to start work the day after tomorrow."

"Demolition?"

Josie nodded her head and her mop of red curls flew in all directions. "And lots of it. I'll go over to the house in the morning and mark what's going and what's staying, make sure the Dumpster's in place. . . . Maybe she could meet me there? That is, if she really is looking."

"I'll get on the phone and call right now," Fern offered.

"Wonderful." Josie shoved a large calico cat away from her plate. "This animal is overweight," she announced. Since her office was well known on the island as a haven for runaway and unwanted felines, no one else was surprised by the animal's presence or its condition.

"Don't you want someone to go over to the house with you tomorrow?" Betty asked, tossing an empty beer can in the plastic recycling receptacle next to the makeshift planters.

"You want to see it?" Josie asked, grinning.

"I've wanted to see inside that house since I was a kid," Betty admitted. "I used to ride my bicycle six extra blocks on the way to and from school just so I could go by it. We called it the house of hearts."

"I suppose all that gingerbread appeals to romantic young girls," Kristen said, tossing away the empty chip bag.

"You don't like it?" Betty sounded incredulous.

"All those hearts on the woodwork are a little fussy, if you ask me," Kristen answered. "I like things streamlined and practical. I mean, it's fun working on old houses, but give me a modern house every time. I prefer good closet space to charm."

"No way," Betty protested. "Think of the history of that house. It was built as a honeymoon cottage by a man in love with his bride. The next owner was a famous hostess. Diamond Jim Brady was supposed to have visited there with Lillian Russell. The couple who owned it when I was a kid were Broadway producers. There were huge parties there almost every single weekend from Memorial Day to Labor Day. How can closets compare with that?"

"The Van Emberghs are going to have closets as well as history once this remodeling is finished," Josie explained. "They're modernizing everything. It's a huge project."

"You have the blueprints?" Kristen asked.

"Yeah, I'd love to see them," Fern spoke up.

"Go ahead and look at them if you want. They're on the top of the filing cabinets."

"I can't tell you how glad I am that we got the job," Betty confided when she was alone on the deck with Josie.

"You're surprised, aren't you?"

"Innovations and Renovations has a fabulous reputation."

"They're bigger than we are, not better."

"Oh, I agree," Betty insisted, her eyes wide. "You know, I wondered why you were there the other day."

"Where?" Josie had lost track of their conversation and wondered if the beer was going to her head.

"Over at Innovations and Renovations' office. I saw you going in the front door."

"When?"

Betty thought. "The day before yesterday."

"You're kidding. I can't remember the last time I was there." Actually, Josie did remember. But it had been over a week before and she saw no reason to tell anyone about it. She had been admiring I and R's new fleet of dark green Broncos.

"I was so sure I saw you there. . . ."

"Where?" Kristen appeared with a long tube underneath her arm.

"I thought I saw Josie at Innovations and Renovations—at their office the day before yesterday, and she says she wasn't there."

Before Josie could protest that she wasn't lying—about this at least—Kristen explained everything. "You must have seen the Josie Pigeon look-alike. Fern and I were talking about her just the other day."

"The who?"

"The Josie Pigeon look-alike. You know. Your double."

"I didn't know I had a double."

"Boy, do you," Fern said. "I was down at the hardware store the other day and I saw this mop—well, a head of long red hair—on top of a pair of overalls striding down the aisle ahead of me and I just assumed it was you. But when she didn't answer—"

"Didn't answer?"

"I thought the woman was you and I called out to her. But she wasn't you, so she didn't answer," Fern explained. "But I didn't know she wasn't you and I figured you were just having a bad day, so I decided to go around the corner to another aisle and then I'd run into you—face-to-face, you know?—and then, when I did, I realized it wasn't you. I mean, the clothes and the hair were you, but she was someone else. Someone older. And not pretty like you are." Fern had apparently decided that her description might have offended her boss. She frowned. "Am I making any sense at all?"

"There's someone who looks like me on the island who shops in the hardware store and hangs out at Innovations and Renovations' office."

"Works *for* Innovations and Renovations," Betty said. "I heard all about her at the health club last night."

Josie squinted at Betty. "You joined that new health club? You work all day doing physical labor and you felt you had to join a health club?" Her idea of a perfect evening after work was to lie on the couch in front of the TV. No wonder Betty had such a fabulous figure.

"No, I'm dating one of the instructors there," Betty explained. "He has unlimited guest passes."

"You go to that snazzy health club where all the summer people go—and what everyone is talking about is someone who looks like me?" Josie asked. "I thought the discussions around there would be about things like whether the new Lexus has more comfortable seats than the old Mercedes or where to shop to find the most darling little diamond earrings."

"I don't think Sam would be interested in either of those things," Betty said. "He prefers classic sports cars and doesn't seem like the type of man who'd get his ears pierced."

"Sam goes to the health club?" Josie asked. "Sam Richardson?" She barely managed to stop herself from adding a possessive pronoun before his name.

"Yeah. He was on the stationary bike next to mine the other night. He told me he'd just started. He's been training on the Nautilus equipment and doing some free weights."

Good-looking, slim, intellectual Sam Richardson? *Her* Sam Richardson working out in a sweaty gym? That was what she wanted to ask. Instead she asked: "Are you telling me that Sam Richardson was talking about me down at the health club?"

"Not about you actually," Betty began reluctantly. "He was talking about this other woman who looks so much like you. He said that he thought it was interesting that there was another carpenter on the island with the same red hair."

Josie remembered how Sam had always claimed to admire red hair, especially hers. And perhaps this other woman had other attributes he would admire as well. "Is this other woman built like me?" she asked Fern before she could stop herself.

"I don't know. I mean, it was hard to tell. She was wearing overalls when I saw her, after all."

The embarrassed expression on Fern's face answered Josie's question more than her words. The other redhead was slim. And probably hard-bodied—like Sam was going to be if he worked out regularly.

"But you should be glad that she doesn't look too much like you—if what she's saying around the island is true," Kristen added.

"What is she saying?" Josie asked, not terribly interested in anything that didn't have to do with Sam Richardson.

But Kristen's next words riveted her attention. "She says someone is trying to kill her."

THREE

JOSIE PIGEON'S NEXT day was busy, with little time for introspection—or even lunch, she realized around one o'clock, leaning back against a wall and admiring the morning's accomplishments. The old plaster walls, cracked from age and the barrage of moisture and winter freezes that life on a barrier island threw at its buildings, displayed Josie's graphic interpretation of the blueprints nailed onto the foyer wall across from the front door. New doorways, walls destined for removal, windows to be enlarged, ceilings to be replaced, every bit of change had been delineated with swaths of black spray paint.

"Nice work. But you'll never compete with the kids under the overpasses in New York City," Betty Patrick said, joining her boss to contemplate the words and lines that now covered the walls on the second-floor landing.

Josie grinned. "They have more interesting tags than 'Out.' "

"True. On the other hand, they just write on the walls, you actually get to knock them down. Say, how did you get here? I thought the truck needed servicing."

"It does. I dropped it off at the service station late last night. Kristen's been driving me around."

"Oh, I thought maybe Sam—"

"No, definitely not Sam."

Betty seemed to realize it was time to change the subject. "Do you mind if I look around?" she asked, beginning to do so.

"I'll go with you. I need to review everything before tomorrow morning. I'm getting nervous over just how big a job this is," Josie admitted.

"But what a house . . ." Betty breathed, walking into a bedroom.

"What a doorway," Josie muttered, looking up at the lintel. One end dipped almost three inches and the top of the door had been altered to fill the space.

"This must be the master bedroom." Betty glanced around the large area. Two windows, one with a shabbily built-in window seat, looked out over the water. At one end of the room another window peered into the next-door neighbor's tri-level cedar deck. The other end was entirely mirrored with a doorway cut through to what seemed to be a walk-in closet and another window. "Strange decorating," she continued, looking at the golden wooden sconces mounted across the Victorian woodwork and the navy-blue wall-to-wall carpeting. "Any idea what's under the carpet?"

"Very worn fir flooring. And the decor gets even stranger. Wait until you see the chandelier in the turquoise bathroom."

But Betty was already heading in that direction, through the doorway built in the mirrored wall. A few minutes later she was back in the bedroom, a wide grin on her face. "Just another example of more money than taste, isn't it?"

"Hey, I'll bet someone paid a decorator big money to

come up with this elegant scheme," Josie answered. "And it probably looked a lot better with furniture."

"Not if the same person who chose those light fixtures picked out the furniture," Betty argued. "Funny, the master bedroom taking up the entire front of the house. Are there other bedrooms on this floor?"

"One more—and one more bathroom. But the Van Emberghs are changing the entire layout of this floor—and they're taking out all the gold shit and wall-to-wall carpeting and returning the house to its original look—lots of white beaded wainscoting, woodwork around the windows, new wood floors. And this space is being cut in half"—they both looked down at the double lines she had painted on the floor to indicate just where this was to be done—"and made into two bedrooms. Both will face the water. And the wall at the end of the hall is going to be removed so the window there will bring light into the hallway."

"This wall covered with the mirror?" Betty called from outside the room.

"There are lots of walls covered with mirrors," Josie answered. "And they're all being removed."

"Good thing. This place keeps making me want to comb my hair or put on some mascara."

"I know what you mean." Actually, it made Josie think about that diet she kept promising herself to go on.

"Hey, come here a second," Betty yelled, and Josie followed the sound of her voice to the back of the house. Betty was kneeling on the floor and looking out the bathroom window. "There she is," she said, pointing out to the street.

"Who—oh, I see."

"She does look like you, doesn't she?"

"Sort of. Thinner, though." Josie leaned closer to the window. "What do you think she's doing?"

"Staring at the house."

"But why? Why would she be staring at the house?"

"I have no idea. We could call and ask her," Betty suggested, struggling to open the warped window.

"That's okay. The company van is in the driveway. She

knows someone's here and she can come up to the house if she wants to talk to one of us. Let me show you the rest of the building and you can tell me if my instructions are clear."

Betty glanced at the large block letters spray-painted on the mirrored wall in the bathroom. "I don't see what could possibly be clearer than 'Rip Down.' "

"I've put blue tags on the things—lighting fixtures and stuff—that the Van Emberghs want us to save. We should check through them, too. I don't want to get this project off on the wrong foot. If they come down this weekend and ask to see the brass wall sconces that hung on either side of the mirror in the living room, we should be able to find them immediately. And we need to make sure that everyone knows about the jade mantel in the living room."

"Jade mantel? You mean that green thing over the fireplace? I thought it was poorly dyed marble."

"That's exactly what we don't want anyone to think! It's worth a lot of money. Let me show you—oh, damn." The bright red beeper she wore on the hammer loop of her overalls went off. "Let me see. Where did I leave that phone?"

"I saw it in your truck outside when I came in. Want me to get it?" Betty offered.

"Thanks. I hope this is the carpenter Fern recommended. She left a message on the phone at the office saying she would call today, but I haven't heard anything. I was hoping she'd just stop by. I'd really like to sign her on."

"Not without meeting her?" Betty looked surprised.

"I was thinking of it," Josie admitted. "She sounds like a nice person—moving here to take care of an ill relative. Fern seems to think highly of her and . . . and . . ."

"And that means she's a competent carpenter?"

"Not necessarily, of course. But we could give her a tryout period of a week or two, don't you think?"

"If you're desperate." Betty was looking out the window again.

They were, but Josie admitted it only to herself. She had spent over an hour last night calling her list of available carpenters on and near the island and they had all been either busy or out of town. It was, after all, peak building season. This woman Fern had met was as likely to be competent as any other unknown person. Besides, Josie reminded herself, the only thing they knew about her was that she'd disrupted her entire life to care for an ill relative. That was more than a little positive, wasn't it? She noticed that Betty was waving to someone out the window. "Is she waving back?"

"She?" Betty seemed to realize who Josie assumed she was signaling. "No, your look-alike is gone—wandered off down the street or around the back of the house. I was waving to Sam."

Josie felt a painful thump in her chest, but decided it was probably—almost certainly—a manifestation of hunger. "Is he here?" she asked as casually as possible.

"No, he just drove by and waved. He's always driving by, isn't he?"

"I hadn't noticed. I've been busy, you know." Josie pulled her beeper out again and glanced at the message printed on it. "I'd better make this call."

Betty repeated her offer to fetch the phone.

"No, I'll do it." Josie hurried from the room, thinking to catch a glimpse of Sam driving down the street. But when she reached her truck there was no sign of the classic MGB tooling down the road. With a sigh, she pulled the phone from the red truck and made her call. It was answered on the first ring.

"Yeah?"

"Ah . . . I'm calling for . . . for . . ."

"This is Alma Snapp." The woman on the other end of the line supplied her name.

"You're the person I'm calling for," Josie said, relieved. "I'm Josie Pigeon. I own Island Contracting."

"Yeah. Hang on a sec."

Josie heard a loud public-address system blaring in the background.

"Sorry about that. For a moment there I thought my aunt was through with her treatment."

"You're at the hospital!" No wonder she was so

abrupt. Certainly talking on a public phone in a hospital waiting room would cause anyone to sound abrupt.

"I'm always at the hospital these days."

"But you're looking for a job."

"Sure am. I even have a practical nurse lined up for my aunt. The woman spends all her spare time knitting and reading gossip mags. My aunt will love her. So, if you hire me . . ." Alma sounded uncertain for the first time in their conversation.

Josie reminded herself to be professional. "Do you have references?"

"Yes, but my last job . . . hell, let's be frank. I was involved with my boss on my last job, but he was a real bastard, so I broke it off with him, and I don't think he'll give me what you might call a glowing reference, if you know what I mean."

"You sound like the type of woman Island Contracting needs," Josie said firmly. Problems with men . . . ill relatives . . . this woman deserved another chance. "But we need someone to start right away."

"I can be on the job first thing tomorrow."

"That would be wonderful. There's paperwork, but—"

"I can fill out everything at lunchtime. It only takes me one hand to eat," Alma assured her.

"Great. The address is—"

"I know where you're working. The house with all the hearts, right?"

"Yes, but—"

"That girl Fern told me about it and I made a point to drive by last night. Just curious, you know. Interesting house."

"Yes, it is and it's a big job, so I'm glad you'll be helping us out."

"Yeah, well, I gotta get. My aunt needs me."

Josie was startled to hear the click indicating she had been hung up on. But she'd never, thankfully, spent much time in hospitals, so who knew why Alma had to get off the line so quickly—and there was no time to think about it. The woman everyone was calling her look-alike had returned and was walking toward her.

Josie turned off the phone and smiled awkwardly. "Hi."

"You're Josie Pigeon, aren't you?" the other woman said, tugging on the red bandanna that was holding her hair out of her eyes. Now that they were close together, Josie realized that it was really only the hair, their coloring, and their clothing that caused people to think they looked alike.

"Yes." Josie didn't know what else to say.

"Are we alone?" She looked up at the windows on the large house nearby. A family of six was walking over the dunes on the path from the beach. They looked tired, hungry, and slightly sunburned. Josie's double waited for them to pass before speaking.

"I've been thinking," she began abruptly. "Someone's trying to kill me. But there's no reason for anyone to hate me that much. So I've been thinking," she repeated, her hair flying around as Josie's did, as if it had a life of its own. "It could be a mistake."

"A mistake?"

"They might want to kill you."

Josie shook her head and tried to think. What was this woman saying? Was she sane? "Why do you think they want to kill me rather than you?" she asked, realizing that she wasn't making sense either.

"Because no sane person would want to kill me. So I thought I should warn you," the other woman answered, turning.

"Hey, where are you going?" Josie cried. "You can't just come here, say something like that, and leave."

"There's nothing more to say."

"There must be more to say! For instance, why do you think someone is trying to kill you? You don't seem to be full of bullet holes or . . . or anything." Josie realized she sounded foolish, but she was tired and hungry—as well as shocked.

"You don't believe me? I just came here to help you—maybe to save your life."

"Then tell me why—"

"Because I was hit on the head and almost killed a few weeks ago. I had a headache for days. Then last night I was leaving the hardware store late and someone grabbed me from behind and tried to drag me into an alley. If some stupid teenagers hadn't been smoking pot back there, I'd probably be dead."

Josie didn't know about that, but she saw no reason to argue. "But why do you think that this person might be after me instead of you?"

"Because both times I was attacked from behind. And we do, you know, look alike from behind. Everyone mentions it."

Josie couldn't argue with that.

FOUR

WHEN SHE WAS just eighteen years old, Josie's family had shrunk from two (parents) to one (son) after she dropped out of college and became an unwed mother. Over the next fourteen years she had become resigned to the situation and she delighted in her child (although recently there had been signs of adolescence rearing its ugly head). But Tyler attended boarding school in the winter and was, right now, enjoying a summer camp, to which he'd won a scholarship, in Pennsylvania, so she felt herself lucky to have a caring landlady with a strong maternal instinct. In addition, Risa was a talented cook, trained in her hometown in Tuscany, and usually more than willing to share a pot of polenta with mushrooms or a seafood risotto.

Tonight, however, Risa appeared at Josie's door empty-handed. "How are you feeling?" she asked anxiously, worry wrinkling the firm brow beneath masses of dark hair.

Josie grimaced. Her landlady seemed to think she should be swooning on the chaise since the breakup with Sam. "Hungry," she answered abruptly, hoping Risa would take the hint. "I was going to have some toast—or maybe open a can of tuna," she continued. Often the very mention of processed food sent Risa dashing down to her kitchen for fresh ingredients.

"You've probably lost your appetite—from grief."

Josie headed for her kitchen cabinet. "I don't think so. Island Contracting just got a big contract. We're doing a complete remodel of the house with the heart-shaped gingerbread up at the other end of the island. I probably won't have a moment to spare between now and Labor Day."

Risa's dangling earrings flashed as she nodded. "Bury your sorrows in your work. You Americans are so industrious. So practical. So—"

"If I don't work, I don't eat. And you will have to wait for the rent."

"No matter . . ."

"And I won't be able to afford the new dirt bike Tyler is hoping to get for his birthday."

Risa backed out the door. Josie was her friend, but Tyler was her joy. Anything that might deprive him of something he wanted was to be avoided. "You enjoy your meal. You reminded me. I was going to write a letter to Tyler tonight. Oh, you got a postcard from him. I noticed it with your mail this morning."

Since Tyler was as aware as his mother of Risa's interest in the mail, Josie knew any message he wrote on a postcard was meant for both of them. "What did he say?"

"He says that he still hates camp. And why you Americans send your children to these camps that they hate so much I don't know."

"It's good for them. And he doesn't hate it. He just

thinks his counselor is an idiot," Josie said abruptly. Going to camp had been Tyler's idea and he had earned his scholarship—but she had earned the money to pay for the expensive clothing that the camp insisted he bring along. "What else did he say?"

"He says he understands if you are too busy to come up for parents' weekend—he has made other arrangements."

Josie chuckled. "Knowing Tyler, he's probably become best friends with the richest kid in camp so he can share in the goody boxes the parents bring." But she was glad to hear that he had accepted her possible absence. She had spent all day thinking about it and she simply wasn't going to be able to take off and visit her son. They had discussed this possibility before he left home, but she hoped he would understand now that it was a reality.

"He has moved up a level in his swim classes. And he has made you a present—but it is a surprise and he will bring it home with him when he comes."

Josie remembered the plastic lanyard she had made for her father her first year of camp and didn't get unduly excited at the prospect. But the other news . . . "That's wonderful. He was so disappointed to be put in the intermediate swim group. Now he'll be able to swim out beyond the float in the middle of the lake."

"But he might drown!" Risa cried, genuinely alarmed. "He should not be allowed to swim out so far alone! Why does he want to go there anyway?"

Josie smiled. "He won't be alone. I'm sure the camp has a firm buddy system. And apparently he wants to swim beyond the float to get closer to the girls' camp that's on the other side."

"Ah. The little darling!" Risa didn't understand athletic prowess, but she understood the needs of men. "I will write him right away." And she vanished out the doorway and back down the stairs to her first-floor apartment, leaving only the scent of imported perfume in her wake.

There was, in fact, a can of tuna in the cupboard and Josie shared it with Urchin, the dark brown cat her son had adopted a few years before. She glanced at the television while she ate, wondering once again why there was nothing to watch when she wanted to watch and an interesting show on when she had to work. Just as she was ready to give up and return to her paperwork, she discovered an early Tom Cruise movie on. Well, she'd seen it before, so maybe she could work and watch at the same time.

There probably are people who find numbers more interesting than Tom Cruise, but after half an hour Josie had to admit that she wasn't one of them. She turned off the set and got up, wondering if a hard wooden chair, a cup of coffee, and some cookies would keep her awake long enough to understand the columns of figures before her.

"Or maybe a nice ride to the grocery," she said to Urchin, who had leaped onto the countertop, as interested in the contents of the cupboard as Josie was. "Now all I have to do is find my keys. . . . Here they are," she cried, surprised by her own efficiency. She'd be home in less than half an hour at this rate. She trotted down the stairs and out of the house toward her truck.

The island was only seven miles long, its largest grocery store near the middle. Despite low speed limits, the round-trip took less than five minutes. Although there was the evening rush of tourists desperate for ice cream, potato chips, and sunscreen to contend with, Josie filled a small basket, checked out, and was back in her car in less than ten minutes.

So, she realized, Sam certainly hadn't waited very long to see her. His little MGB zoomed off down the road as she turned the corner to her street. Risa was standing on the front step doing what Josie realized must be referred to as wringing her hands. She pulled into the driveway and, grabbing her bag of groceries, jumped down from the cab of the truck, locked the door behind her (necessary in the summer, but not in the winter), and approached Risa. "Was that Sam I saw?" she asked, trying to sound casual.

"You know it was." Apparently Risa didn't feel it necessary to answer unasked questions.

This seemed to be a day when Josie was going to learn the reality behind a number of clichés. She swallowed her pride and asked another question. "Was he looking for me?"

"You know he was."

Two people could play this game. "I am going to go upstairs and finish my work," Josie stated as abruptly as possible and started on her way.

She wasn't surprised when Risa couldn't resist the opportunity to express her thoughts about the situation. "He is brokenhearted, you know. He was devastated when he did not find you here."

Josie bit her lips and didn't answer.

"The man is in love and he is alone. That is not natural for a man."

Josie sighed loudly. "Did he say why he wanted to see me?"

"He could hardly speak when he found you were not here. It was obvious that he was brokenhearted . . . deeply wounded . . . distraught. . . ."

Enough was enough. "If he wanted to be with me, he shouldn't have broken off our relationship," Josie insisted. And before she had to listen to anything else, she headed on up the stairs to her apartment. Once there, she closed the door with relief. She was well aware of the fact that she had left a very surprised Risa in her wake. Everyone assumed that she had broken up with Sam rather than the reverse. And, out of pride, Josie had allowed that misunderstanding to remain, knowing Sam was too kind to correct it. Of course Risa's ability to keep a secret was probably less than—

There was a gentle knock on the door. "Josie, my lamb? Are you there?"

The question had to be rhetorical. The only alternative would have been going out the window and climbing down Tyler's favorite pine tree. "Yes, of course."

"I did not know that it was your heart that was broken, my little lamb." Risa seemed to think it appropriate to whisper and Josie had to strain to hear the words. "I will leave you alone—but you must promise to call if you need anything. Anything at all."

"I will," Josie agreed, wondering if it would be opportunistic of her to suggest Risa's homemade cannoli as balm for her "broken heart." But she heard Risa tiptoe down the steps before she had a chance to utter the thought. There was nothing to do but put away her groceries, make a cup of coffee, and get back to work.

But it was difficult to concentrate when she couldn't stop wondering why Sam had stopped by—and why he hadn't waited to talk. Then it occurred to her that perhaps Sam was missing her so much he drove by merely to be near—like that song from *My Fair Lady*. It was a nice thought, but reason prevailed. If he wanted her back, he'd just call and tell her that he understood. It was that simple. And what other reason could there be for him to drop in?

She was back where she had started. Angry at herself for wasting time and energy and becoming depressed on this day when she should be happy about landing Island Contracting's biggest job since she'd taken over, she gulped down her coffee and forced herself to stare at the papers she had brought home from work. When the phone rang a few minutes later, she was thrilled. She had to answer; it could have something to do with work. . . . Or, she thought, panic defeating fatigue, maybe it was the camp and something was wrong with Tyler Clay. Maybe that buddy system she had been extolling to Risa was nonexistent. Visions of her son's pale body floating facedown in the middle of a vast body of water caused her to leap to the phone.

"Hello? Hello?" She was talking before the receiver reached her ear.

Silence.

"Hello? Tyler?"

"Good evening, madam, am I speaking with the lady of the house?"

"Yes, but I—"

"Have you ever considered the amount of time you spend shopping for meat? We here at Frozen Flanks are aware of your dilemma—whether to shop for the best cut at the best price or whether to—"

Josie slammed the receiver down and tried to keep her heart from exploding. She had been so afraid that the call had to do with Tyler. The vision of her son drowning was merely paranoia. . . . She should get it out of her mind and take a much-needed shower.

The way the day was going, it shouldn't have surprised her that the phone rang just as she began to rinse the shampoo out. Or that she managed to dash to the phone in time to hear the click as the caller gave up waiting for her to answer.

"Shit!" Josie slammed the receiver down and stared at the path of wet footprints her feet had made across the floor. She dashed back into the bathroom to keep the dripping to a minimum, knocking over the magazines piled on her kitchen counter as she passed. The magazines slid underneath the still partially filled bag of groceries, which followed the reading material to the floor. Urchin, curious as ever, nosed around the mess. Josie, feeling shampoo getting into her eyes, ignored it all and fled to the shower.

Eyes burning, she rinsed her hair and felt around for the cream rinse that was usually on the edge of the tub. She had installed hundreds of shelves in bathrooms over the years. Why, she asked herself for as many times, didn't she do something about her own? She hit something and heard the dull thud of a plastic Tame bottle strike the linoleum floor.

"Shit!" Could shampoo still be seeping into her tightly closed eyes? Josie grabbed for a washcloth with one hand and leaned out of the tub to find the cream rinse with the other. One hand made contact with a mildewed square of terry cloth that had been lying in the corner of the tub. The other hand hit what felt like a leather boot . . . and Josie hadn't been wearing boots when she entered the bathroom.

She opened her eyes and found herself staring down at a

heavy black leather boot. She gasped and stepped back, slipping on the soapy bottom of her tub and, feeling herself falling, grabbed at the torn fish-printed shower curtain. The curtain was surprisingly strong and didn't rip, but it did pull the heavy metal rod out of the wall. She hit her head on the soap dish protruding from the wall, the curtain rod smacked her in the mouth, splitting open her lip, and she realized that her ankle was painfully twisted beneath her. But the worst part of the experience was the realization that Mike Rodney, police officer and son of the island's chief of police, was staring down at her naked body. If she'd had the energy, she'd have blushed. Instead she just repeated what seemed to have become her favorite word.

"Tsk. Tsk. Tsk. Such language!"

"You are such a—" She stopped herself from saying "shit." It was becoming a little repetitive, and besides, she was busy rearranging the shower curtain so it covered her.

Mike stuck out his hand. "Want me to help you up?"

"What I want is to know what the hell you're doing in my home! I didn't hear you knock! I didn't let you in!" Josie realized she was becoming slightly hysterical.

"That's the thanks I get for dashing over here when Sam Richardson called? You think I just wanted to see you buck naked? I have a girlfriend now. Or haven't you heard that Barbie Douglas and I are dating?"

Josie was beginning to feel nauseous. Of course, Barbie Douglas did that to some people. But he had mentioned . . . "What does Sam have to do with you being here?" she asked weakly.

"Sam called the station and insisted that you shouldn't be left alone right now. So Dad and the others"—Josie knew he referred to the officers straight out of the state police academy that the island employed during the tourist season—"headed straight to the crime scene and I jumped in my car and got the hell over here."

"What crime scene?"

"That house with all the hearts. The one with the brand-new Island Contracting sign out front."

"What crime?" Josie managed to get the words out. And she thought she heard the answer as the blackness that had been circling her peripheral vision closed down to a pinhole of light before all was darkness.

"Murder. That girl who everyone says looks like you was murdered on your construction site."

FIVE

THE FIRST THING she noticed was the pungent scent of basil. And someone was whispering. She was pretty sure she was in bed—her bed, she guessed from its familiar contours—and she seemed to be both dry and dressed. She ran her hand down her thigh and felt an unfamiliar stiff fabric. But if she opened her eyes, she realized, she might be expected to say or do something, and she wanted to think. She needed to think.

If only she could think! Her head ached, her left wrist ached, and her right ankle was throbbing. She moved gently, but that seemed to be the extent of the damage. And maybe, if she listened carefully, she would recognize the voices of the other people in her bedroom. . . .

"Looks like she's coming to."

"You should have called a doctor immediately. A concussion can be serious."

Josie didn't recognize the first speaker, but the second was definitely Sam Richardson—and he sounded concerned.

"See! She's just fine. She's smiling." And that, dammit, was Mike Rodney. . . .

"I wouldn't have fallen down if you hadn't scared me!" Josie cried. "And I wouldn't have fainted if I hadn't fallen, so that's your fault, too. I still don't understand what you were doing in my bathroom anyway!" she angrily continued to Mike Rodney, still unwilling to look at either man.

"I told you. I was guarding you. Sam called the station and insisted that someone come over here right away. He was worried that someone might want to kill you."

"A lot of good you did. You could have killed her!" Sam dropped any pretense of keeping his voice down to "sickroom" levels.

"I only did what you told me to."

Josie opened her eyes.

"See—her eyes are open. She's fine."

"Just a minute." Sam leaned over, lifted Josie's eyelid, and stared into her hazel eyes—or in this case, eye.

"What are you doing?" Her head felt like it was going to split in half—or had that already happened?

"Her pupils are dilated. It's a concussion. We should call a doctor."

"At the department we usually call the county coroner when we need a doctor—and he's busy with the body right now."

"I don't need a doctor."

"She could go to the emergency room," Sam suggested, ignoring her statement.

"You want to drag her all the way off-island? You think that's wise?"

"That emergency-care place in town, then," Sam persisted.

"The doctors there don't do much more than take splinters out of the feet of kids who go barefoot on the boardwalk. Treat sunburn. Tourist injuries," Mike Rodney said scornfully.

"It's a common concussion—not a mysterious tropical disease," Sam insisted.

Josie had been moving about gingerly. "Actually, I think it may be a sprained ankle. It's my ankle that hurts," she explained to the men still standing above her.

Mike grabbed for the sheet that was covering her, but she beat him to it. "Hey, don't I deserve some privacy?"

"How do you think you got dressed?" Mike asked with a leer.

"I . . . ? Who . . . ?"

"You were lying naked in the bathtub," Sam said gently. "We just grabbed the first thing we could find, put you in it, and got you onto the bed."

That explained it. Josie had been trying to figure out what she was wearing and she now realized it was her Miss Piggy nightshirt—a present from Tyler for her last birthday. It usually hung in the position of honor on the back of the bathroom door. She wore it only when Tyler was around to notice. She appreciated the thought her son had put into the gift, but she didn't feel that wearing the life-size portrait of a large pink pig with weird hair improved her appearance. Although she probably hadn't been terribly appealing lying bent and naked, half-wrapped in an old moldy shower curtain. She closed her eyes. Maybe, if she was lucky, she would pass out again and when she woke up she'd be alone.

"Look, she's going to faint again. We'd better get her to a hospital."

"No. Really, all I need is a good night's sleep," Josie insisted, keeping her eyes firmly closed. "Or maybe something to drink. Coke?"

"You need sleep, not caffeine," Sam insisted.

"That Italian lady who lives downstairs brought you some spaghetti of some sort—it has green stuff on top of it."

"Risa brought up some pesto," Sam translated Mike's words. "She said something about you feeling better—I don't know how she knew you had fallen, but—"

"That's okay," Josie said, opening her eyes. She didn't think Sam needed to know that Risa was worried about her emotionally rather than physically. She wanted him to think she was doing just fine, thank you very much. "I'm not at all hungry." Even Risa's fabulous pesto couldn't tempt her right now.

"Say, maybe she really is sick. It's not like Josie to reject food."

Josie wondered if Sam would turn her in to the authorities if she slugged Mike Rodney. Probably, she decided. And it didn't matter, she was too exhausted to defend herself. . . .

When she woke up again it was the middle of the night, and someone had turned out the lights in her bedroom. She was still thirsty—and needed to go to the bathroom. She moved Urchin off her chest and swung her legs over the side of the bed.

"Oh no!" The pain shot up her leg.

"Josie! Josie! Are you okay?"

"Who—"

"It's me." Sam Richardson appeared in the light coming in the doorway. "You yelled. Are you okay? You shouldn't get up alone . . . . You might faint."

"I have to go to the bathroom."

"I'll help you." And without waiting for her consent, he put his arm around her waist, and with his support, Josie limped to the bathroom.

"I can manage from here," she insisted, squinting in the bright light of the room. She realized Sam had been busy while she slept. Not only was the ruined shower curtain neatly folded and stuffed in the banged-up tin she had found at a garage sale and decided would be an attractive wastebasket once it was painted (and perhaps, when she got around to painting, it would be), but there was other evidence of Sam's neat habits. Shampoo, soap, sponge, and razor were lined up on the windowsill in the tub. Towels were folded over towel bars, her green chenille robe was on the correct hook, and the tub and sink appeared to have been wiped clean. "I said I was okay," she repeated when he didn't leave her side.

"You shouldn't be alone. You might faint and hit your head—again."

"I need to be alone to do what I have to do," Josie

insisted. "You can wait outside the door. Then, if you hear my head hit, you can dash right in and rescue me."

"Josie . . ."

"Sam, please leave me alone."

He sighed. "I'll be right outside the door. If you feel like you're going to black out—"

"I'll yell," she promised, reaching out and slamming the door in his face. Her needs had become too urgent to worry about manners.

A few minutes later she was back in the hall, again thankful for Sam's support. "I'm not going to pass out. It's my ankle that's hurting." They both looked down.

"It's swollen—and looks like an ugly sprain—or else the bone is broken. I think we should get you to an emergency room and have it X-rayed."

Josie allowed herself to bask for a moment in the warmth of his concern—but only for a moment. "I need to get back to sleep. Tomorrow is going to be a big day."

"You don't plan on working tomorrow!"

"We're starting the biggest project of my life tomorrow!"

"Josie, look at the ankle. Look at your wrist. Look at your face."

"My face?" She limped over to the dresser mirror. Sam reached out and turned on the overhead light. She gasped. "I look terrible!" There was a large lump on her forehead and the skin under one eye was black-and-blue. "I can't believe this."

"You can't go to work looking like that."

"Oh, yes, I can! I'm a carpenter, not a fashion model. It doesn't make any difference what I look like, for heaven's sake!" Her headache was returning. "I need to go back to bed. I have to be up early."

Sam sighed loudly. "You are one of the most stubborn women I've ever known. If that ankle is seriously hurt, you could do more damage by walking around on it."

"I'm trying to go to bed," she reminded him.

"Fine. Just let me bandage it up for now. You can

always go to the emergency room tomorrow morning if you can't get around on your own."

"Right." She hobbled toward her bed.

"I don't suppose you have an Ace bandage?"

"I do. Tyler twisted his ankle at his school's field day in June and he was sent home with a few. They're in the medicine cabinet."

"Don't move."

Josie leaned against her headboard and sighed loudly. "I'll be right here waiting for you," she assured him.

Sam came back with his hands full in just a few minutes. "You seem to have lost the little metal fasteners that go with this, so I had to scrounge around in your drawers for a safety pin."

"Lucky you found one."

"Yeah. Lucky."

Josie opened one eye and peeked at Sam. He seemed strangely quiet and there was a serious expression on his face. But she had other things to think about. Why, oh why hadn't she had the time to shave her legs before Mike appeared in her bathroom? Sam was frowning as he wound the pink elastic around her leg and she didn't blame him. Between the swelling and the spiky hairs, her ankle was especially unappealing. Josie took a deep breath and closed her eyes.

"I'll be in the living room if you need me," he announced, standing up.

"What?"

"I said—"

"I heard what you said," she answered impatiently. "I was just surprised."

"Why? Didn't you realize that I was sleeping on your sofa? Josie . . ."

"I'm fine, Sam." She wasn't; she was near tears, but she didn't want him to know. Any fantasies she had been entertaining about them getting back together had vanished. "Just let me go to bed. Please."

"Fine. And you'll call if you wake up and don't feel well?"

"Yes, please, I just want to get back to sleep."

"Will the light in the living room bother you if I stay up for a while?"

"No . . ." She fell asleep before she could suggest that he close the door.

And she slept so soundly that she wasn't aware of the hours he spent pacing her living-room floor. Only Urchin, curled up on the empty couch, kept him company.

SIX

JOSIE TRIED TO get a word in edgewise. "You said there was a telegram."

"You appear looking like that and all you're worried about is some telegram?"

"What happened to yo—"

"You look like you were mugged. . . . Did you call the police?"

"Does this have anything to do with the death of the woman who looks—"

"Shut up! I need to know exactly what the telegram said. And who sent it! Right now!" Josie rarely yelled at her employees—unless it was the only way to make herself heard over their work and then everybody yelled—but she didn't seem to be able to get their attention any other way.

And it worked. The women had been hauling stuff from their storage shed to the truck. They were getting ready to set up at the work site. Betty dumped a pile of drop cloths on the ground. Fern, who had been lugging two crowbars, a pickax, three shovels, and a couple of sledgehammers to the pickup, stacked everything on the ground and squatted next to her pile. Kristen, who was walking into the shed, stopped to listen.

"I'm going to make this short and then we have to get on with it," Josie announced. "First, Betty, you said a telegram arrived at the office before we all got in. Who was it from and what did it say?"

"It was from the Van Emberghs and it said that the fax machine has been ordered and will be arriving later today."

"Where?"

Betty shrugged. "At the office, I guess. That's all the telegram said."

"Did it say why Island Contracting needed a fax machine?" Josie asked. "Or who was going to pay for it?"

"It didn't say anything else," Betty repeated. "Now you tell us how you got hurt."

"I fell in the bathtub."

"That's all? That's all you're going to tell us? That you fell in the bathtub?" Betty asked.

Josie remembered her embarrassment at being found by two men, how they had dressed her and put her to bed. How Sam had spent the night and nagged at her to go to the emergency room again this morning while he fixed her breakfast and cleaned out one of her kitchen cabinets. "That's all there is to tell," she insisted. "I fell in the tub. I'm fine. The shower curtain is a total loss."

"There's—" Kristen began.

"I don't want to hear anything else," Josie insisted. "It's time to get to work. Now—" She stopped before she could say anything else. It was obvious that everyone was watching something behind her. Josie bit her lip. If Sam had come to pester her about going to the emergency room again . . . Forgetting about her injured ankle, she started to spin around—and fell down, her heavy key ring digging painfully into her hip.

"Damn!"

"I'll say. That must have hurt. You should be more careful."

"I wasn't trying to fall," Josie snapped back before realizing that she was talking to a stranger. "And who the hell are you? And what are you doing here?"

"Hell, I don't need a job this bad."

Fern dropped her load and ran down to Josie. "Josie, this is the woman I told you about. From the hospital. The carpenter," she explained further. "You know, the one you were thinking about hiring."

"The one she hired," the other woman answered. "Not that I expect people to keep their promises necessarily. I just thought working with women might be a bit different than working with a bunch of asshole men, if you know what I mean."

Josie tried to clear her head. "You're Alma Snapp?" She was unable to go on. *This* was the woman Fern had suggested would be appropriate for Island Contracting? she wondered, staring. Certainly her muscles promised powerful work, but the tattoos that covered those bulges were more than a little disconcerting. Josie knew many women with tattoos, discreet hearts on shoulders, bands around ankles and wrists, even lilies outlining a young breast, but this woman was covered! Cartoon characters, flowers, sayings, two snakes that Josie counted before she realized she was staring and looked away.

"Something bothering you?"

"I . . . um . . ." Josie had no idea what to say. This woman would look right at home riding a large Harley-Davidson, but on a contracting crew?

"It's the body art, isn't it? Don't worry. I'm used to it. Everyone reacts that way at first. Go ahead and stare. There's a story behind each and every one." The young woman standing over Josie flexed her biceps and grinned down.

Josie found that she had to work hard not to feel intimidated.

"So? Are we gonna work together or not? Maybe now that you've seen me, you don't need another carpenter so bad. Maybe Island Contracting isn't so different from other companies."

That did it. "We *are* different and I want you on board. Why don't you start work this minute and we can get your paperwork filled out over lunch?"

"Yeah. Well, okay. I do have some errands I wanted to run during lunch, though."

"Then we'll do the paperwork tomorrow. But let's get on with this job," Josie insisted, so proud of her decisiveness that she didn't notice the concerned looks the rest of her crew were exchanging. "This is Alma Snapp, everyone."

"Al."

Josie looked up at the woman and then realized what she was suggesting. "You mean your friends call you Al?"

"Everyone calls me Al."

Josie could believe it. "Well, everyone can introduce themselves as we work," she suggested. "Fern, why don't you show Al where the stuff is to go and then drive on over to the site. Al can help you unload there. That way you'll get to know the layout of the project," Josie continued to the new woman.

"We gotta lug our own stuff around? On most of the crews I've worked on people were hired to do that stuff. You know, unskilled people," Al said, moving only a few steps toward Fern.

"This is a small company. We all help out," Fern explained before Josie could speak. "Come on, I'll show you where everything goes."

Al shrugged her illustrated shoulders and followed in Fern's wake.

"What the hell was that?" Betty asked, offering Josie a hand to help her get up.

"That was your new coworker," Josie said, refusing the offer and getting up by herself. "She needs a break and Island Contracting is going to offer it to her."

"But she doesn't stay if she doesn't work out, right?" Kristen added, and then blushed. "I mean, you wouldn't keep me on the job if I . . . didn't get along with everyone or get my work done . . . or something like that." She ended slowly, obviously embarrassed.

"She is taking care of an elderly aunt," Josie reminded them both. "I think that says something very positive about her, don't you?"

"Yes, of course," Kristen agreed quickly.

Josie realized that Betty wasn't being quite so obliging. "You don't agree?" she asked her.

"I know you're right—that we should give her a chance and all—but there's just something about her. . . ."

"Look, I don't find so many tattoos all that appealing, but I don't think we should judge women any differently than we judge men and men have been getting those things for years. Let's just give her a chance."

"Fine," Betty agreed briskly. "What are you going to do about the fax machine? Shouldn't someone go back to the office and wait for the deliveryman? Maybe we could talk the people who deliver it into hooking it up for us."

"I can hook it up easily," Kristen said. "But you're going to need a new phone line strung if you want to be able to receive messages all the time."

"Fine, another expense." Josie sighed. "Well, I guess it can't be helped. Go on over to the office. While you're waiting for the delivery, you can review the blueprints and get the electrical order ready. If the machine doesn't arrive before lunch, I'll be over and we can decide what to do then."

"Great." Kristen hurried off to do what Josie asked.

Josie noticed that Betty was still frowning. "What's wrong?" she asked, thinking she already knew.

"You look like shit."

"Thanks for the compliment."

"Look, I'm not stupid enough to criticize my boss for no reason at all. I'm worried about you and I don't buy that story about falling down in the bathtub."

"It's not a story. It's what happened," Josie assured her. "Really. Why doesn't anyone believe me?"

"You come to work covered with bruises the day after your look-alike is murdered. What do you expect people to think?"

Josie bit her lip. She'd been so involved in getting started this morning (and was still suffering from a dull headache, although she had no intention of admitting it) that she completely forgot about the murder. "I don't think that had anything to do with me," she insisted, hoping she sounded more confident than she felt.

"You're telling me that a woman who looks like you was killed in a place where anyone would expect you to be and you're not concerned?" Betty asked.

"I—" Josie stopped suddenly, the impact of what had happened suddenly dawning on her. "Shit! You don't think the police have put up barricades to keep us off the property, do you?" She had, in the past, crossed similar barricades herself, but she certainly couldn't expect everyone on her crew to do so.

"I passed by there when I was out jogging this morning and they did have that yellow tape strung up—but out back of the house—around the pool house. I don't think it's going to interfere with our work."

"I hope not." Josie frowned at the ground. Her headache seemed to be growing.

"Look, your truck is full. Why don't you head on over there and check it out," Betty suggested. "I don't mean to be stepping out of line or anything, but—"

"You're not and thanks for the suggestion. You can stay here with Kristen and wait for the delivery."

"Don't worry about that. I'll leave a note for the UPS man."

"But if the machine has to be signed for . . ."

"Then he can bring it over to the house. Don't worry," Betty continued. "I know the delivery guy. I used to date him, in fact."

Josie smiled. There were few single men on the island Betty couldn't say that about. "Thanks. I think I'll go over, then."

After checking to make sure her load was packed securely, Josie climbed slowly into her truck and drove up-island to the house. It was just nine A.M. and the morning light shimmered off the golden stucco walls and, less charmingly, illuminated the mildew staining the white woodwork and underside of the roof of the wrap-around porch. It also shimmered on the island's three police cars parked on the street, but only their presence suggested a nearby crime scene.

There was, she noted, no sign of the truck Fern and Al had driven off in before her departure. She hadn't passed them on the way, so where could they be? There were always last-minute things to pick up, of course—maybe Fern had stopped for something at the island hardware store. Josie frowned. It wasn't like her to forget small details at the beginning of a job. And it wasn't like Fern to take time off during the day without asking permission.

The men coming around the corner of the large house reminded Josie that she had other, more immediate problems.

"Miss Pigeon," a heavyset middle-aged man called out as he recognized her. "I want to speak with you immediately."

Josie wasn't surprised. Mike Rodney's father always assumed everyone was at his beck and call. She supposed that came with being the chief of police. She had always gotten the feeling that he didn't like her. He hadn't liked her when she dated his son. He hadn't liked her when she broke up with his son. And his refusal to call her "Ms." was annoying. But she put a smile on her face. "Good morning," she began, when he was close enough to address without yelling.

"Yeah. Good morning. You got another body, you know."

"It's not my body," Josie responded without thinking.

"Yeah, well, she's sure thinner than you, but she's got your hair. It was a mistake anyone could make."

"What was a mistake?" Josie asked, dreading the answer.

"Well, your boyfriend thinks she got killed instead of you."

"If you're talking about Sam Richardson, he's not my boyfriend," Josie insisted.

Chief Rodney looked at her curiously. "Yeah, I heard you two had broken up. News didn't surprise me. The guy's too old for you. Too sophisticated, too. Guess he finally realized that there's lots of younger women on the island."

"We were talking about the woman who looks like me," Josie reminded him. "Why does everyone think she was murdered?"

"Someone shot her. Shot her in the back, too. Besides, the woman has been running all over the island saying that someone was trying to kill her."

"You mean she asked the police for protection?"

"Nope. No way anyone's gonna pin any professional negligence on us, Miss Pigeon. She talked, but not to the police department."

"So . . ."

" 'Course we don't know what she wrote in her note," the police chief continued.

"What note?" Josie asked, momentarily distracted.

"The note we found in the pocket of her overalls. It's in an envelope. And guess whose name is on the envelope, Miss Pigeon. Yours."

"Mine?"

"Says Josie Pigeon right there in the middle of the envelope."

With each word, her headache got worse.

SEVEN

"TO ME? SHE wrote a note to me?" Josie asked. "What does it say?"

"Won't know till it's opened, will I?"

"And . . ."

"And you can't open it now, can you?"

What was with this family? Whenever she was around one of them, she had to work hard to resist smacking them. "Why not?" she asked as sweetly as possible.

"It's police property right now. Has to do with the investigation of Amy Llewellyn's murder."

"Then why don't you read it and tell me what it says," Josie suggested, making a note of the dead woman's name.

"Well, I don't know if I should—say, why are you so anxious to read that note? Is it possible you know what's in it?"

"If I knew what was in it, why would I be so anxious to see it—not that I'm all that anxious to see it," she added, realizing that she was making a mess of this discussion. Luckily, the arrival of another truck from Island Contracting interrupted it. Fern jumped out of the driver's seat and Al followed more slowly. Josie couldn't resist taking a peek at Chief Rodney to see his reaction to Al's tattoos. She was rewarded by the sight of his mouth dropping open in a most unappealing manner. But her smile faded when she saw the scowl on Alma—Al's—face. And Fern's usually cheerful demeanor was absent also.

"Cops? Have we got problems with the cops?" Al asked abruptly.

"There's been a death," Josie muttered, realizing she hadn't answered the question.

"Oh, well, I guess you want us to start unloading the truck," was Al's surprising reaction.

"Why don't I show you where everything is supposed to be stored," Fern offered.

"No one crosses the yellow crime-scene tape out back," Chief Rodney announced.

"My crew is smart enough to know that," Josie insisted, hoping Amy Llewellyn had been considerate enough to get herself murdered in an unused corner of the property. Then she had another thought. "The body isn't still around, is it?"

"Nope, she's been chilling off-island—in the hospital morgue—since late last night."

"Who found her?" Josie asked, glad that she had resisted the temptation to check out the work site one last time the day before. It wouldn't help Island Contracting's reputation if its owner was known to be a person who stumbled across dead bodies.

"You don't know?"

"I wouldn't ask, if I knew," she answered.

Chief Rodney seemed delighted to tell her. "Your old boyfriend. Sam Richardson found the body."

Josie was stunned. "Sam? What was he doing here?"

"According to him, he came here to meet you. Guess that's one alibi gone to hell, though."

"What do you mean?" Josie was having a difficult time digesting all this.

"Stands to reason that if he was meeting you here, you would know about it. Right?"

"If that's what Sam said . . . But maybe there was a misunderstanding. Maybe he called and left a message for me to meet him here and I didn't get it and—"

"And so he ran into the woman everyone on the island is calling your look-alike and he was so furious with her for not being you that he killed her."

"What? That's nuts! Sam would never kill anyone—and especially not just because I wasn't them . . . or her . . . or . . . dammit, you know what I mean!"

"Yeah, I know what you mean." Chief Rodney's grin was huge. "Word around town is that the two of you have broken up. You sure seem worried about his lying to the police. Guess you still have feelings for the man, Miss Pigeon."

Josie opened her mouth and then, with what she thought was an extraordinary amount of self-discipline, immediately shut it.

The island's chief of police confined his response to a chuckle.

"I assume there are going to be policemen around here for the rest of the day?" Josie finally said.

"We'll need to question everyone on your staff, of course. Can't imagine anything else at the beginning of a murder investigation, Miss Pigeon, can you?"

Since Josie had had exactly the same experience of murder investigations as the island's police force—one—her opinion was worth exactly as much as his. "I think I should go do my job and you should get on with yours."

"Sounds good to me. 'Course it's gonna be easier for you to do your job now, I suspect."

"Why?"

" 'Cause now you won't have to be looking over your shoulder wondering if whoever was trying to kill Amy Llewellyn might make a mistake and kill you."

"I—"

"On the other hand, it might just not work that way at all."

"Wha—"

"Just might be that the person who killed her made a mistake and wanted to kill you in the first place. If that's so, it's sure possible that he's gonna be real mad. And you know what that means."

"What?"

"That he's gonna be even more anxious to kill you."

"There's just one problem with your analysis, Chief." Josie finally managed to get more than a word in.

"What's that, Miss Pigeon?"

"There's no reason for anyone to want to kill me."

"Well, that may be true, but there's one thing you should remember, Miss Pigeon."

"What's that?"

"That's just what Miss Amy Llewellyn said to me yesterday morning."

Josie was glad the arrival of Betty and Kristen gave her an excuse not to reply—especially since she had absolutely no idea what to say.

"The fax machine arrived," Betty announced. "He's connecting it up now."

"Who is he?" Josie asked.

"I told you I'd dated the UPS deliveryman, didn't I?"

"Yes, but—"

"He's working for a promotion and has learned how to

work all the office equipment, so he volunteered to do it. He'll lock up when he's finished."

What's done was done. Josie knew you couldn't change the past, so she hoped the man was as honest as Betty seemed to think, and went on with her day. "Did the refuse company leave a message on the machine?"

Betty nodded. "There'll be a Dumpster here first thing—in fact, there it is." She pointed over Josie's shoulder, but Josie didn't need directions. She could hear the roar of the large semi-tractor trailer hauling the Dumpster to its location. "Do they know where to . . . ?" she yelled the beginning of her question to Betty.

"Up the drive and at the side of the house," Betty screamed back, waving to the handsome young truck driver. "Don't worry. Everything's taken care of." The driver was motioning for her to join him. "Do you mind?" she asked Josie.

"Not if you make it short."

"Don't worry," Betty said, running off toward the truck.

Josie didn't. Betty always got done what needed to be done. And her good relations with subcontractors often earned Island Contracting preferential treatment.

"Looks like everyone's here," Kristen commented, hauling her toolbox from the floor of the front seat.

Josie just nodded and started back to her truck.

"Look, it may not be my place to say anything. . . ."

Josie stopped. There was no mistaking the concern in Kristen's voice. "Go ahead."

"I . . . I should be old and wise enough to know when to keep my mouth shut. Ignore me."

"Kristen, we're starting the biggest project Island Contracting has had since I took over, there are new people on the crew, and that means we all have the normal adjusting to do—and now there's been a murder. If you have a problem, speak up, otherwise—"

"I'll shut up," Kristen interrupted. "I'm just one of those people who worries about every little thing. Ignore me. Besides, it looks like you have a visitor."

She surprised Josie by turning around abruptly and heading up the path to the house at a brisk jog.

"Guess she doesn't want to see us."

It was a man who spoke from behind Josie and she frowned. More talk with cops was something she didn't need, want, or have time for. "You know, it's not my fault this woman was murdered on my job site," she began, turning around as she spoke. And realizing immediately that the two men she was speaking to were not representatives of the police department. The elder was Joe Ellis, owner of Innovations and Renovations; the younger was one of the best-looking men she had met in a while—or maybe in her lifetime, she decided as they walked toward her.

"Hey, I'm not here to hassle you," Joe replied, a serious expression on his face. Josie suddenly remembered he had just lost one of his workers—and possibly a friend.

"Joe, I'm so sorry about . . . about Amy's death," she began, relieved that she had remembered the victim's name.

"Yeah, me, too. Hard to find a good finish carpenter this time of year. All the good ones are working."

Josie hoped he hadn't arrived to steal one of her crew. "Yes, I know. Are you here to look at the place where she was found?"

"Not really. We're here to pick up our stuff."

"Your stuff?"

"The police said Amy had some of I and R's tools with her—they suggested we come pick them up," the good-looking young man interjected.

"This is David Sweeney. Josie Pigeon." Joe introduced his companion.

"It's nice to meet you." Josie offered her hand, wishing she had the time, the money, or the type of job that allowed for manicures and soft skin. Her hand met calluses that matched her own—and a nice firm grip. She resisted glancing to see if David wore a wedding band.

"Nice meeting you."

David's dark good looks were enhanced by a confident smile. Josie gave up and peeked at his left hand. Eureka! No ring! "It's very nice meeting you, too," she repeated warmly.

"It's David's tools that Amy took," Joe explained.

"Yeah, I loaned her some things. She just moved to this part of the country and not all her stuff had caught up with her," David explained modestly.

"I'll show you where the body was discovered," Josie offered. "I haven't been there myself, but Chief Rodney said it was by the pool house."

"Lead the way," Joe suggested.

They started up the path that wound around the side of the house, Josie trying to think of something intelligent—or clever—or sensitive—to say. But Joe spoke first.

"Looks like this murder isn't going to interfere with Island Contracting's job," he commented, glancing up at the large heart-trimmed house.

"Good thing. We were lucky to get it," Josie said, trying not to sound smug.

"Yeah. The owners asked for bids a little late in the season. I and R's summer jobs had been booked for months."

"But I thought . . ." Josie began, wondering where she had gotten the idea that I and R had been her company's strongest competitor for the job.

David spoke up. "It's an interesting house. Are the hearts going to go?"

"The hearts?" Josie glanced up at the white gingerbread trim. Tiny birds were fluttering around it. "No. Why? Don't you like them?"

"They're a bit much, aren't they?" Joe suggested.

"Yeah, a little feminine," David agreed. "The way they're hanging in the corners, they could be replaced easily."

"Well, I like them. And as far as I know, so do the Van Emberghs," Josie commented as they arrived at the yellow-taped area. As promised, a pile of tools stood over to one side. David walked toward it and Joe headed to the group of policemen standing together just inside the taped line.

Josie stopped, looked around, and realized that she wasn't wanted anymore. Once again, she'd evidently made less than a great first impression on an attractive single man. Well, she had work to do, she thought, striding back to the house.

She would have been surprised to realize the amount of attention David Sweeney paid to her departing figure.

EIGHT

THE VAN EMBERGHS were leaving the main floor of the house pretty much the way it had been for years (except for the small powder room off the foyer; in Josie's experience people with money rarely chose to live with dark fifties bathrooms). A previous owner had installed a large professional kitchen in an ell added to the main building and the first thing Fern and Al had done after arriving at the house was drape layers and layers of heavy plastic in the kitchen doorway. Imported appliances didn't thrive in plaster-dust-laden air.

The second floor was being gutted, its two bedrooms and baths reconfigured to include such amenities as walk-in closets and whirlpool tubs. The third floor was to be gutted then turned into one large room with an adjoining bath. Summer residents seemed to like dormitorylike bedrooms for their children—until they lived with them and realized that the noisiest child needing the least sleep controlled the lives of the others. But Island Contracting had made some much-needed money turning bunkhouses into bedrooms, so Josie wasn't about to complain.

The house was also getting new wiring and heating systems, and all windows and doors were being custom-made in a small factory in New Hampshire. But the first few days were going to be devoted to demolition.

Demolition is a very satisfying task. Sam Richardson, arriving to pick Josie up for dinner early in their relationship, had watched her crew slam sledgehammers into brick chimneys, smash walls, and pry up floorboards with crowbars, and concluded that it was obvious why the employees of Island Contracting didn't need psychiatrists. Josie suspected her crew simply couldn't afford mental illness—or at least, professional help for their problems.

Josie was thinking of Sam now as she tore layers of cracked plaster from the attic ceiling. Spiders, mice, and raccoon nests fell to the floor, where Betty scraped them up and shoveled them onto a wooden slide attached to the window. Before everyone left for home that day, the mess on the ground would be neatly stowed in the Dumpster. Josie was focusing on her last date with Sam—what he said, what she answered. What she should have answered. What she wished he had said . . .

"Hey, watch out! You're going to break right through the roof," Betty yelled in her ear.

Josie dropped the sledgehammer and lifted the dust mask covering her nose and mouth. "What?"

"I just wondered if there was a reason you were trying to smash a hole in the roof?"

Josie wiped sweat from her forehead and glanced down at the Timex on her wrist. "We've been at this for four hours. Why not take an early lunch?" She realized she wasn't explaining her anger.

"Do you want me to collect orders and pick up lunch?"

"Good idea. And would you stop at the office and see if the fax machine is working?"

"No problem. And doesn't Al need to fill out her employment records?"

"Yes, but she said she had something else to do during lunch. She probably wants to check in on her aunt," Josie added a little uncertainly. Al certainly didn't seem to be the warm, loving person she had envisioned—but that was judging by appearances, she reminded herself. "She can do the paperwork after five—or tomorrow."

"Fine. So what do you want me to pick up for you?"

Josie placed a large lunch order (after all, she had been working hard all morning) and then, replacing her mask, returned to her task. By the time Betty took everyone's order, picked up the food, and checked at the office, she'd probably have the ceiling demolished. And maybe she'd also manage to stop thinking about Sam.

But he had been so sweet this morning, filling her thermos with fresh coffee and insisting she take it. And he'd dashed out at dawn to buy doughnuts for their breakfast. And he hadn't been angry when Urchin licked the frosting from one doughnut and sprinkled a few dark hairs on the rest. (Josie had eaten them all anyway.)

Of course, Sam wasn't always so sweet and obliging, she thought as she swung the hammer and the last few square feet of plaster fell to the floor. Sometimes he was stubborn, demanding, unreasonable. . . .

On the other hand, she could think more about Sam when she was alone. Right now David Sweeney had joined her. "Hi. Can I help you?" she asked, flipping up the dust filter. She had started the day with a scarf covering her long red curls, but, as usual, had pulled it off hours ago and the plaster dust in her hair now flew everywhere. She closed her eyes and sneezed.

"Here. Will this help?"

Josie opened her eyes to the sight of an immaculate pressed linen handkerchief. "I don't think I need . . ." She hated to think of wiping any part of her sweaty, dust-streaked body with that snowy-white cloth.

"Yes, you do." David gently slid the soft fabric across her cheeks.

Josie felt her knees grow weak and leaned her weight

against the sledgehammer she had propped up on the floor.

"You've had a busy morning," he commented, glancing around the space as he tucked the handkerchief back in his jeans pocket.

"Did you find all your tools?" she asked, wondering why he was still there.

"Not really. I'm looking for my spirit level, in fact. It's a big one and you know how expensive those things are."

"It wasn't out back?"

"Nope."

"And you think she—Amy—might have brought it inside? I don't think that's possible. I know the house was locked up last night and I don't see how she could have had a key—"

"I just thought someone might have found it outside and brought it in. It was marked, but no one here knows me."

"Marked with your name?"

"Initials. D.S. in bright red paint."

Josie frowned. Smart workers marked their equipment carefully. Tools were borrowed back and forth all day long, but most people made sure to get their property at the end of the day. At Island Contracting, both Betty and Kristen used red paint to identify their property. Betty painted a tiny heart on her tools, and Kristen's sported an upper-case *K* and some sort of squiggly design. Josie didn't think either symbol could be mistaken for David's initials.

"I gather you haven't seen it around here."

"No. Have you checked with the women downstairs?"

"Not really." He paused for a moment. "To be completely honest, my level isn't the only reason I came up here."

Josie just waited for him to continue.

"I was wondering if you were going out with anyone. And if you would consider going out with me."

It must be something in the dust. She had to be hallucinating. This couldn't be happening to her.

"Maybe we could go to the movies? Or to dinner some night?"

"We're working pretty late these days," Josie said, hoping he wasn't the type of man to discourage easily.

"So are we. So how about a late supper? I could pick you up around eight-thirty, we could get something to eat—and I'll have you back home well before eleven. I promise. I need a full night's sleep myself. Ask anyone who knows me—I'm always in bed by eleven and up by six."

All alone? she wanted to ask. But she just said, "Sounds great." *What night? What night? What night?* she wanted to cry out.

They must be simpatico. "How about tonight?" he suggested.

"Fine. I'd like that," Josie admitted, hoping she sounded casual.

"Is eight-thirty okay?"

"Sure. Do you know where I live?"

"Yeah. Someone pointed it out to me once," he said, starting toward the stairs. "I'll be there on time."

"Fine . . . And I'll check around about your tool."

"My what?" He seemed startled by her statement.

"Your level. To see if anyone has seen it."

"Oh that. Don't go to any trouble. See you tonight."

Josie didn't bother to answer. Now that his mission was accomplished, David seemed anxious to leave. He turned and ran down the stairway. Josie headed over to the window and was rewarded by the sight of the sun gleaming off his hair as he leaped into a black Grand Cherokee parked by the curb.

As he started his car Betty and Kristen drove up in the Island Contracting Jeep. It was hot and both women had stripped down to skimpy tank tops. Josie was thrilled that David didn't even slow down and glance in their direction.

She was also thrilled that lunch had arrived, but as she watched she noticed that the first things to be taken from the back of the Jeep were not paper bags from the deli, but several sheets of paper covered with what looked like diagrams. Betty rolled the papers into a cylinder and, after tucking them in the back pocket of her jeans, grabbed two of the five bags and started up the walk to the house. After a quick look down the road where David had disappeared, Kristen followed with the rest of the food.

Josie dumped her tools on the floor, pulled the dust mask off her head, and clumped down the stairs to join her crew. "Hey, where is everybody?" she called.

"The roof," came the answer from outside the building.

Josie entered the nearest bedroom. She spied Fern climbing out the window onto the porch roof. Josie skirted the rubble piled in the middle of the floor to do the same. In this room all three windows had been removed from their frames. There was no reason for Island Contracting to make work for themselves—and climbing up a ladder to the porch roof and using the windows to enter and exit would save the stairway's treads and banisters from the wear and tear of construction.

The porch roof was flat enough for comfortable perching and the view over the beach and out to sea was superb. Kristen was handing out cans of soda and tea. Fern was sorting through wax-paper-wrapped sandwiches. Betty had ripped open a bag of potato chips and was eating them absently as she examined the papers she had brought with her. Josie joined her, grabbing a handful of chips as she did so.

"What are these things? They're terrible!" she cried.

"Baked potato chips. They're fat- and salt-free."

"And damn near tasteless," Josie said, accepting a can of peach iced tea and sitting down at Betty's side. "And what's with the paper? Those aren't Al's records, are they?"

"No. They're faxes. From the Van Emberghs. They're for you." Betty passed over the pile and stuck her hand back in the bag of chips.

"Betty bought those chips, but there are regular chips and guacamole-flavored tortilla chips here, too," Kristen explained. She passed her boss another bag, but Josie was too busy going through the fax sheets to open it.

"Anything wrong?" Fern asked as she handed Josie two oil-stained bags.

"Not really," Josie replied, staring at the sheets.

"Something must be wrong," Kristen said. "You're not eating your lunch. I mean, I'm starving," she added, ripping the paper surrounding her hoagie and taking a huge bite.

"Those messages are something, aren't they?" Betty commented.

"That's a polite way of putting it," Josie agreed, continuing to read.

"Something wrong?" Fern asked quietly.

"Nothing we can't handle," Josie said briskly, folding the sheets and tucking them in the top pocket of her overalls.

"It's not easy to work for clients who make changes once a project is begun," Betty said.

"True. But we haven't really started on the remodeling of the house. And if the Van Emberghs want nickel fixtures from Italy in their bathroom instead of the chrome they chose initially, now is the time to let us know."

"Will they get here in time to be installed?" Betty asked.

"It says they're being air-freighted in. They might actually get here before the ones on order from our supplier," Josie answered. "I'd better remember to cancel that order when I get back to the office tonight."

"I don't understand," Fern said. "Where are the Van Emberghs and where are these fixtures coming from?"

"Italy," Betty answered.

"That's where they are and where the plumbing supplies are coming from," Josie added. "Apparently the Van Emberghs like to spend their vacations shopping."

"For faucets?" Fern asked.

Josie shrugged. "Guess so."

"Italian faucets?" Kristen asked.

"Yes . . ."

"I wonder if those things couple with American piping," Kristen continued.

"Yeah, I do, too," Betty said, and Fern began to tell a story about a job she had worked on where the owner insisted on combining Mexican and Italian tiles—and the disaster that had resulted.

Josie didn't join the conversation. Sitting near the edge of the roof, she could see around the corner to the little white pool house by the azure pool as well as out to the deeper blue sea. And she was wondering what Al was doing climbing over the yellow crime-scene tape—leaving, not entering, the crime scene.

NINE

IT HAD BEEN a long and productive day. The Dumpster was half-full. The second and third floors were almost empty. The supplies from the lumber company had been stacked neatly by the side of the driveway, then covered with large blue tarps. Island Contracting's employees had left the site almost an hour earlier and Josie was sure most of them had showered, had a drink or two, and were now eating dinner. She hoped they all went to bed early because tomorrow was going to be another busy day.

Josie was regretting her enthusiasm over David's invitation. She was exhausted. She ached all over. And she had to go back to the office and do some paperwork. When she inherited the company, she also inherited an excellent relationship with many of the local suppliers. That was important and she maintained it by paying bills on time and handling orders and returns in as professional a manner as she could. So if the Van Emberghs were sending the hardware for the master bathroom, she had to amend an order she had sent in yesterday. She sighed. She hated paperwork and never felt entirely confident in her ability to do it. Changes could be difficult. She tried not to remember the time Pella had delivered double the order she thought she had made. Those custom windows were still taking up much-needed room in the storage area Island Contracting maintained off-island.

She looked down at her wrist. Less than half an hour remained before her date with David. Not a lot of time if she was going to head back to the office and call the supplier before going home to shower and change. Even less time if she was going to check out the place where Amy Llewellyn's body had been discovered.

The police had left in the middle of the day, but the crime-scene tape was still in place. She had warned her crew about crossing the line and had said nothing to Al about seeing her cross it. She had been thinking about the murder all day long. Amy Llewellyn resembled her and she had been murdered on Island Contracting's job site. Remembering Amy's warning, Josie wondered if perhaps she really was in danger. Except that she couldn't think of a single reason anyone would want to kill her. Of course, Amy had said the same thing, hadn't she?

That was the thought she couldn't get rid of, no matter how hard she worked. It wasn't that she necessarily thought any answers were waiting for her on the other side of the yellow tape . . .

But where else was she to look? she asked herself as she leaped over the tape. And tripped, bringing the tape down to the ground. Shit! Josie looked around, trying to figure out what had been holding the tape up so she could reconnect it. There were some stakes stuck in the ground, but she wasn't sure how the tape had been tied to them. . . .

Fifteen minutes later, fifteen minutes that she couldn't spare, the tape was back up. Now there was no time for a look around. She absolutely had to get to the office.

No one who didn't want a ticket risked speeding on the island during tourist season, but it was a small island and Josie was at the office in less than five minutes. She dashed in the door—and stopped dead. A new machine stood in the middle of her desk. A pile of paper lay on the floor beneath it. As she watched, the gray machine extruded more paper. A tiny calico kitten jumped hysterically into the air to grab the sheet as it fell. Another cat, a large tiger, leaned over the side of the machine, staring intently at the papers on the floor. As Josie stood there the machine stopped suddenly and a loud beeping sound filled the air.

Oh good. Another machine she didn't understand had come to live with her. Josie hurried over to her desk, wondering if a sign was hanging over the door that she couldn't see: WANTED—STRAY CATS AND SUICIDAL MACHINES. What else possibly could explain this scene?

It took a few minutes (and a can of cat food) to disentangle the felines from the faxes, but less than that to understand why the Van Emberghs had bought Island Contracting a fax machine: they were, apparently, fax addicts. Merely reading through the top few sheets convinced Josie that she had a major problem. And one that was not going to be solved in a few minutes. She gathered up the papers, checked to make sure her strays had water as well as dry food, and headed home. She had just enough time to shower before David was due. Unless he arrived early, she thought as she drove up to her home.

There was David, standing in front of the house talking with her landlady, a smile on his attractive face. Risa was smiling back, but Josie realized that the expression was forced. Clearly, Risa did not like David.

Josie grabbed the fax sheets, jumped from her truck, and trotted up the sidewalk. She knew she looked tired and dirty, but she was a carpenter and David was just going to have to get used to it . . . if he ever wanted to see her again.

"Hi, David. Hi, Risa. I see you two have met."

"Yes. I have met this young man." Risa, as usual, was swathed in lengths of flowing fabric. Without moving, she managed to give the impression of wrapping it more tightly around her shoulders.

"I'm sorry to be late," Josie began.

"No problem," David assured her.

"Your phone has been ringing all afternoon," Risa said accusingly.

"The answering machine is broken," Josie said.

"I thought, perhaps, this charming young man—" Risa began.

"Nope. I was working all day long. No time to call," David admitted cheerfully.

"Then perhaps it was Sam."

"I'm sure if it was Sam, he'll call back. Besides, it was probably just someone trying to convince me to buy something." Josie turned to David. "Do you mind if I take a few minutes and shower?"

It was a stupid question. No man in his right mind would want to take out a woman as filthy as Josie was. But David's manners were as nice as his looks. "No problem. Take your time."

"Come on up. There's beer in the refrigerator—I think," Josie said, hurrying up the stairs to the second-floor apartment she rented from Risa.

"Don't worry about me," David insisted, following her to her apartment.

There was a pile of mail on the counter outside of the door. Risa had left it, but Josie also knew her landlady would have gone through it and mentioned anything interesting, so she just picked the pile up, and taking it into the apartment with her, tossed it on the coffee table in front of the couch. She was embarrassed to realize that Sam had neatly placed the extra blanket and pillow he had used the night before on one end of the couch. But if her date noticed, he didn't say anything.

"The refrigerator is over there," Josie said, pointing to the compact kitchen at one end of the large room. "I'll just go shower. I won't be more than a few minutes."

"No problem," he assured her as she hurried into her bedroom. She carefully closed the door behind her, pulling off her clothing and tossing it on her bed on the way to the bathroom—where she realized that showering without a curtain was going to be a challenge. Standing there naked, she pursed her lips. Tomorrow she would find the time to buy another shower curtain, but right now a little improvising was in order.

Fifteen minutes later she returned to her living room, excited despite her fatigue. David was such a good-looking man. . . . And they had a lot in common. . . . And who was he waving to out her front window?

"Hi. I'm ready. Finally." She announced her appearance.

David spun around from the window, a serious expression on his face—that he changed to a charming smile when he saw her. "Wow! You look wonderful!"

"Thanks. Who's outside?" she asked, starting over to the window.

"I was just waving to the kids. You know how it is, the parents are sitting on the deck of their rental house drinking gin and tonics and the kids are riding bikes and playing in the street."

Josie joined him at the window. "Summer vacation," she said quietly. "I remember it from when I was little," she added. "My parents used to come here for two weeks every August. It was a completely safe island then and I was allowed to run wild with whatever kids were also on the block. We'd stay up late at night, playing kick the can in the street and burning punks to keep away the mosquitoes."

"So how did you come to live here as an adult?" David asked politely, holding the door open for her.

"It's a long story. And not a very interesting one," Josie answered. "We'd better get going. I really have to get home to bed at a reasonable hour."

David smiled. "Nothing like dating a workingwoman. Don't worry. I have to get up early, too. You won't believe the problems we're having with this new project."

"You're kidding. The best architect around designed it and I understood the owners have plenty of money and are willing to spend it."

"If they could only make up their minds what they

want to spend it *on*," David said. "These people have picked out four different tiles for the master-bathroom floor . . . and there are three other bathrooms in the house that they haven't even thought about!"

"Did they buy I and R a fax machine?" Josie asked, and then explained what had happened that afternoon.

They were still trading tales of employers and remodeling jobs when they entered the restaurant David had chosen. "I hope you like Italian," he said as the scent of tomatoes and garlic enveloped them.

"Love it." Risa was the best Italian cook on the island, but Josie didn't mention this.

David greeted groups of friends at the bar as they walked to the tables in the back. "You seem to know a lot of people here," she said, sitting down in the chair he pulled out for her.

"I and R kind of uses this place as a hangout," he answered, nodding to a friend at a table on the other side of the room.

"Have you all worked together a long time?"

He gave her a curious look before answering. "Well, I came to the island less than a year ago, of course, but the rest of the crew has been pretty stable for the past few years."

"Except for Amy Llewellyn."

"True. She just joined us a few months ago."

"I'm starved," Josie said, taking the menu that was offered.

"Good, because the portions here are large. I can recommend the lasagna and the cheese ravioli."

She scanned the menu and chose the lasagna, ordering as soon as their waitress reappeared—and then spent the next five minutes wondering what it was going to take to get that waitress back to the kitchen to place the order. The girl didn't look old enough to be out of high school, but she was definitely old enough to appreciate David Sweeney's good looks. David himself finally set her on her way with a request for water.

"Would you like some wine? Or a beer?" he offered.

"A glass of Chianti would be nice."

"Ah, a wine drinker. I guess it's all the time you and Sam Richardson spent together. You couldn't date him and not learn a lot about wine, I guess."

"I guess. . . . So, where did you work before you came to the island?" she asked, trying to change the subject.

David looked at her curiously. "You mean you don't know?"

"No . . ." She wondered why he thought she would. Then the answer occurred to her. He was a good-looking single man; he had lived on the island for a while; he had undoubtedly dated Betty. "I mean, there's no reason I would know," she continued. "We talk while we work, but we don't tell each other every small detail of our lives."

"I didn't think a marriage was a small detail," he protested.

"A marriage? You were married to Betty?"

It was David's turn to look confused. "Who mentioned Betty? It's Kristen I was married to—for almost ten years, in fact."

TEN

At least it had been a short evening. Once she realized she was dating the ex-husband of one of her employees, relief replaced Josie's annoyance each time their giggling waitress appeared. She couldn't help but wonder what Kristen would think when she found out that Josie was dating David. Not that one date could accurately be called dating. . . .

It was midnight and Josie was lying in bed, desperately trying to sleep. She was exhausted, but there was too much to think over. Maybe a cup of warm milk with some sugar and nutmeg, she thought, getting up and padding to the kitchen. It was her grandmother's recipe and usually worked—especially with the addition of brandy or bourbon.

But she didn't have brandy or bourbon. There was a bottle of single-malt Scotch that Sam loved to drink. . . . And that gave her something else to think about, she realized, standing over the stove and stirring the mixture in the saucepan.

As bubbles rose around the side of the pan, she found a clean mug stamped with the assertion that CARPENTERS DO IT WITH HAMMERS. Tyler had given it to her when he was too young to understand the slogan. In fact, Josie wasn't sure what to make of the words herself, but it was clean and the rest of her dishes weren't, she realized as she turned off the gas.

Some of the milk spilled down the side of the chipped mug and Urchin enthusiastically lapped it from the countertop. Josie yawned and flopped down on the couch, placing her mug on the cluttered coffee table before her. Foam rubber poked from one of the cushions and she picked at it as she sipped her drink and scanned the day's mail. There was a postcard from Tyler's camp that excited her for a moment until she realized it was from his counselor notifying her of the upcoming parents' weekend. She spent a few minutes regretting a life that kept her from seeing her son. She missed Tyler. She missed Sam. She hoped the date with David wouldn't upset Kristen. She wondered if the Van Emberghs were going to become the "clients from hell." But most of all, she wondered what Al had been doing behind the crime-scene tape.

Peripheral thinking—a complete waste of time—she should be sleeping. Who knew what tomorrow might bring? It was up to her to set an example for her crew. Sleepy workers caused accidents and made mistakes. . . . In the middle of her own lecture, she dropped off to sleep on the couch.

Maybe it was the couch, or maybe the warm milk

didn't settle properly in her stomach, or maybe it was the dream about someone sneaking up behind her and shooting her in the back. As she fell to the ground she heard a man's voice say, "Oops, wrong woman." It wasn't a peaceful thought and it wasn't a peaceful dream and she woke up at a little before five A.M. feeling terrible.

Everyone has his or her cure for a bad morning. Betty, Josie knew, ran a few miles on the beach. Sam swore by fresh-squeezed orange juice and a handful of vitamin pills. Josie usually headed straight for the local doughnut shop. She didn't know if it was the sugar or the fat, but she was firmly convinced that cream doughnuts were a wonderful cure for a bad night's sleep.

And the local bakery was owned by a neighbor who just might be convinced to open a little early for a friend, Josie decided, putting on her clothing and heading for the bathroom.

As David had promised, the lasagna had been more than ample, but she was starving, she realized as she drove up to the bakery. The back door was open and the scent of yeasty dough wafted through the screen as she climbed from her truck.

"Hi, guys! Guess who's here?" she called out.

"Hey. It's Josie Pigeon! Come on in, Josie. I think about you every time I shower. Island Contracting really did a great job with that bathroom!"

Josie pushed open the screen door and entered the large busy room. The slanting early-morning light illuminated particles of flour in the air. Half a dozen young men and women stood around long tables, cutting out and forming elaborate shapes from various kinds of dough. A heavy red-haired man was poking a huge wooden paddle into the largest mixer Josie had ever seen. He pulled it out and flipped on a switch that set the beaters whirling and, a large welcoming smile on his face, came over to greet his guest. "How are you? The entire island is talking about you."

"About me?"

"Sure, you know we're all worried since this woman who looks like you was killed."

"I don't think—" Josie dashed in to reassure this kind man and then realized that she actually had come here hoping to benefit from that concern. "It has been difficult," she admitted quietly.

Her landlady was good friends with this man; one of the beliefs they shared was the conviction that food, if not actually the solution to life's problems, greatly helped in smoothing out its bumps. Of course, Risa believed in pasta. Johnny Mahoney believed in Irish soda bread, and almond-studded brownies, and cream-filled doughnuts. He shoved a large tray of the latter across the table between them. "Here. Tell me about it."

"I don't know how much there is to tell that you probably haven't already heard," Josie began, her mouth full of delicious cream and fried dough. She knew how information traveled across the island, passing from resident to resident seemingly faster then the ever-present laughing gulls flew.

"Well, we know that this young carpenter named Amy Llewellyn was shot behind the house you're rebuilding—and that she had been running around the island saying someone was trying to kill her. And of course everyone knows that she looked remarkably like you from behind. And then there was the note to you that was found in her pocket."

"That's right! I had forgotten the note," Josie cried, swallowing. "I don't suppose your information goes so far as to know what is in the note?"

"Have another. The ones on the right are raspberry jelly. Pretty good, if I do say so myself."

"They're wonderful and you know it." Josie took one and tasted it. "Really wonderful." Like Risa, Johnny expected a lot of appreciation for his cooking. She took a larger bite before continuing. "Do you have any idea where that note is?"

"Nope. But one of the kids was saying something about evidence bags a little while ago." He glanced around the room at his workers, none of whom had stopped working, but all of whom were listening.

"It was me, Mr. M." A young African-American man, long dreadlocks pulled off his forehead and into a huge ponytail, spoke up. Mahoney's bakery was a good place to work. He was a good boss. He paid well. And the workers got off at noon each day to spend time on the beach. Josie knew he had his pick of the college students who, having summered on the island with their families as kids, now returned to live in dormitories full of their peers, all trying to earn money and have fun at the same time. Anyone working here was a good student and a responsible person, so she listened carefully.

"I'm prelaw at Yale and my uncle is also the coroner in New Haven, so I know a little—a very little—about collecting evidence."

"And he was down at the police station yesterday afternoon when the police were coming in from the crime scene," a young woman called out. She held large trays of Danish in her hands.

"Paying a speeding ticket," the young man explained.

"But tell about the way the island police collected evidence," someone else suggested. "That's the funny part of the story."

"I know a bit about the police on the island," Josie added, seeing the reluctant look on the young man's face. "Nothing you can say would surprise me—and the murder could really damage my business."

"Josie once solved a murder on this island. You can go ahead and tell her what you saw," Johnny suggested, winking at Josie.

Josie knew most islanders assumed Sam Richardson had done most, if not all, of the detecting that ended in a member of her crew being arrested for murder, but she was determined not to get sidetracked. "I really would love to hear about it," was all she said.

"Well, I was down at the station yesterday after work, and after I paid my ticket, I was on my way out when two men came in from the crime scene. They were talking about what had been found and I . . . well, I was curious and so I stopped to read the notices on the bulletin board and do some eavesdropping."

"And tell her what you saw!"

The young man chuckled. "I guess I was pissed about the ticket—after all, I was only going thirty-five in a twenty-five-mile-an-hour zone and—"

"You're going to be a rich lawyer if you charge by the hour," someone called out from the rear of the room.

"Okay, I'm just trying to explain that I was near enough to get a pretty good idea of what I saw."

"So spit it out already!"

"Evidence collecting on the island is pretty casual—"

"Tell her how casual!"

"Look, I don't want you to think I'm telling tales. . . ."

"I wouldn't be surprised at anything the police do," Josie assured him.

"Well, the younger cop—the one who is the chief's son—dropped something on the dispatcher's desk and said something about locking it up in the evidence locker. And the dispatcher asked what it was. He said a note to Josie Pigeon that was discovered on the body. She—the dispatcher—picked up this Baggie sandwich bag and held it up to the light and asked why the note was covered with greasy stuff."

Josie realized that everyone in the room had already heard this story and many of them were giggling in anticipation of the punch line.

"And he said he hadn't been carrying any regular evidence bags, so he just pulled the tuna sandwich out of his lunch box, ate the sandwich, and used the Baggie for the evidence. He thought maybe some of the mayo and pickle relish had been left behind."

"I gather that's not the way evidence is usually stored," Josie said.

"No, usually anything found at a crime scene is picked up carefully and placed in a heavy sealed plastic bag, then it's printed and photographed at the station. That way it's protected from contamination."

Johnny was enjoying the story as much the second time as he apparently had the first. "I guess a little tuna fish might smear up any fingerprints that were on the note." He chuckled.

"Definitely."

"You said it was going to be placed in an evidence locker," Josie reminded him, wondering if she could get a look at that note. It was, after all, addressed to her.

"Yeah. If a used Baggie is an evidence bag, what do you think the evidence locker is?" someone called out.

"Maybe someone dumped out their tackle box and they used that," someone else suggested.

"Or maybe a bait bucket."

The entire bakery got into the act, each young person trying to top the outrageous suggestion of the person before him. Josie chuckled and said her good-byes after accepting two large bags of doughnuts for the crew.

She was glad she'd gotten up extra early; she had just enough time to stop at the police station before heading to the office. There probably weren't a lot of people around yet and maybe she'd be able to wrangle a peek into whatever was being used as an evidence locker.

Except no one seemed to be there. The police station was connected to the fire station, which was the right arm of the building that served as the island's municipal center. The fire department, composed entirely of volunteers, was empty. It was too early for anyone to be in the municipal offices. The woman who sat directly inside the doorway of the building, directing traffic and selling beach passes to visitors, wouldn't be in for another two hours. But surely the police department was manned all the time. Who took care of emergency calls? Who guarded prisoners in holding cells? Who answered the doorbell that Josie pushed and pushed?

Apparently nobody, she decided, after the first dozen rings. She peered in the glass on the door and saw a desk covered with a messy pile of twigs and feathers. She buzzed a couple more times, wondering vaguely if the bell could be heard in the rest rooms. But she finally gave up, returned to her truck, and drove to the office.

Seeing Al casually ignoring the crime-scene tape yesterday had caused her to wonder if maybe she should insist the woman fill out Island Contracting's employment forms. There might be something about Al that she should know. And there wouldn't be any more excuses if Josie brought the forms along with the doughnuts this morning. She'd slip into the office, feed the cats, pick up those forms, and arrive at the work site right on time—even if it took her a while to find the papers in her less-than-organized desk drawer.

But her desk was no longer the messiest spot in the room, she realized as she stepped inside. The spot on the floor underneath the fax machine won hands down. The pile of papers looked to be six or seven inches high. And judging from the contented looks on the faces of the two sleeping cats, it was the most comfortable spot in the room.

ELEVEN

"SO WHAT DO they say?" Betty asked, taking another doughnut from the bag Josie was passing around the group.

Josie stared down at the stack of unread faxes in her hand. "I don't know. But I suppose I have no choice but to read through them," she muttered, picking up the top sheet. "Who knows what changes—oh, no."

"What's wrong?" Betty asked.

"They've been shopping again." She glanced around the room. "I forgot to bring the cell phone, didn't I?"

"You did. But I saw it on the desk and picked it up," Kristen said.

"You stopped at the office?" Josie was surprised.

"Yes, that's why I was late."

Kristen paused and Josie was afraid she knew what was coming. "You dropped off more kittens, didn't you? Look, I hate to think of these animals abandoned on the street, but we have to make a concerted effort to find them homes."

"No, you don't understand. I went to the office to get a kitten. One of my neighbors just happened to mention that she was looking for a kitten for her son and I thought I should give her one of ours before she changed her mind."

"Hey, an adoption! Congratulations. Anyone can build a house, but finding a good home for an Island Contracting orphan kitten is a real accomplishment," Betty cried out, getting up.

"It *is* a good home, isn't it?" Josie asked. "I mean some children aren't very responsible—and boys can be rough."

"It's a wonderful home. The mother is a nurse . . . and the little boy has some sort of disease. He's crippled and really needs the company of a pet," Kristen explained.

"You took the little calico?" Josie asked, still reading through the papers.

"Yes. Maybe I could find a home for the adult."

"I think I'd like to keep the big cat. We need a mascot down at the office. And we don't have to worry about her being lonely."

"Why not?" Fern asked.

"She has the fax machine to keep her company. Listen, it's time to get to work. I just have to make a few phone calls."

"We know what to do," Fern said, and getting up, the women scattered to their various jobs.

"The second-floor blueprint—" Josie began.

"—has been nailed up on the wall in the guest bedroom,"

Fern called out as she headed down the hallway. "Next to the chimney."

"Great."

"But I have a question." Fern reappeared just as Josie had finished dialing the company that supplied tiles.

"Sure."

"I have a doctor's appointment at noon. Can I take my lunch break a little early?"

"Of course."

"I'll work late tonight to make up any time I miss," Fern added, and then left the room before Josie could protest that such a gesture wasn't necessary.

It *was* necessary, however, if they were going to finish this job on time, Josie thought. And they'd all have to stay healthy, too. She wondered how she could ask why this doctor's appointment was necessary. But she had calls to make, and when that was done, she discovered that she had another problem.

Sam Richardson.

Old habits die hard and she couldn't help smiling as he walked in the door.

But he didn't return her smile. "I have something important to talk over with you."

"I thought we weren't going to talk about that."

"It's about Tyler. I received this postcard from him."

Josie took the rectangle of cardboard he held out. It was one of the dozen she had sent to camp with him. Postpaid, she had written her own address on each one, thinking that if Tyler only had to supply a message, she might hear more about his life. Tyler had crossed out her address and written in Sam's. No wonder she wasn't hearing from him as frequently as she had hoped!

She read through the short message before handing the card back to him. "So?"

"So? Aren't you concerned?"

"About what? Tyler has been complaining about his counselor since the second day of camp. And he's just asking about the parents' weekend because I had told him

I probably wasn't going to be able to go. I called and left a message about it yesterday. What are you so worried about?"

"It sounds like he's planning something."

"Sam, you know Tyler. He's always planning something." Josie loved her son, but he had been amazing her since nursery school, when it was discovered that he had taught himself to read. The elementary school on the island was good, but his teachers had a hard time keeping up with him. It wasn't so much that he was intelligent, but that he was active and creative—and always what Josie's mother used to call "up to something." The inheritance that had given Josie control of Island Contracting also allowed Tyler to attend an excellent boarding school.

"But this could be different." Sam's voice was serious.

"It's always different with Tyler. Do you remember when he started an alternative newspaper at his school the first month he was there? Or when he talked the harbormaster into letting him build a clubhouse under the public dock? Or the series of letters he wrote to the island newspaper?"

"This is different," Sam insisted. "Here on the island everyone knows Tyler, and if he's allowed to get away with some things it's because he's a responsible kid. And that school he goes to encourages him to express himself creatively, but this is just an ordinary camp you've sent him to and they probably aren't prepared to deal with one of Tyler's brainstorms."

Josie frowned. He had a point. "But the camp is out in the wilderness in Pennsylvania. What can he do there? Besides, he knew if he went to camp, I might not be able to get away in the middle-of-the-summer building season. He said it didn't matter. You know that he was prepared for me to remain on the island."

"That's one of the things that worries me. It sounds to me like your son has a plan. And you know what that means."

She wasn't going to think about it.

"Besides, since when is there wilderness in Pennsylvania?" he added.

"He's taking a class in wilderness skills," she protested. "It says so right on that postcard you keep waving in my face!"

"Josie, think about it. Tyler goes off to camp knowing that there's a good possibility he's going to be one of the only kids alone on parents' weekend. He signs up for a wilderness-skills course when there are classes in computers, archery, marksmanship, for heaven's sake—which is what he planned on taking when he signed up for the camp last spring, and now he sends me a postcard telling me—"

"Reminding you," Josie corrected him.

Sam pursed his lips, but continued without commenting on her words. "Reminding me of the antique wooden boat show in New York City this weekend."

"You and he have been talking about finding a small sloop and restoring it for the last year!"

"And you and I were talking about spending a weekend in the city ourselves, if you'll remember."

"But Tyler doesn't know about that!"

"He probably assumes we're spending a lot of time together . . . unless you wrote him that our relationship had changed." He raised his eyebrows in a way that caused Josie's heart to thump.

"No. I didn't think . . . well, I thought maybe . . . I mean . . ."

"Yes, I know what you mean. I haven't mentioned it either."

"Oh . . . Well, good." Josie was both confused and relieved that she hadn't revealed her hope that they'd be a couple again before her son returned home in August, and that Sam hadn't guessed her meaning. Then she realized the import of his last words. "You've been writing Tyler?"

"That surprises you?"

"So you have been."

"Josie, your son and I are friends. I thought you appreciated that fact."

"Well, I have in the past, but now . . ."

"You didn't expect me to write Tyler and say that since his mother and I are having trouble with our relationship, he and I could no longer be friends? I'm not that type of man, Josie."

"I know." And she did. "I just wasn't thinking. . . . So what has he been telling you about camp?"

The look of concern on Sam's face deepened. "He's been writing you, hasn't he?"

"Just postcards."

"Fourteen-year-old boys are pretty private, you know. I mean, it's what psychologists call age-appropriate behavior, isn't it?"

"I suppose so. . . . But, you know—" She stopped talking and moved closer to the doorway. "I think someone is yelling for me."

"You don't mind if I call Tyler's camp director, do you?"

"Why?"

"Josie, I just told you that I was worried."

"Sam. Someone is calling me. I've really got to get back to work."

"Fine. I'll let you know if I find out anything disturbing."

"Okay . . . What do you mean, disturbing?"

The voice yelled again.

"Josie, haven't you heard anything I've—"

A distinctive buzzing sound could be heard from above.

"What was that?"

"That," Josie replied as she dashed out the door, "was the sound of someone turning off the power the hard way."

"The hard way?"

"By touching a live wire with a metal tool . . . or an unprotected hand . . . or . . ."

Sam couldn't hear the rest of the sentence. He stood still, silently waiting until a whoop of laughter could be heard from above. Then, sure nothing serious had resulted from the accident, he turned and walked out the door, frowning as he slipped Tyler's postcard in the pocket of his pressed chinos.

Josie, standing at the top of the stairs, watched him through the hall window. Sam's small green MGB was parked at the curb, so she was surprised when, instead of heading to it, he turned and marched toward the back of the house. Toward, she realized immediately, the place where Amy Llewellyn's body had been found. Something about that spot seemed to draw people to it. And, she realized, she herself hadn't been one of them.

She waited inside the house until Sam finished his mission and was driving off before she started out to trace his steps. "I'm going to head out for a few minutes," she called over her shoulder to the top floor.

Kristen stuck her head around the corner of the doorway. "Where are you going?"

"Just out back. I want to check out the stuff stored there and all. I'll only be a few minutes," she repeated.

"Oh, I wanted to talk with you."

"When I get back," Josie said, heading for the door. Kristen hadn't mentioned Josie's date with her ex-husband and Josie was hoping to keep it that way for as long as possible. She ran down the stairs and out of the house.

TWELVE

NOTHING WAS THERE. No scene-of-the-crime tape. No marks on the ground. Nothing to indicate a murder had taken place here less than forty-eight hours ago. There was, however, a strange geometric shape made from rocks and twigs on the floor in one corner of the pool house. Josie knelt down beside it, feeling a chill, despite the hot day. The symbol looked familiar. She'd seen it before—on a television show about satanic cults that she had dozed off in front of just last weekend.

Josie stood and checked out the entire area before returning to the small pile of rocks and twigs. There was a broken champagne bottle in one corner, nothing else. What did it mean? Teenagers might have been using this place as a hangout, but would they have risked a confrontation with adults, especially the police, by tampering with a crime scene? Unless, of course, they had something to do with the murder. It was an interesting idea. . . .

It was an old habit that didn't seem to want to die, but she wondered what Sam was thinking. He must have been as surprised as she to find the crime-scene tape gone. And he might have noticed the shape on the floor. She made a decision. She would call Sam. The fact that they were no longer dating didn't mean they couldn't discuss a problem or two. He certainly hadn't been shy about coming over with Tyler's postcard.

She'd call right away, she decided, turning and trotting back toward the house.

And running straight into Chief Rodney as he rounded the corner.

"I understand the crime scene has been tainted, Miss Pigeon." As always, his emphasis was on the *miss*.

"How do you. . . ?" she began, deciding there was no reason to quibble with his refusal to address her as Ms. right now.

"I got an anonymous call to come over here and look at it. The caller insisted I would find something interesting. And by the scared look on your face, whatever is back there is more than interesting." His expression suddenly became serious. "Not another body, is there?"

"No. Of course not. There's nothing . . . absolutely nothing. That's why I'm upset. I knew you wanted everything left in place . . . and someone has cleaned up . . . and I was afraid you would blame one of my crew when I know for a fact that none of them has been near the crime scene."

She paused to consider the lie she had just told and Chief Rodney took the opportunity to ask a question. "How?"

"How what?"

"You sound a little like an Indian in one of those old black-and-white movies, Miss Pigeon," he stated. "How do you know no one on your crew has been out there moving stuff around? Or anything else?"

"Because . . . because I told them not to."

"And you know all those women so well? Even the tattooed lady?" he asked sarcastically.

Josie didn't get as angry as she might have, since, after all, he had mentioned the person she was worrying about. She knew for a fact that Alm—Al had crossed the yellow tape. On the other hand, unless Al was a murderer, she needed each and every one of her crew on the job each and every day—and not in jail awaiting trial.

"Every single one of the people who work for me has undergone extensive background checks." She hoped she was saying the right thing—it sure sounded official to her. As though she had actually checked out all the application forms. As though Al had even filled out one of the damn things. Just as long as no one asked to see . . .

Josie felt as if Chief Rodney had read her mind.

"I'd like to see the employment records of those women on your crew, Miss Pigeon."

"Well, I would have to gather them."

"Just get them to the police department before I go home tomorrow night. And murder investigation or no murder investigation, I go home at five P.M. on the dot." With that, he stomped off toward the road.

Josie had an urge to ask which dot—the one after the *P*

or the one after the *M*? But she sure didn't want the conversation to continue, so she kept her mouth shut. She had real problems here. She had no idea what sort of order her personnel files were in—and she was positive she hadn't verified any of the information on the forms. How would one go about checking that out anyway? she wondered, following Chief Rodney back around the side of the house.

It was, she realized, watching the policeman get in his brightly marked patrol car, another reason to call Sam. Now all she had to do was find out where Kristen had put the phone.

Her luck must be changing; Kristen was coming down the stairs just as Josie entered the house.

"Hi, where did you put the cellular phone?"

"I left it upstairs in the bedroom next to the blueprints. But I think the last time I saw it was in the south-facing bathroom on the second floor. Check with Fern. I know she was calling about some wiring order that arrived incomplete."

"Oh, fine. I guess I'd better call about that, too," Josie began.

"Don't worry. Fern said everything was okay. And I need just a moment of your time," Kristen insisted.

It couldn't be avoided any longer, so the sooner they got to it, the sooner they could all get back to work. Josie took a deep breath. "Okay, I'm sorry I dated your ex-husband. I didn't know or I would never have done it." She looked carefully to gauge Kristen's reaction. To her surprise, Kristen looked puzzled. "What's wrong?"

"It's not your fault. I lied on my application form. It was stupid, but I didn't know you at all well and I didn't know the politics—or whatever you call it—about living and working on the island. I was afraid you wouldn't hire me if you knew."

Josie pushed her red hair up off her neck, twisting it into a ponytail and then letting it fall back down. The truth was, she just didn't pay that much attention to

Island Contracting's paperwork. She read everything through, of course, but very little seemed to sink in. Once she had taken care of health insurance, workmen's comp, social security, and the like, she just put the papers away and didn't think about them again. "I don't mean to sound like an idiot, but I don't know what you're talking about."

"I thought if you knew that I was divorced from a man who worked for I and R, you might not hire me."

"Why not?"

Kristen looked at Josie curiously. "I just thought you wouldn't like it," she answered quietly. "You know, we might talk and then information about Island Contracting would be known at I and R."

"How long have you lived on the island?"

Kristen looked startled. "Almost six months . . . Why?"

"So how come you don't realize yet that keeping a secret is almost impossible around here?" Josie asked, thinking about her breakup with Sam.

"You mean Island Contracting doesn't have many secrets from I and R?"

"I doubt it."

"You don't mean that personally . . . like the people on the crews surely have secrets from each other."

"Oh, of course." Josie wondered exactly what Kristen was trying to keep from her ex-husband—not that it was any of her business. And they were losing valuable work time. "I was just thinking of professional things. You know, Betty has dated men on I and R and no one thought a thing of it. So you didn't have to worry."

"And you don't mind that I lied on my employment form?"

"Not now that I understand why you did it," Josie assured her. "So why don't we get back to work?"

She stood up, stretched, turned around . . . and found herself looking right into Sam Richardson's face. The expression on it was not a happy one.

"Hi, Sam," Kristen said before heading for the door as fast as she could go.

"I cannot believe you just did that," Sam stated flatly.

Josie had no idea what he was talking about. But she wasn't going to admit it. "Are you criticizing the way I run my business?"

"I assume you've read the forms all your employees fill out."

"Yes, of course I've read them. I've even filled one out myself."

"Even the bottom line that informs the employee that anything less than truth on the form will be grounds for dismissal?"

She was on less sure ground here. "That doesn't mean I have to fire someone who lies, just that I can. Right?"

"Yes, but . . ."

"Well, then?"

"Josie, we have to talk. Why don't I take you to dinner tonight? Nothing personal. Just business, and I still think we need to do something about Tyler."

"Did you call the camp? Is he okay?"

"As far as I know. I spoke briefly—very briefly—to the director of the camp, who said that if there was a problem with one of the campers the counselors would let him know immediately. It was a singularly unsatisfactory conversation."

"You don't think—"

"Look, he claims to have a system in place so he is informed immediately of any problems. I don't have any reason to disbelieve him. I did manage to extract a promise that he would check with Tyler's counselor and make sure everything was fine. He obviously thought I was an overprotective parent—"

"You told him you were Tyler's father?"

"I did not. He assumed."

"Fine." Josie sighed. "Look, I have to get back to work. Where do you want me to meet you for dinner?"

"I could pick you up."

"No way. Risa would see you and assume we were

back together and you know how she can be. She would start driving me nuts."

"Fine. How about the Beachcomber at eight?"

"Make it nine. I have to work as long as there's light."

"Okay. See you at nine."

She had a thought. "But Basil might be there."

"It's a small island. We can't avoid everyone who might make an incorrect assumption or two."

"Fine." She'd said she needed to work and she'd better get going. "See you at nine," she repeated awkwardly.

"Yeah." Sam started to leave, then turned back. "Did Chief Rodney give you any idea why he had taken down the crime-scene tape so soon?"

"No. No one has said anything to me." It wasn't the truth, but it wasn't exactly a lie either.

"Your crew hasn't been questioned?"

"Why should they be? They weren't here when Amy was killed."

"You know your crew is suspect. She was, after all, killed here. The location may not have been an accident."

"Or it may have been," Josie protested. "Besides, there's only one person that I know of who's a suspect."

"Who?"

"You." And she spun on the heel of her work boot and stomped off, wondering just why that hadn't been a satisfactory ending to an unsatisfactory conversation.

THIRTEEN

"I TOLD YOU this would happen. Now Basil is going to tell everyone on the island we're dating again." Josie leaned across the blue sailcloth covering the round table and hissed the words at Sam Richardson.

"Do you want me to go find him and tell him this isn't a romantic dinner?" Sam asked, moving a goblet of water out of the reach of Josie's elbow.

"No, that would only make it worse. . . . What's this? Did you order champagne?" A waitress had appeared with an ice bucket and wine.

"No."

"Compliments of the management." The young waitress made the official announcement and then leaned down to continue the message in a whisper. "Basil was jumping all over the place he was so thrilled to see the two of you together again."

Josie leaned back in her chair with a thump. "I don't believe it."

Sam didn't speak until he had tasted the champagne, nodded his approval, and the waitress, after filling two glasses and smiling, had left, promising to return to take their orders shortly.

"Sammmmm." Josie realized she was very close to whining.

"Have some champagne."

"Now you really are going to have to tell Basil that . . . that . . ."

"That we accepted his champagne under false pretenses?" There was a smile on Sam's face.

"Whatever." She picked up her glass and drained it.

"Hey . . ."

"I work hard. I get thirsty."

Sam took a small sip from his glass and studied the menu. "Any idea what you want?"

"Yes. I want to start with the fried calamari and then the pasta with broccoli rabe."

"Calamari? I remember when you refused to think of squid as anything but bait."

"So I've become a sophisticate in my old age." She knew she sounded bitchy, but she couldn't seem to stop.

"Look, I can't sit and talk all evening. I have to be up early tomorrow."

"I know—"

"No, you don't know. You don't know at all. Apparently you think the only reason I have a job is so that I have an excuse not to spend the night at your house! As though I might not have a perfectly good reason to want to spend the night in my own bedroom."

Sam leaned toward her across the table. "If you speak a little louder maybe the people waiting for seats outside will be able to share this moment, too."

Josie glanced around. Everyone seemed to be either leaning toward their table or working hard to avoid looking as though they knew she existed. Basil Tilby was standing in the open doorway to the kitchen, a huge grin spread across his face.

"Do you want to order or do you want to leave?" Sam continued.

Josie sighed. "Let's order and hope everyone else leaves. I don't think I can bring myself to walk past them right now." And besides, she was, as always, starving.

"Fine." Sam waved at their waitress and she scurried toward them.

Josie drank another glass of champagne while Sam placed their order. It didn't seem to be affecting her at all tonight, she decided, pouring herself another glass.

"You know—" Sam began.

"Why were you so annoyed when you came in this morning?" Josie interrupted.

"I wasn't annoyed when I came in, I was annoyed . . ." He shook his head and his straight blond hair fell into his eyes in an appealing manner. "Let me begin again. I was upset and worried when I heard what you were saying."

"About what?" The day had been long and the morning seemed to be more than twelve hours ago.

"About lying on your employment forms, Josie."

"I didn't lie—oh, you mean Kristen lying."

"Exactly . . . Or not so exactly. My concern is over the fact that you acted like it didn't matter."

"But once I understood that she was embarrassed about her ex-husband's job on a competing contracting company . . ."

"Is that what she told you?"

Josie was busy sipping and peered at Sam over the top of her glass. "Why? Do you have any reason to believe she was lying about her lie?" she asked, and then, realizing how foolish that sounded, began to giggle. Maybe the champagne was making her just a bit tipsy. . . . But the appetizer had arrived and she was sure food would help. She picked up her fork and attacked the pile of sweet fried rings. She was halfway through the plate before she realized Sam was making a point. "What?"

"Josie, as much as I enjoy watching you eat, I'd appreciate it if you would listen to me at the same time. I am a lawyer, after all."

"I know." Now, what did that have to do with anything?

"Look, you have every right in the world to fire someone who lied on their application form."

"I don't want—"

"I wasn't suggesting that you either wanted to or that you should. I'm just telling you your rights. Now tell me, what's your procedure when you hire someone?"

Josie reached for her glass and didn't answer.

Sam's charming and crooked smile appeared on his face. "You don't *have* a procedure, do you?"

"It's just that I don't exactly know what you mean." She defended herself with her ignorance.

"Every time someone new is hired and fills out their application form, what do you do?"

"Well, I talk with our insurance agent, of course."

"After or before you check references?"

She'd had a feeling it was going to come down to this. "You know, Island Contracting is a little different from other companies."

"Please don't tell me you don't check references."

"The obvious answer is 'okay I won't tell you,' isn't it?"

"Josie, how do you protect yourself? How do you protect Island Contracting? You could be hiring people with—" He stopped.

"With what? With illegitimate children? With prison records? With cancer? We've done all that, and you know what—Island Contracting is thriving! This job is the biggest we've gotten since I took over and it's an indication of how well—"

"Josie, I know how well you've done in the past year. And I give you all the credit in the world. You know that. But once again, the company is involved in a murder, and even if you didn't carry out full background checks on your employees, the police are going to. And it's always best to be prepared. You want to find out if there are any skeletons in anyone's closet before that idiot Rodney does."

Josie grinned. "Which idiot Rodney?"

"They're both idiots and you know it. But Kristen sounds to me like the person to start with."

"Why?"

"Simple. She has a connection with I and R—and so did Amy Llewellyn."

"But Amy Llewellyn had no connection to Island Contracting!"

"She was killed on your site. She looked very much like you from behind."

"Did you ever see her?"

"Actually, yes."

Hearing the uncharacteristic hesitation in his voice, Josie remembered that Sam had discovered the body. "When she was alive? Did you ever see her alive?"

"Yes."

"I suppose you're one of the people who ran into her from behind and mistook her for me?"

"Well, actually, it was a little more than that. We actually spoke on a few occasions."

"You what?"

"There are people who would say that since we're no longer together, it's no business of yours who I spend time with."

"It is when you find her body at my job site."

"Can I get you another bottle of champagne? Or perhaps a portable microphone so the people eating in the back of the room can hear your argument without straining?" The flamboyant Basil Tilby stood at their side.

Josie felt a flush spreading across her cheeks. It almost matched the silk scarf tied casually around Basil's neck.

"I'm afraid we accepted the champagne under false pretenses," Sam admitted.

"Where there's life . . ." Basil said, ending the phrase with a shrug.

A young man, working for the summer as a busboy, hurried to the table, a chair in his hands. He placed it between them and Basil promptly sat in it, propping his elbows on the table and his chin in his hands. "You don't mind if I join you." It was a statement, not a question.

Josie, who once had found Basil's pretentiousness more than slightly irritating, had grown in the past year to appreciate him—as well as the exotic food served in the restaurants he owned. "Of course not," she said sincerely. "Have you heard anything about what the police think about the murder?" she asked. Basil had his ear to the ground—or, more accurately, to the sand—on the island.

"You don't think the Rodney boys have suddenly become competent, do you?"

"It's their incompetence that scares me." Sam spoke up. "Those men are incapable of filling out a speeding ticket correctly. And remember how they almost screwed up the last murder investigation on the island."

"I remember who solved it," Basil added.

Both men looked at Josie.

"And I sure hope you're hard at work on this new problem," Basil added.

Josie shook her head. "I already have a job. Besides, solving that last murder didn't exactly make my day." In fact, finding out who the murderer was had been more than a little painful and both these men knew why.

"But it did save Island Contracting," Basil said gently.

"Island Contracting isn't actually involved in this murder. It just happened to have taken place on the property we're renovating—not even in the main house. The Van Emberghs weren't even planning on doing anything to the pool house. Our instructions were to leave it alone until the end and then it would be painted to match the main house."

"I was listening to some of the Van Emberghs' friends in the bar earlier. They were discussing how to get hold of the Van Emberghs so they could let them know about the murder," Basil explained gently. "That's what I came over to tell you."

"Shit!"

"That *is* bad news," Sam agreed in a more mannerly fashion.

"I guess the phone lines between France and the island have been pretty busy," Basil commented.

"Amazing how easy it is to call overseas these days," Sam started.

"France? Did you say France?" Josie interrupted.

"Yes. Well, they said France. Paris, Nice, and Saint-Tropez, to be exact."

"Those cities are all in France?"

"Saint-Tropez is still more a resort town than a city, but yes."

Josie started to pull on strands of her long red hair. "They're in Italy."

"No, France."

"I mean the Van Emberghs. The Van Emberghs are in Italy."

"Are you sure?"

"Definitely. Their faxes are coming from Italy. And that's where they bought the fixtures for their master bath."

"Fixtures? They're shopping for toilets on vacation?"

It was a thrill to know something one of these sophisticated men didn't. But she was too worried about what Basil had reported to gloat. "No. Faucets and towel racks—things like that. They're in Italy and they're shopping."

"Did you say you'd gotten a fax machine?" Sam asked.

"The Van Emberghs sent one. From an office supply store in New York City. They had another phone line installed, too."

"At their expense?"

"Well, I haven't seen any bills. You don't think they would do something like that without asking me and then expect me to pay for it, do you?" Oh, fine. A new worry.

"I don't know. You're their friend."

"I'm not their friend. I'm their employee. I don't know them all that well."

"That's the least of her problems. If the Van Emberghs hear about the murder, they could cancel their contract," Basil said.

"They can't do that! They can't, can they?" Josie cried to Sam. "It's a contract. I have some legal rights here, don't I?"

"You have a lot of rights. But the Van Emberghs could refuse to make their quarterly payment. Then you'd have to take them to court. And that could take months. And"—Sam reached across the table and took her hand—"if you're in the financial shape you usually are, it could be the end of Island Contracting. You have lots of money tied up in supplies at this point, I would imagine."

Josie felt the comfort of his gesture and didn't move out of his reach. "You're right. I guess the only thing to do is to try to solve this one by myself, too."

"By ourselves," Sam corrected her.

"Anything I can do to help?" Basil offered.

"We should investigate the people on your crew," Sam insisted. "It's what I was saying earlier. We want to know the facts so the Rodney boys can't spring any surprises on us."

"Don't you want to start with the victim? With Amy?" Basil asked.

"True. Something in her life might lead us right to the murderer," Josie agreed. "All we need to do is find someone who knew her personally."

"Sam."

"Excuse me?" Josie wondered what Basil was talking about.

"You can start with Sam. After all, he'd been dating her."

Josie snatched her hand back and reached for the champagne.

FOURTEEN

SHE WOKE UP early, her headache made insignificant by her anger. Sam dating Amy Llewellyn! And then he didn't mention it to her. What had he said? Something like he had talked with her? Josie wondered exactly what had gone on besides talking. Not that she wasn't perfectly aware of the fact that this was none of her business. Unless, of course, it had something to do with the murder. . . .

She rolled over and squashed the cat.

"Oh, damn. I'm sorry, Urchin."

Urchin jumped off the bed and strolled casually from the bedroom. If her feline feelings were hurt by Josie's behavior, she wasn't going to show it.

"Smart cat," Josie muttered, pulling the old T-shirt she slept in over her head and grabbing for the knob on her underwear drawer. It came off in her hand. The dresser was an old maple one that Josie had bought last fall at an estate sale. She had been planning to refinish it ever since. The magazines were full of old furniture which, after a few coats of paint had been applied, looked wonderful. But it was easier to look at the pictures than pull out the paintbrushes. And even Tyler had pointed out that the furniture's appeal was increased by the expensive antiques that surrounded them in most of the photos. He had offered to paint the dresser for her, but Josie knew there were lots of things he'd rather do during his short vacations and had turned down the offer.

She sighed and wondered what Tyler was doing at this moment. Probably sleeping in a bunkhouse full of fourteen-year-old boys. Sweaty fourteen-year-old boys whose parents were not around to nag them into cleanliness. Ugh. She pried open the drawer with a plastic hair clip.

Josie had promised to meet Sam for an early breakfast at the all-night diner on the highway off-island. She wanted to kill him, but there was a murder to solve and she knew she needed his help. Sam's years as a prosecuting attorney had given him access to police-department files as well as the world of private investigation. And she was a big girl, she reminded herself. There was no reason she couldn't maintain a professional relationship with a man she no longer had a personal one with—was there?

And he'd never know how angry she was, she decided as she put on her clothing and rushed out of the house. The first challenge of the day was to keep Sam from knowing exactly how she felt—both emotionally and physically.

She was early, but Sam was waiting in a booth at the

back of the room. She had spent the drive over thinking up a cute opening line.

"Why is it that when we start investigating a crime, we spend so much time in restaurants?" She hoped the smile on her face didn't look forced.

"We need to talk. We need to eat. We're both busy people." Sam shrugged, apparently immune to her charming manner. "Want some coffee? It hasn't improved since the last time we were here."

"As long as it has caffeine, it's just what I need. And some water," she added.

"Yes. Me, too. I'm afraid I drank a little too much last night. Thank goodness Basil has all those young people around who are willing to drive his patrons who overindulge home."

Josie vaguely remembered a young man chauffeuring her in her truck. "Then how do they get home?"

"Someone follows in Basil's car. Of course, it's not as though either of us was really drunk—but as Basil said, neither of us wants any extra attention from the police right now."

"Extra attention? Does that mean you've been interviewed about the murder already?"

"Of course." Sam looked down at the heavy white cup in front of him. "I think you're the only person on the island who didn't know I had been dating Amy."

"And, of course, you found her body." She paused. "That must have upset you."

"Of course. Finding someone murdered is very upsetting. But, Josie, I didn't have any deep feelings for her. We were just dating. You know."

"Look, why don't you tell me about it. All about it." She noticed the surprised look on his face. "Unless you were . . . ah . . ." She didn't know how to continue.

"We had three dates. I know it's the nineties. But we weren't sleeping together. And we weren't going to. I wasn't that interested in her and she wasn't that interested in me. In fact—and this is the truth—I asked her out because she reminded me of you."

Josie realized he was embarrassed. "Because she looked like me from behind?"

"Well, I've always been attracted to women with red hair. And she was a carpenter as well, of course."

"I can't believe you've always been attracted to carpenters."

"It's true that the man who built the bookshelves in my apartment in New York City was a little heavy for me—he must have weighed at least two hundred and fifty pounds. Do you know what you want to eat?" he continued as a waitress in a dirty pink uniform appeared.

"Hmm." Fine time for him to mention weight—oh, the hell with it. They'd never get back together no matter what she weighed. "Two eggs fried over, bacon, hash browns, and rye toast."

"I'll have the egg-white omelette with chives and red peppers. No potatoes. Whole-wheat toast. No butter. No jam."

Just one more reason they hadn't succeeded as a couple. "Are you going to be embarrassed to tell me what you know about Amy?"

"Not really."

"So?"

"To tell you the truth, I'm just beginning to realize how little I knew about her. Let me start at the beginning.

"I met her at the store. She was shopping, standing in front of the California varietals. As you said, from behind she really did resémble you." He shrugged. "So I went up to her. I don't remember what I said, but she turned around and laughed. Apparently I wasn't the first person to confuse the two of you.

"Anyway, we got to talking. You know, general stuff about the wines that interested her."

"You're telling me a carpenter is interested in fine wine?"

"Just because you look a little alike doesn't mean you *were* alike."

Touché. Her fondness for any wine that was in a jug had mainly to do with the price, though. She might have developed fine tastes, too—if she hadn't been a single mother struggling to pay the bills. "And so you asked her out."

"Well, it was late. Almost time for the store to close. And we had been chatting about the new Merlots. . . . So I offered to open a few bottles and some of the cheeses we're now carrying and stage an impromptu wine tasting. She agreed."

"So you did all the background stuff then?"

"What do you mean?"

"The what are you doing on the island? Are you single? Divorced? You know."

"I guess so. She was single. Never married."

"How old was she?"

"Mid-forties. I'm not sure of her exact age. When a women seems less than anxious to talk about her age, I don't push."

Of course that was because he usually dated women much older than Josie. "How did she end up being a carpenter?"

Sam chuckled. "She was a hippie in the late sixties or early seventies. Dropped out of college, went back to the land, and joined a commune. She spent quite a while there—four or five years, I think. Anyway, she discovered that she hated the land—could have cared less about growing food, be it animal or vegetable—at least that's how she put it. But she loved building things. She said she started with a repair to the henhouse because the rain was coming in and collecting eggs was a rotten job without having to get wet while doing it. And she did it so well that the community began asking her to do all the repairs. That turned into her job for the next four years. She actually built a day-care center and a stable by herself before she left."

"Impressive." Josie was trying hard not to think so. "And without any training?"

"Well, she had been an engineering student in college, so I guess the actual design work was something she had a theoretical background in."

More sophisticated. Closer to Sam's age. More educated. She and Amy Llewellyn had less and less in common. The waitress delivered their breakfast. She looked down at her eggs and bacon, swimming in grease, and then glanced over at Sam's austere plate. Amy would, no doubt, have preferred his meal.

Sam might have been thinking the same thing. "She was a good cook as well," he added. "I had dinner at her apartment the next night. She invited me."

Josie poked her egg yolk with a corner of her toast and watched the yellow flow onto the plate. "I didn't think you just barged in. Italian food?" She and Sam shared an affection for this cuisine.

"No. Oriental—I suppose you would say she specialized in Pacific Rim cuisine—you know, Japanese, Thai, Vietnamese with a French colonial influence. It's very chic in the city right now."

Just something else she didn't know. And how was Sam keeping up with these things? He'd moved to the island over a year ago. Apparently once chic, always chic. "Amy was from New York?" Certainly there weren't any rural communes in the city—unless Central Park was bigger than she thought.

"I don't know where she was from. She went to college in Oregon—and the commune was somewhere east of Seattle. And after she left, she stayed in the Seattle area."

"That explains the rain in the chicken coop."

"Yes."

"Why did she leave the commune?"

"I don't know. I got the impression that it just disbanded. She said something about living with another woman from the group after she left. These things happen. People are young, idealistic, enthusiastic. And then they get older, more practical. They want something more for themselves and their children than that type of environment has to offer."

"And she and this other woman just moved to somewhere around Seattle and Amy set herself up as a carpenter?"

"I don't know. We were just chatting—getting to know each other. I wasn't quizzing her about her past. I do know that you and she have something else in common."

"What?"

"She worked for an all-female contracting company."

"Really?" She was interested in spite of herself. "Out west?"

"Yes. In Seattle. They were called something really cute. Building Broads. Contracting Cuties."

"Yuck!"

"No, that's not right. Working Women. That's it. Working Women."

"So how long did she work with that company?"

"I have no idea. She talked like it had been a long time—like she had some sort of loyalty to the company."

"So how did she end up here?"

"On the island?"

"Yes."

"I have no idea. She never explained—but I don't remember asking, so it's not like she had something to hide."

"Not necessarily."

"True. Not necessarily," he conceded.

"How long had she been here?"

"Since early in the spring." He paused to drink some coffee. "I think she said something about March . . . or was it April? I don't really remember."

"And she worked at Innovations and Renovations ever since she arrived?"

"I don't know. But that type of thing shouldn't be hard

to find out. You know people on the I-and-R crew, don't you?"

"A few men—but Betty probably knows most of them."

He chuckled. "Yes, I'm sure she does."

"But there are going to be some things harder to find out—harder than the dates she started working and all."

"Such as?"

"What was she like?"

"You're asking me?"

"Well, you dated her."

Sam put down his fork and stared at the remains of his omelette. "I don't think I actually know. She was always cheerful and fun to be with."

"You mean she was flirting with you?"

"If you want to see it like that. I suppose you could say she was flirting."

She really wanted to know if he had flirted back, but there was no way to ask. So she continued with her investigation. "You must have gotten some ideas about her. Besides the fact that she was a hippie dippie in her youth."

"I got the impression that she was idealistic when she was young," he corrected her. "I can understand that. I was, too."

And she had just been a poor unmarried college dropout trying to support her illegitimate child. This conversation was a lousy way to start the day.

FIFTEEN

THEIR CONVERSATION SEEMED to have gone nowhere. Sam finally admitted that he knew little about Amy. The fact that she had told Josie as well as other people that someone was trying to kill her was interesting—especially since she hadn't mentioned anything about it to Sam. He thought that could be significant. Josie thought it only meant that Amy couldn't flirt and worry at the same time. They had left the diner, agreeing to spend any spare time during the day collecting information. They would meet at Island Contracting's office in the evening.

Breakfast had replaced Josie's hangover with a case of heartburn. "You look lousy," Fern commented, walking in the doorway of the office. "Is that what's making you sick?" She pointed to a pile of fax paper on the floor beneath the machine.

"That and some very greasy bacon . . . or maybe it was the fried potatoes. . . . What's that?" Josie looked at the tablets Fern was holding out to her.

"An antacid tablet."

"Do you think I should take one? Does your doctor prescribe them? They're not too strong? Or addictive?"

"They're over-the-counter stuff—you can buy them at every drugstore and grocery in the country. I get upset stomachs just like everyone else. It has nothing to do with the cancer or chemotherapy."

"Oh, thanks, then." Josie accepted the tablet, unwrapped it, and popped it in her mouth. "I thought you were done with chemotherapy—not that I'm prying."

"I am. You're not. But you never know."

"Whether the cancer will come back?"

Fern nodded and bent down to pick up the faxed messages.

"You're really wonderful about all this," Josie commented.

"No, I'm not. I don't have any options. I either learn to live my life with cancer, or . . . or I suppose I kill myself."

Josie was shocked to hear the brutal words. "How can you say that?"

"I say it because it's the truth. I don't see myself as being brave, or adaptable, or anything. I'm just a human being struggling to live as good a life as I possibly can. Period. Everyone's opportunities and disabilities are different and most are not as dramatic as cancer, but we're all doing the same thing—except for the people who sit alone moaning 'woe is me.' "

"I think, if someone told me I had cancer, I might do just that."

Fern shrugged. "For a while maybe. But then you'd just want to make the most of the time you have left—and make the time you have left as long as possible."

"Then you think you're a better person for having cancer?"

"No way. I think I would have been a better person if I had been born brilliant, beautiful, and with a silver—no, a gold—spoon in my mouth. But I didn't have any choice."

Josie smiled. "Yeah, but those gold spoons can be taken away pretty easily. Believe me, I know."

"So here I am. Most of the time I don't think about the cancer returning—but sometimes . . ."

"You get frequent checkups?"

"Of course. And I try to take care of myself. And I'm involved in a wonderful support group—it's made all the difference in my life."

"That's how you met Al, isn't it? Through your support group?"

"Sort of. She was looking for a group for her aunt—reading the bulletin board in the waiting room at the hospital and chatting with other people waiting for their tests. Cancer patients and their families get a lot of practice waiting. So I told her about the group I go to. And we got to talking. . . . You know how it is."

"Hmm." Well, it was a chance to learn something, after all. "Did you meet Al's aunt? Is she like her niece?"

Fern grinned. "Well, she doesn't have any tattoos

except for the ones the doctors give you when you're getting radiation treatment."

"You're kidding!"

"No. When you get radiation you also get your choice of a rose or a snake—you know, to cheer you up. Hey, don't look like that! I'm kidding—sort of. The technicians tattoo tiny little dots on your body to show the limits of the radiation."

"Really?"

"Really. They always kid about adding flowers and stuff. It helps make those lab places just a little less grim." Fern frowned. "Maybe we should look at those faxes—it's getting a little late, isn't it?"

"Yeah." Josie picked up the pile. "I appreciate you talking openly about your cancer," she said gently.

"I appreciate you listening. It makes my life a little more—I don't know, more normal, I guess. . . . What's wrong? Is it bad news?"

Josie ran her free hand through her hair and sighed loudly. "Good news and bad news, I guess. The good news is that the Van Emberghs are in Greece, so I guess all attempts to find them in France are bound to fail. On the other hand . . ." She sorted through the dozen or so sheets.

"On the other hand?" Fern prompted.

"They're still shopping."

"What have they bought this time?"

"Tiles. Floor tiles for the small bathroom on the first floor. And accent tiles for the guest bathroom on the second floor."

"That might not be too much."

"And granite for the master-bathroom floor!"

"Granite? Can't they get that here?"

"Apparently they want this particular granite. How long does it take to get things like rocks here from Greece?" she asked, thinking of the bonus she was depending on.

"I don't know. Months probably. A cousin of mine used to go to school in Austria and we were told to mail her Christmas presents right after Halloween—unless we paid for airmail. And no one would airmail ceramic tiles and granite, would they?"

"Probably not." Josie sighed loudly. "I guess there's nothing we can do about it now, is there?"

"No. We can just do that part of the job sometime in August—two months from now. Why worry?"

Josie knew very well why, but she didn't explain about the bonus—which was looking less and less generous. If the Van Emberghs were making all these changes, it was a safe bet that there'd be no extra percentage for Josie and her crew. "Yeah, I suppose. Do you want to ride over to the house with me?"

"Sure. I was going to wait around for Kristen, but it looks like she's going to be late. Or maybe she forgot about me and she's there already."

Josie realized Fern was protecting Kristen, trying to cover for the fact that she was late. "That's probably it. Kristen is a good worker," she added. "Maybe she had a hot date last night and overslept this morning."

"Lucky Kristen," Fern muttered.

"Yeah," Josie agreed.

"But if she's in the middle of a hot romance, she's sure keeping it a secret. Maybe she's fallen in love and she'll get married! That would be something new, wouldn't it?"

"What do you mean?" Josie asked, folding the faxes and sticking them in the back pocket of her overalls.

"Well, I was thinking about it last night. We're all single. And we all date men—I mean, I don't think anyone is gay. So I was wondering if women carpenters just weren't considered marriage material for some reason or another."

"Lots of women who've worked for Island Contracting in the past were married. And I know that Betty could have her pick of dozens of men."

"Yeah, well . . ."

Josie grinned. "So who are you interested in?"

"Is it so obvious?"

"I'm so glad to see that someone else blushes." Josie chuckled, realizing she had stumbled on Fern's secret. "So who's the lucky man?" she asked again.

"It's stupid. I mean, I'm too old to have a crush on someone—"

"So who is he?"

"His name is David . . . and he's a carpenter." Fern paused. "I really feel like a fool. He works for I and R, in fact."

"Oh . . ."

"What's wrong?"

"Not David as in David Sweeney?"

"You know him!"

"Yes." Josie decided it wasn't necessary to admit to dating him—in so many words, at least.

"We just went out a few times—nothing serious. I told you this was merely an adolescent crush—a little late. Or maybe I'm not going to have a long life, so this is my midlife crisis."

Josie was horrified. "Don't say that!"

"I'm sorry. I should reserve my black humor for other cancer patients. Why don't we get going?" Fern suggested.

"Fine." Josie glanced toward the three file cabinets in the back of the room. She had been hoping to go through the personnel records this morning, but it could wait until after work. It would give her something to do if Sam began nagging her about her slipshod ways.

"You won't say anything about this, will you?"

"You mean your feelings for David?"

"They're not really feelings. It's just a crush," she repeated.

Josie wasn't going to argue. She, too, had always thought that after thirty she'd stop having crushes. So far at least, her assumption had proven to be wrong. It was embarrassing. She could see Fern was embarrassed as well. "Time to get to work," she repeated.

Fern hurried out to the truck, and after one last pat to their lone cat, Josie followed her.

"Strange to have just one cat around, isn't it?" Fern asked as Josie put the key in the ignition.

Josie realized Fern was anxious to change the subject.

"Oh, I suspect there'll be more. But it was good of Kristen to find a home for the little calico." She paused as she pulled her truck out into the island's morning rush hour—two cars and fifteen sunburned people pedaling bikes down the middle of the wide road. "Did you ever talk about David in front of Kristen?"

"Probably. You know how we talk."

"Yeah." Josie chuckled. They worked long hours and they talked and talked. And men were the favorite topic. But since she and Sam had broken up there seemed to be less bantering in her presence.

"She may not have known who I was talking about, though. Betty and I talk about a lot of men—she's dated a lot of guys on I and R's crew, but Kristen didn't join in except to kid us about how optimistic we were."

"Yeah . . . What did she think we were being too optimistic about?"

"Finding the right man. Kristen seems pretty bitter about relationships."

"A bad one can do that to some people," Josie commented.

"Yeah . . . I guess no one knows what goes on in a marriage."

"Guess not," Josie agreed. "I certainly don't. I've never been that close to getting married."

"Really? I was . . . once."

"What happened? If you don't mind me asking," Josie added.

"I don't know. . . . Things. Life. You know how it is."

"What you were saying earlier is interesting," Josie said, determined to make this conversation pay off. "About all of us not being married. What about Al? Do you know if she's been serious about anyone?"

"She said something about the asshole she used to work for. I got the impression that her feelings about him were personal rather than professional."

"Hmm. She mentioned that they had dated." That had been Al's excuse for not offering the standard references. But what was her excuse for not filling out the standard forms? Josie wondered as they pulled up to their destination. Today she was going to get those forms completed or know the reason why.

Just as soon as she discovered what those men were unloading right in the middle of the sidewalk.

SIXTEEN

PEOPLE TRAVEL FOR many reasons: to learn, to relax, to explore. The Van Emberghs apparently saw the world as a large unenclosed shopping mall. Thus a truck had just delivered an antique chandelier that was to be hung in the foyer of their remodeled summer home. Hanging it was the decorator's problem, not Island Contracting's—although it had to be stored safely for the next few months. Josie insisted that the deliverymen take it to the closed-off kitchen. They refused until Betty appeared, clad in cutoff jeans and a skimpy batik halter. For a while it looked like the men would never leave, until, that is, they discovered that Betty had attended grade school with the truck driver's fiancée. After that revelation, they vanished in a puff of diesel exhaust.

"Men!" Betty exclaimed, walking back to the house. "Do you believe that? He would never have mentioned being engaged if I hadn't started talking about going to school here on the island."

"Men are scum," Al insisted. "Can't trust them as far as you can throw them." She flexed her muscles as if to show exactly how far that might be.

"Damn right," Kristen contributed to the conversation.

Josie and Fern contented themselves with irritated expressions on their faces. In her early twenties, Betty was almost ten years younger than anyone else on the crew. But few single women reached their third decade without collecting at least a few stories of male betrayal or deceit.

"There are days when I think we'd be better off without men," Josie muttered, getting back to work.

"Oh, that reminds me," Kristen said. "Sam Richardson called. He said he has something very interesting to tell you and could you please call him as soon as you have a moment."

"When did he call?"

"Just before you got here."

Josie was puzzled. She'd left Sam no more than an hour before. "And he didn't say why he wanted me to call?"

"Nope. I'm sorry. I should have mentioned it earlier."

"Don't worry about it. I just had breakfast with the man. How much could have happened since then?" Without waiting for an answer to her rhetorical question, she stomped off to the phone.

"Breakfast? Did she say breakfast?" Betty repeated.

"I can't believe it! She didn't say a word to me at the office," Fern cried. "Do you think this means they're back together?"

"She didn't seem all that positive about the opposite sex," Kristen said, picking up her hammer.

"So who the hell is?" Al commented, following the rest of the crew back into the house.

Josie, meanwhile, had found the phone. Sam answered on the first ring. "Hi. It's me. Josie."

"Well, it took you long enough."

"I just this second got your message!" Josie cried, indignant.

"I'm sorry. It's just that Basil was waiting for me at the store this morning and he told me a very interesting story. It seems he was doing some early-morning fishing and he ran into one of the men from Innovations and Renovations. And guess what."

"What?"

"When Amy came to the island she was a blonde."

"So?"

"That doesn't strike you as interesting? Think, Josie."

"It doesn't strike me as the least bit interesting. Why should it?"

"Because she dyed her hair to match yours! She was trying to look like you!"

"Sam, if I had said that, you'd have gone nuts. You're always telling me that I'm jumping to conclusions. What do you think you're doing?"

"Why else would she dye her hair red?"

"I can think of lots of reasons. Because she liked red hair. Because she heard you liked red hair and she was hoping you'd ask her out."

"That's only two reasons. And I really can't believe the second one could possibly be true."

"Sam . . ."

"Josie, she didn't just dye her hair red, she dyed it the exact same color as your hair. Now, what are the odds of that being an accident?"

"I don't know."

"Unless your hair is Clairol's most popular color."

"Sam! My hair is completely natural!" She reached up into the tangled mass. Perhaps a bit too natural . . .

"Well, I don't know about that, remember," Sam said with a scowl that was audible across the phone lines. "You're telling me you think she just happened on your exact color?"

"It's just possible you can buy dye the color of my hair," Josie said. "Besides, why would anyone want to copy my hair color?"

"That's a very good question. A very good question."

"And do you have a very good answer?"

"I just hope it's not the answer I'm thinking of. Josie, promise me one thing."

She knew what was coming. "What?"

"Promise me you'll be careful."

Well, at least he cared. Not enough to accept all her decisions, but . . . Time to think about something other than their defunct relationship. "Where did you pick up Amy when you were dating?"

"Where? At her home, of course. We didn't try to hide our relationship, if that's what you're thinking."

"I was just wondering if she'd found a place to live. The island can be difficult during the season."

"You want her address. She lived at eleven-forty-five Twelfth Avenue. Three blocks in from the beach. Second floor. Why?"

"I was just curious about whether or not she was living on the island," Josie repeated.

"The police were there when I drove by this morning."

So he had been thinking of checking out the apartment, too! "Are we still on for tonight?" was all she asked.

"Sure are. How late do you want to meet?"

"We're starting to frame in the second floor. Why don't I give you a call when it looks like we're wrapping up here?"

"Super."

But Josie had something she wanted to do after work that evening. And she wasn't going to call Sam until it was done. Instead of phoning him at the end of the day, she headed for a small shopping center near the bay at the less wealthy end of the island.

The shopping center was used mainly by full-time residents. It contained a small convenience store that sold hoagies and prepared salads; a shop aimed at the island's teenagers, well stocked with audiotapes, CDs, T-shirts, posters, and comic books; a small florist's shop; a newsstand; and a tattoo parlor. This last was Josie's goal. She parked her truck in one of the spaces out front and glanced around quickly. Then she smiled at herself. Why was she so embarrassed about going into a tattoo parlor? To judge by the bodies on the beach these days, over half of the people under twenty-one seemed to have chosen to permanently adorn their body in some way. It was chic . . . it was nineties . . . it was—Josie opened the door, entered the shop, and gasped—it was done by this huge ugly man?

"Whaddaya want, lady?"

"I just . . ." The walls were covered with tattoo patterns. "Are these the designs you do?" she asked quickly, moving over to a naked lady with an improbably large chest—and then moving just as quickly away.

"We do everything. Whaddaya want?" he repeated.

Before she could answer, an elegant hand pushed aside the cloth curtain covering the doorway to the back of the shop and a good-looking, well-groomed young Oriental man with glasses appeared. "She's not a crusty old sailor, George. There's no need to act like that." He smiled and greeted Josie. "I must apologize for George. He's a product of the days when people got tattoos to prove their manhood."

"And why do they get them now?" she asked politely.

"Decoration. To make a statement—a fashion statement usually."

Josie glanced at another naked woman posed on the wall.

"Some fashion statements are more tasteful than others," the young man conceded. "Maybe you'd just like to look around for a while?"

"Yes. That would be great."

"Then we'll leave you alone. Just call us if you need anything. And if you're interested in getting a tattoo . . ."

"I'm not sure."

"Well, you should just know that we can do any design at all."

"We?"

"Me, actually. I'm well qualified. I graduated from the Rhode Island School of Design last year." He noticed Josie's glance at George, who had kept himself busy during their conversation by picking at a pimple on his hairy shoulder. "George just hangs around for color," he added. "Come on, George."

Josie wandered around, looking at the walls, feeling foolish. All she had to do was push aside the curtain, walk to the back of the shop, and explain her problem. So why didn't she?

She took a deep breath, glanced around once more—and noticed Al Snapp on the sidewalk outside.

Damn, the last person in the world Josie wanted to see right now. She ripped aside the curtain and entered the back room of the shop.

When she left, fifteen minutes later, Al Snapp was nowhere in sight. Josie dashed home to feed Urchin, change her clothes, and give Sam a call. Maybe by the time she'd done all that and driven back to the office, her blushes would have faded.

SEVENTEEN

"YOU'RE NOT TELLING me this is normal—you don't get this many faxes every day." Sam stared down at the pile on the floor. The cat, of course, was asleep in the middle of it.

"Not every day—every few hours. I picked up a dozen or so this morning. Then Kristen stopped by at lunchtime and she brought back at least that many. And you can see for yourself what's here now. I keep wondering if these people ever sleep."

"Apparently not at the regular time." Sam glanced at his watch. "It's past midnight in Italy right now."

"Greece," Josie corrected him.

"What?"

"They're in Greece now. Is it in the same time zone as Italy?"

"I haven't the foggiest." Sam picked up the cat, glanced through the top two sheets, and then replaced the animal. "So let's get to work."

"Where do you want to begin?"

"With the personnel files, I think." He headed across the room to the computer.

"They're in the file cabinet."

"I thought . . ."

"I said I'd enter all the information into the computer when I had a chance and I haven't had one." Why was she becoming so defensive? It was her business and she was running it to the best of her ability. She didn't have to answer to anyone.

Sam contented himself with a sigh and began to sort through the file drawer. "Alphabetical order, right?"

Josie scowled. "What sort of disorganized person do you think I am?"

"I'm not touching that one with a ten-foot pole."

Sam had his hands fulls of files, so Josie resisted hitting him. She didn't want all those papers mixed together on the floor now, did she? "What exactly are you looking for?"

"I thought we might start with your newest employee—Alma Snapp."

"She's been too busy to fill them out yet. But she did

answer a couple of questions I needed for my insurance carrier—I insisted on that," Josie added, feeling very professional.

"And is she all that busy?" Sam asked.

Josie frowned. "Do you think she's just been looking for an excuse not to fill them out?"

"Isn't that possible?"

Josie tugged at her hair as she considered the question. "Not really," she said finally. "If there's something she's trying to hide, she could just lie, couldn't she?"

Sam thought for a moment. "She'd probably expect you to check out what she put down—most people would."

"I—"

"Josie, I'm not here to criticize the way you run your business." Sam put his hand on her arm. "It's not my way; you're more than a little, uh, casual for me. But I give you a lot of credit. You've kept Island Contracting going. And getting this new job was a real accomplishment. I just need to know how you'd normally handle this type of thing."

"It's simple. New employees fill out the forms—they're the same ones Noel used. I use that information to fill out all the OSHA forms, the social-security forms, the insurance forms, and then I send everything to the appropriate person in the appropriate office. And that's that."

"What about references?" Sam was still going through the papers. "Did you call all these people that"—he paused to find the name at the head of the application—"Kristen listed here, for instance?"

"No. I felt a little embarrassed about doing that—and I knew that Noel didn't even ask me for references when he hired me," she added quickly, assuming Sam might think this was rather lackadaisical on her part.

"Well, then we know where to start."

"You mean you want to call all the names that were given for references?" Josie glanced at her watch. The crystal had been cracked recently and it was difficult to read. "It's almost eight-thirty. Not many people will be at their offices this late."

"So we'll call the personal references first. We can leave messages at the other places. We can give my number at the store instead of here and I'll take the return calls there."

Josie thought for a moment. "Okay. Fine. I'll go get the cellular from the truck and we can call at the same time. Give me Kristen's folder."

Sam tossed her a manila envelope. "Great. But the first call I'm going to make is to the pizza parlor. I'm starved."

"Get a couple cans of Mountain Dew for me," Josie added, reading through Kristen's file. "Here is where Kristen doesn't admit to having been married. She marked single."

"Hmm. And she did have the option of checking divorced or separated—if the divorce hadn't actually gone through when she arrived here. Kind of a strange thing to lie about, don't you think?" He reached for the phone.

"Maybe she just didn't want a lot of questions about her past," Josie said. There had been a time in her life when she had felt the same way—and there were still things she didn't want to discuss, as Sam knew well.

Apparently he was thinking the same thing. "Yeah. Well," was his only comment before placing an order for a large pepperoni-and-mushroom pizza with extra garlic.

Josie, listening, smiled in spite of herself. There were some things they could still agree on.

". . . and two cans of Mountain Dew and a bottle of Pellegrino."

She frowned. And some things they were never going to agree about. She headed out to her truck for the phone.

It took two hours, the entire pizza, the soda, bottled water, and a bag of baked (not fried!) salt-free potato chips (Josie assumed the only reason people bought them was that real cardboard was unavailable) before they finished making the calls. They'd worked independently. Now it was time to compare notes.

"So what did you find out from Kristen's references?" Sam asked, raising his arms over his head and stretching.

Josie resisted the warm feelings that his ruffled hair and tired eyes were producing. She paused, trying to put her thoughts and the notes she'd taken down in some sort of order before she told him the story. She had spoken with both the personal references Kristen had listed as well as the last employer of her and her ex-husband. He had been working late, going over some paperwork, and was happy to give Josie the information she requested—as well as exchange views about the humongous amount of paperwork it took to run a contracting business these days.

It hadn't been like that fourteen years ago when Kristen and David first came to work for him. They'd met on the job, in fact. Their courtship, as he explained it, had taken place between the two-by-fours of a new split-level. Their engagement was spent remodeling an old abandoned elementary school. That was a long project, and by the time sixteen smelly classrooms had been turned into seven luxury condominiums, David and Kristen were honeymooning in Bermuda. Their son had been born less than a year later.

He was dead before his eleventh birthday. Some sort of sports accident, Josie had been told. The marriage survived the death by less than a year. The man Josie spoke with was surprised to hear that David and Kristen were living on the same island. His comment had interested Josie. He said he'd been under the impression that each found the other's presence acutely painful. Other than assuring Josie of what she already knew—that Kristen was an excellent carpenter—he didn't offer anything new.

Kristen had listed her ex-landlady and her next-door neighbors at the apartment she'd rented for two years as personal references. All of them agreed that she was everything a Girl Scout should be—polite, honest, quiet, good. None of them seemed to know her very well.

"You know, her son's death might explain why Kristen wanted everyone to think she'd never been married," Sam suggested when Josie finished relating her story.

"Because if she had to explain her divorce, she would have ended up mentioning his death," Josie said, nodding. "I thought of that, too." Of course, what she'd thought about the most was how she'd feel if she lost Tyler, a possibility she couldn't bear to consider. "So what did you find out about Fern?" she asked quickly, needing the distraction.

"Fern is one amazing young woman," Sam began.

"That she is," Josie agreed. "And an extraordinary electrician, too."

"Her last boss, whom I was unlucky enough to catch at the office, seems to have been one of the world's worst bastards," Sam surprised her by continuing. "He hired her because, as he put it, she 'was cute and some dyke bitch was threatening to sue him for discriminatory hiring practices.' "

"He didn't really say that."

"He did. And it gets worse. The bastard fired Fern immediately after being told she had cancer."

"Mean son-of-a-bitch."

"First class. I felt like slamming down the phone, finding the bastard, and beating the crap out of him."

Josie had a hard time not smiling. This wasn't like Sam at all. It was, she thought, an improvement on his usual calm lawyerly demeanor. "So much for professional references. Did you learn anything from her other references?"

"Quite a bit. Partially by default."

"Huh?"

"Well, Fern listed three personal references instead of

two. The first . . ." He shook his head. "Why don't I tell you about her second."

Josie had no idea what he was talking about. "Fine."

"Okay, her second reference was a macrobiotic cooking teacher and dietician. Apparently Fern started attending her classes hoping that a macrobiotic diet would improve her health. The diet part wasn't a success—Fern's fondness for french fries is apparently akin to heroin addiction, but she and this woman did become close friends. So, naturally, she had only good to say about Fern."

Josie suspected some of her friends might be less generous if asked about her. "What about the third reference?"

"That was a rather strange conversation—and a serious misjudgment on Fern's part."

"What do you mean?"

"The third reference apparently hated her."

"You're kidding."

"I'm exaggerating, yes."

"So tell me about it! Who was this person?"

"Fern's ex-roommate. A woman named Miriam. They shared a rental house for over two years—until Miriam moved in with her boyfriend." Sam chuckled. "She didn't have anything good to say about him either."

"But what did she say about Fern?"

"Well, she started by referring to her as 'that bitch.' "

"What? I've never known anyone less bitchy, less—"

"Do you want to hear this or would you prefer to emote for a while longer?"

Josie remembered how irritating Sam could be. "Tell me," she said tersely.

"It took a while to get to the crux of the problem. Miriam seemed to enjoy having a captive audience to hear about how badly life had treated her. She insisted on a recital of the low points of an exceedingly dull and self-centered life before she would tell me anything about Fern."

"That must be when you ate the last piece of pizza," Josie said.

"After that she mainly wanted to complain."

"What exactly did she complain about when she was talking about Fern?"

"She seems to feel like that man who gives the famous soliloquy in *The Matchmaker*."

"Do go on," she said sarcastically. "You know how I love literary references."

"The point of the soliloquy is that unless you have one fault, you're in danger of turning your virtues into faults—which is what Miriam apparently thought. According to her, Fern is too sweet, too kind, too cute, too neat, too"—he paused to look down at his notes—"smart, too happy, too polite, too pretty—"

"I get the idea."

"Living with all these virtues was a bit much for our Miriam—it brought out a lot of insecurities. Anyway, she had nothing good to say about Fern—a fact which I find interesting, of course."

"Why of course? This Miriam is probably awful. That's all there is to it."

"What I find interesting is that Fern put her down as a reference. It's the type of thing a person would do if they didn't want to get the job—or didn't' expect anyone to check their references."

That thought was a new one for Josie. "You don't have any reason to think that's true, do you?"

"I have no idea. What was Fern doing before working for Island Contracting? There's almost a year between the time she left her last job and when she started to work for you."

"You're kidding. Are you sure?"

"Unless she got her dates confused," Sam answered. "People do, of course, write down 1996 for 1997 or whatever."

"But if she wrote it all down correctly—" Josie stopped, unable to decide what it might mean.

"Who knows? It's certainly something to think about, though." He stopped and made a note on the paper he was reading.

"You said something about another reference," Josie reminded him.

"That's the strangest thing of all. I have no idea what to make of it. The other reference was the minister of the church she grew up in—which she still attends when she is home visiting her family."

"Please don't tell me that he thinks she's an agent of Satan or something."

"Not a chance."

"A saint?"

"No. He thinks she's a charming young woman. Very good to her aging father—"

"And her mother?" Josie interrupted.

"Died almost six years ago. But Fern *is* good to her father—who is also an electrician."

"She's mentioned that. And he didn't like the fact that she wanted to follow in his footsteps to begin with—according to Fern," Josie amended.

"That's the story the minister told me, too. Apparently it was quite the talk of the town. The high school had never had a girl who insisted on taking vocational classes. Especially a girl whose father was a part-time teacher in the program and didn't think her choice of career was appropriate. Apparently there was quite a to-do over it, according to the local paper." Sam chuckled. "Fern's mother supported her daughter's decision. I got the impression that the minister found the entire event amusing."

Josie smiled. "Must have been interesting. And not surprising when you think about it. Fern is a very determined woman—that's probably one of the reasons she's dealt with her cancer so well. Did that come up while you were talking with the minister?"

"That's what's so strange. You see, he didn't know about the cancer."

"Not at all?"

"Nothing. At first I thought he might just be avoiding mentioning it—because Fern had given his name to a possible employer and he didn't want to decrease her chance of getting the job. So I came right out and asked about it—and he was shocked."

"What did you say, for heaven's sake?"

"I merely asked him if he thought she had handled her cancer well—or something like that—just to bring up the subject. And he thought I was nuts. I had to convince him that I knew what I was talking about. And it was obvious that I'd shocked and worried him."

"Why worried?"

"Fern's mother died from cancer. When he spent some time thinking about it, he decided that perhaps Fern was trying to spare her father by not telling him about her disease."

"Makes sense to me."

Sam shook his head. "It doesn't to me. Of course, you know Fern and I don't, but would she hide something like this from her family? Could she hide it for any length of time?"

"Why not? To protect someone she loves? It's not as though she still lived with her family after all."

"Well, maybe," Sam said, but he sounded doubtful.

EIGHTEEN

JOSIE LIVED LESS than a mile from her office and tonight, exhausted, that seemed like a long commute. She had left Sam making out lists of questions, things he felt it was important to discover about Island Contracting's current employees. As full of questions as he was, Josie wondered why they weren't asking about Amy Llewellyn first—and if Sam's choice had anything to do with his feelings. It was the sort of question Josie could have tossed and turned and worried to death all night long.

If it hadn't been for the satanic symbol left just outside her apartment door. . . . Josie knelt down and examined it carefully. It was identical to the small construction she'd found in the pool house; she was sure of it. Wondering what to do, thinking perhaps she should call Sam, she heard footsteps coming up the stairs behind her. Josie turned quickly and, losing her balance, stepped right in the middle of the design. The fragile twigs were crushed beneath her work boot.

"Damn!" She stepped back right into the curvaceous form of her landlady.

Risa pulled the layers of gray and lavender silk that served as a bathrobe closer to her shoulders. "Another of those silly piles of twigs and feathers, *cara*? Ignore the mess. I will sweep tomorrow. Tell me about your date with Sam."

"It wasn't a date." Josie knew the words were futile before she got them out of her mouth. Risa had a romantic, optimistic nature—she preserved it by not allowing little things like the truth to spoil her fantasy life.

"*Cara,* Sam Richardson is a handsome single man who once again has come to help you in your distress. He loves you. What else could he mean?"

Josie frowned at the ground. How much should she tell Risa about what was happening?

"And stop worrying about those twiggy things. I sweep them up in the morning. They are nothing. I already cleaned one off the front porch and also one in front of my door."

Josie grabbed for Risa's arm and came up with a

handful of silk. "You've seen more of these things? When? Today?"

"Yes, I tell you."

Josie was now fully awake. "Tell me everything. Where? When? How many?"

"*Cara,* you sound like those foolish men on television."

"Risa, please. It's important."

An elegant shrug caused a thin band of dark lavender to slip from Risa's shoulder. "*Si.* Let me think, *cara.* I fell over one of these little designs early this morning—about ten, I think."

Josie couldn't resist smiling at her landlady's concept of early. "Where was it?"

"They were by the front door."

"There were two of these things?"

"Three . . . nicely spaced. Neat."

"And what did you do with them?"

"Swept them away. What else would I do?"

"Do you recognize the design?" Josie asked. She didn't want to mention the TV show about satanic cults. Things were difficult enough without Risa emoting all over the place.

"I think, *cara,* I have seen similar on jewelry—maybe necklaces. Very attractive, I think."

Josie thought of the heavy metal ornaments hanging around the necks of less-than-clean teenagers with dyed black hair arranged into spikes.

"Do you want to know about the ones I found behind the house?"

"There were more?"

"Two more. One at each corner of the building."

"The same design?" She knew Risa, with her interest in fashion and her aesthetic nature, would be able to answer the question accurately.

"Not exactly. This one was thick, not flat. With points . . . what are those things that American Indians shoot?"

"Arrows?"

"Ah, arrows. There were arrows that go up into the air. Pointed toward your apartment, you know."

"Yeah, I know," Josie muttered, exhaustion beginning to dull her worry. Someone was putting a satanic curse on her. Maybe Amy Llewellyn had been right. Maybe someone did want to kill her. And maybe that someone, after killing Amy Llewellyn, was now planning to kill her.

"Risa, could I—" Josie stopped herself from asking to spend the night in her landlady's apartment. It wasn't much safer than her own and the thought of the emotional Risa in the middle of a real crisis was too much to bear. There was always the office, but that wouldn't be much safer. . . . Josie pursed her lips. There was only one place where she would feel completely safe. She took a deep breath. "Risa, I'm going to go spend the night with Sam. . . ."

Someone did want to kill her. She was suddenly being smothered by yards of filmy cloth and the overwhelming scent of musk.

"*Cara!* My joy! You do not tell me. I stand here and keep you from your ablutions."

"I have to leave right away."

"But you must shower . . . wash your hair."

Josie thought quickly. "I'm going to do it there. Sam is waiting for me."

"Go. Fly. Go to the man you love."

With one last glance at the crushed twigs on the floor, Josie flew as fast as her sputtering truck would take her. It was late and it was dark and by the time she arrived at Sam's house, she was sweating and panicked. She jumped out of her truck, ran up the sidewalk, and banged loudly on the door.

Sam had moved to the island last summer. Busy during the season with the liquor store he owned, he had spent much of the winter months remodeling the fifties ranch house he had bought. This summer he and Josie had planned on expanding the small porch at the back of the home into a wraparound deck. Josie wasn't so panicked that she didn't remember their last argument on the subject.

Sam had insisted that a deck with rounded corners would complement the low lines of his home. Josie had disagreed. But Sam had stubbornly—and wrongly—continued the project his way, she realized, smacking her shins against a wooden post sticking up by the front door. "Damn!"

"Who's there?" The question was accompanied by the sudden illumination of porch lights.

"Sam. It's me. Josie."

"Josie, what the hell—goddamn it!"

Apparently the posts hadn't been in the ground very long. Or, at least, not long enough for Sam to learn to avoid crashing into them himself. Of course, if he had chosen the design she had suggested . . .

"Josie, what are you doing here?"

She glanced over her shoulder into the darkness. "Let's go inside and I'll explain."

Sam hesitated and Josie realized what had happened. "Ah, shit. Someone's here with you. You have another woman here."

"Yes. But, believe me, it's not what you think."

"Listen, you don't owe me any explanations." She started to back away from the door.

"It's not what you think," he repeated. "It's my mother."

"Your mo—" He'd never mentioned a mother to her!

"Sammy, sweetie, what's going on out there?" A tall woman with a gray braid falling down over one shoulder of her plush robe appeared behind Sam.

Despite her fears, Josie was thrilled. "Your mother calls you Sammy Sweetie?"

"There's a comma between the two words," he hissed at her. "Mother, go back to bed. There's a slight problem here."

"Sammy, sweetie, since when is an attractive young woman appearing on your doorstep in the middle of the night a problem? Surely I'm too young to have a son so old he sees this situation as a problem."

Josie was grinning. "I'm Josie Pigeon." She introduced herself, stepping into the light.

"Josie Pigeon! Miss Pigeon! Josie! Come right inside. I cannot tell you how much I've been wanting to meet you." The woman placed her arm around Josie's shoulder and led her into the house. "Watch out for that piece of wood sticking up there. I cannot imagine what made Sammy choose this strange shape for his new deck."

Josie flashed a grin at Sam over her shoulder and allowed his mother to lead her into the house.

"Josie was just beginning to explain why she's here so late," Sam said loudly.

"Why, Sammy, sweetie, how rude of you. It is obvious that Josie is scared to death. What's wrong, dear?" Sam's mother asked. "What can we do to help you?"

Josie took a deep breath before answering. "There are these little piles of twigs around my apartment—satanic symbols of some sort, I think."

Sam's mother gasped. "How dreadful. Absolutely dreadful! Of course, it's probably some poor foolish teenagers who think fooling around with good and evil will bring them power. There was a fascinating special about it on television just last week."

"I saw that! That's why I recognized them," Josie cried.

"Did you see—"

"Do you think—"

"Wait one second!" Sam shouted. "I don't know anything about all this, but it's almost one A.M. Josie begins work in less than five hours and, Mother, you know you'll be prowling around in the kitchen before the sun is up."

"I like to make Sammy special breakfasts when I'm here. I don't think he eats well."

"Mother, I am taking Josie to the spare room. Say

good night, Mother. If you're going to continue to embarrass me, you'll have to do it in the morning." He grabbed Josie's arm. "Come on. I'll find you some clean towels and something to sleep in."

"Good night, Josie dear. We'll chat in the morning. You can tell me what my son really has been doing with his life since he left Manhattan."

"Go to bed, Mother."

"Is he always this impatient, my dear?"

"Mother!"

"Come with me." Sam led Josie down the hall. "Mother's in the guest room, but the bed is made up in the spare room. Towels and washcloths are in the hall linen closet."

"I'll be fine, Sam. But we need to talk. This satanic . . ." She took a deep breath. "Maybe you were right. Maybe I am in danger."

"Not here. You're fine here," Sam insisted. "But tell me about these satanic things. Just don't tell Mother."

Josie explained what she had found, and by the time she was finished, she could barely keep her eyes open.

"You'll be safe here," Sam repeated. "Take your shower and we'll decide what to do about all this in the morning."

Josie did as he suggested, not so tired that she didn't appreciate the thick towels in Sam's well-appointed spare bathroom. She put on a large white T-shirt Sam had offered and fell into bed. And slept exactly two hours. Then she awoke with a start, sweating and breathing hard.

On nights like these she reassessed her life, starting with her wonderful son, moving to her struggling business, and on to personal relationships. But tonight everything was tied to the satanic symbols. What if they were a curse? Whoever had placed them at the murder site had found her house . . . and maybe Sam's house. . . . She sat up in bed, breathing deeply. What was to keep them from finding Tyler's camp? Or Tyler himself?

Sleep was impossible. Josie reached out for the bedside lamp. She'd wake up Sam—he had spoken with the camp director earlier. They could call and warn them that Tyler might be in danger. She pulled on her dirty overalls and stumbled into the dark hallway. There was a light at the end and she headed toward it.

And found Sam's mother standing by the kitchen stove, a pink bathrobe wrapped tightly around her thin, toned, athletic body. "Josie, darling, you're just in time for tea. Earl Grey, Constant Comment, or camomile? Camomile is certainly more soothing. And you're going to need your sleep if you're going to fight this evil thing."

"I woke up worried about my son."

"Of course, Tyler Clay, right? Sam has spoken about him many, many times. In fact, I had begun to think of him as my future grandson. But we won't talk about that now." She patted Josie's shoulder and passed her a cup and saucer. Steam traveled up from the pale liquid. "You are worried about the evil intent behind these designs, aren't you?"

"Yes, I'm—"

"I have a friend who may be able to help us. He studies cults—especially satanic ones. If you can just draw a picture of one of these things for me, we can find a fax machine and fax the picture to him."

"That would be great. I have a fax at the office." Josie looked around the immaculate kitchen.

"You need paper." Sam's mother began opening and closing cupboards. "Here we are." She waved a yellow legal pad in the air. "Sammy always has piles of these things around. Now you just draw the design."

"But, Mrs. Richardson . . ."

"Mrs. Greenbaum. I remarried a few times after Sammy's father died. But none of them were able to hold a candle to Sammy's father. Abel Greenbaum was the last of a line of charming, foolish men. Or perhaps I was the foolish one. Call me Carol."

It was too much for Josie, who had other things to

worry about. “But Tyler. I wanted to call his camp and check up on him.”

The phone rang as if she had cued it.

“Sammy will answer. He has an extension next to his bed. I thought his days of late-night phone calls would end when he left the city. Heavens, what is Sammy yelling about?”

“Josie! Josie. Where the hell are you?”

“We’re in the kitchen, Sammy.”

Sam appeared in the doorway, a pair of cutoff sweatpants the only thing he wore.

Josie started to smile at his suntanned, spare body, but his next words stopped her heart.

“Tyler’s missing. He’s left camp.”

NINETEEN

SHE THOUGHT HER heart would explode, her body melt into the floor, that there wasn’t enough air in the entire universe to keep her from fainting. “How? Where? It was the phone call, wasn’t it?” The three questions were all she managed to say. She stood up and, having no idea where she would go, sat down again.

“Josie . . .”

“We should call the police. The state police. The Pennsylvania State Police.”

“That’s all been done. Everything that could be done has been done,” Sam said.

“What do you mean? Tyler is gone. Kidnapped—”

“No, you don’t have to worry about that. Tyler wasn’t kidnapped. He ran away.”

"He ran away!"

"Josie, calm down. I'll tell you all about it."

She took a deep breath. "How do you know? What did they say? Who called?"

"It was the director of the camp. The same man I spoke with earlier. He called your apartment, and Risa answered and told him you were here with me. He seems to be very competent."

"He lost my son!" Josie was astounded to realize that she was screaming.

"Tyler ran away," Sam repeated patiently. "He packed his backpack full of what he considered necessities. He told his three best friends at the camp that he was leaving—after he swore them to secrecy. He told them he'd be back in just a few days and then he took off."

"Where did he say he was going?"

"He didn't, apparently."

"Sam . . ." Josie wailed her distress.

"Now, Josie, you just calm down." Mrs. Greenbaum put a restraining arm around Josie's shoulders. "Sammy is a very smart man—and that's true even if it's his mother who's saying it. But you have to let him talk.

"Now start at the beginning, Sammy."

"I got a call just now." He saw the storm breaking out over Josie's face and eliminated his introductory remarks. "Tyler has been missing for two days. The camp has been in an uproar over parents' weekend or his disappearance might have been discovered earlier. Plus, he set things up so that it wouldn't be discovered right away. His friends were protecting him. You know, someone would ask where is Tyler and one of the kids would say they had just seen him at the baseball game on field one or something like that."

"Why? Why did he leave? Why didn't someone report him missing? What's wrong with those kids?"

"Tyler didn't tell anyone where he was going, but he did tell his friends why."

"Why? Tell me!"

"He said he had a mission."

"A mission. What sort of mission? Okay, okay. I'm trying to listen," Josie said, taking a sip of tea that she did not really want. "Go ahead. Explain."

"According to the three boys—and there's no reason to believe they're not telling the truth. Apparently they're pretty scared."

"So what did they say?"

"They said that about a week ago Tyler announced that he was going to leave camp for a few days to—and this is their reporting of his words—to do something very important."

"But he didn't say what."

"One of the boys referred to it as a mission, said that's the way Tyler described it to him."

"Any idea where he was going?"

"The boys got the impression it had something to do with the wilderness-skills class that they were all taking."

"Wilderness . . ." Josie couldn't go on. She had visions of steep mountains, valleys filled with rushing water, wild animals ripping poor little Tyler limb from limb.

"Josie, the camp is not exactly in the middle of nowhere. It's only a dozen or so miles from Hershey, Pennsylvania, for heaven's sake. Tyler could be there enjoying himself on the roller coaster."

Josie saw her son lying on the ground, bent and broken, as a screaming ride flashed through the sky. On the other hand . . . "But he doesn't have any money. How could he go on the rides?"

Sam wiped his hand across his brow. "Of course, I wasn't thinking—but the point I was trying to make is still valid. I know you when it comes to Tyler. You're panicking, imagining him dead under the most awful circumstances, but he's probably just fine. He planned this trip. And you know Tyler."

She did. The kid was a real planner and his plans were usually realized. "But why? Wasn't he happy at camp? I know he wanted me to come up for parents' weekend, but he knew before he left home that might be impossible. And Tyler isn't a kid who does bad things without any reason."

"So maybe we don't have to worry so much," Sam said. "Maybe we can rely on Tyler's good sense. He'll do what he has to do and then he'll return to camp."

Josie frowned.

It matched the expression on Sam's mother's face. "I don't know, Sammy. Young boys do some pretty stupid things. I remember when you were fourteen and you—"

"Mother!"

Any other time Josie would have been thrilled to death to discover the cause of the embarrassed expression on Sam's face, but tonight she had other things on her mind. "Should we call the police?"

Sam ran his hands through his hair. "Do you have any reason to think this could be connected to Amy's murder?"

Josie, who would have sworn that her heart couldn't beat faster, discovered she had been wrong. "Why do you think that?"

"I don't. I just thought that was why you wanted to call in the island police."

"I wasn't thinking of them. I was thinking of the state police. In Pennsylvania. New Jersey. New York."

"That's been done. There is a bulletin out from southern Pennsylvania to the Catskills. But, of course, he's probably still within shouting distance of the camp. The camp director really seems to have taken care of everything. But maybe you'd feel better if you spoke with him in person. He suggested that you call him—at any time."

Josie rested her head in her hands. "No, maybe I'll call him in the morning."

"It almost *is* morning. The sun is just starting to come up," Mrs. Greenbaum said, glancing toward the window.

"You need to sleep," Sam said quietly.

"I can't sleep."

"No, of course you can't," his mother agreed with Josie.

"I think I'll go for a walk. On the beach . . ." Josie looked yearningly toward the stretch of sand outside Sam's house.

"I'll go with you," Sam announced.

"I'd like to be alone."

"I won't say a word. I promise."

"Go. I'll stay here in case there's another phone call," his mother said, almost shooing them toward the doorway.

"The bell by the back door—you can ring it if you need to get us back. We'll hear it on the beach," Sam told his mother.

"So will everyone else on this end of the island," Josie reminded him.

"It's an emergency. They'll live. Let's go," Sam insisted, opening the kitchen door for Josie to precede him into the dark. "Watch out for the posts there."

Josie was so distracted she didn't even seize the opportunity to criticize his remodeling. She hurried out the door and down the path through the dunes to the beach.

She wasn't nuts about Sam's house, but its location was wonderful. The houses at this end of the island were farther apart, separated by sand dunes and the white sandy beach, wide even at high tide.

The rising sun created a luminous line where the ocean met the sky and Josie kicked off her shoes and headed toward the water. Sam followed by her side.

"Are you sure you haven't left out anything that damn camp director told you?" she demanded, ignoring her earlier claim to have no desire to talk.

"No. He really doesn't seem to know anything and he didn't get a lot of information out of Tyler's three friends."

"Sam, do you think it would help if I talked with those kids? I'm Tyler's mother. Maybe they would tell me things they might not tell the camp director."

"It wouldn't hurt to try. No one is going to want to wake them up in the middle of the night, but you could call first thing in the morning."

"Good. I'll do that." There was a pause and then she continued. "You know what bothers me the most?"

"No, what?"

"I should have listened when he said he wasn't happy. Risa warned me."

"Josie, you know Tyler better than anyone. Isn't it just possible that this 'mission' he spoke of was simply a way to get away from something he didn't like at camp?"

"Of course, but maybe he was mad at me over parents' weekend."

"I understand he made you something."

"Yes, I don't know what, but he did say he had made me a present."

"Does that sound like something he'd have done if he was angry with you?"

"You think I'm foolish to be worried about him?"

"No, I think you're smart to worry. Tyler is fourteen and one of the brightest and most resourceful boys I've ever met. But that doesn't mean that fourteen-year-olds don't overestimate their abilities and do incredibly foolish things. I think the sooner he's found the better."

"Oh, Sam . . ." Josie found herself in his arms.

"But he's special, Josie. Let's just hope that he can take care of himself as well as he thinks he can."

Josie looked up at him. "What are you thinking?" she asked when he didn't continue.

"I was just wondering what he was learning in that wilderness-skills class. Maybe if we found out what sort of stuff he was doing, we'd get a clue to where he's gone."

"Yeah, you mean like if he was learning to make rafts to ford streams, then he might have headed for water."

"Exactly. Let's go back home and give that camp director a call. Maybe there's something else to find out."

They ran back up the beach to Sam's house, stopping

only to grab the shoes they'd left at the dunes' edge. Josie was panting hard as she followed Sam through his back door.

"I'll call, shall I?" he asked.

Completely out of breath, Josie merely nodded.

"I knew you'd come back soon," his mother said, greeting them, a large steaming cup in her hand. "I didn't think there'd be time for dough to rise before you had to start your day, so I mixed up some quick raisin-orange muffins. Who are you calling at this hour?" she asked her son.

"The director of Tyler's camp. We had an idea," Josie managed to get enough breath back to explain.

"You know, I have a feeling about this," Sam's mother said quietly, turning back to check on the oven. "I've been thinking about what Sam has told me about Tyler Clay—how inventive and smart he is and all—and I have a feeling that he has a plan. And you know how males are—they love to brag about their plans."

Well, that was a thought. "There are his friends."

"But would he have bragged to them? I mean . . . he is fourteen."

Josie wasn't getting the point. "What do you mean?"

"Is this camp coed?"

"No . . . but there is a girls' camp across the water."

"There's always a girls' camp across the water," Sam's mother said, nodding. "And I suppose the camps do get together for official functions, dances. . . ."

"Yes."

"And maybe he's mentioned a girl in his letters home."

"Postcards," Josie muttered. "Tyler only writes postcards."

"And has he mentioned one particular girl?"

"You're right!" Josie grabbed Sam's arm. "Sam, your mother has an idea. She thinks Tyler may have a crush on one of the girls at Camp Sacagawea and he might have bragged to her about his plan."

Sam put his hand over the mouthpiece. "Do you

remember her name? This man is more than willing to check out any leads."

"Katie. Katie Kompir." How could she possibly forget the name that just two weeks ago had given her a twinge or two of jealousy?

TWENTY

SHE HAD TO work. She had to work to support her son. There was nothing more she could do today except wait. Katie Kompir was going to be questioned and any and all information she offered would be immediately relayed to Sam, who'd pass it along to Josie. There was nothing, nothing to be gained by not working.

So why was she sitting here doing nothing?

Sam had insisted she get on the phone with the camp director, who assured her that he would discover what Tyler had been studying in his wilderness-skills class, question Tyler's friends again, find Katie Kompir, and question her himself. Sam's mother had insisted she eat a muffin with her coffee before she started her workday; then she bagged up the rest of the batch and sent Josie on her way with them. Josie told her crew what was going on, listened to their cries of concern, assured them they could do nothing to help. There really was nothing to do but work and wait. But only the waiting seemed to have any appeal.

"Do you want some company?" Fern stuck her head in the doorway of the space that was to be the master bedroom.

She didn't know. Was company what she needed?

"Just tell me to get out if you want. I understand that sometimes being alone is the only way to handle a crisis." Fern smiled gently.

Josie recalled that hers wasn't the only tragedy in life. "You've had a lot of practice, I guess."

"More than most people and less than some—God, I sound like a character in some historical romance novel, don't I? Stop me before it becomes a bad habit. Please."

"You do stay cheerful despite what happens in your life, don't you?"

Fern frowned. "Not really. When I first discovered I had cancer, I ran around and wept on every shoulder I could find. But, of course, people get tired of that. So I went to the other extreme and became so brave that no one could offer a helping hand."

"And now?" Josie asked, thinking about the secret Fern kept from her father.

"And now . . ." Fern sighed. "You know, you can get used to anything. Not that I think you're going to have the time to get used to Tyler being gone. He could be found right now and Sam's on his way over here with the good news."

"I can't tell you how much I hope you're right."

"Me, too." Fern paused.

"Is there something else you wanted?" Josie asked.

"I was wondering if you would help me figure out one of the blueprints. I thought I knew where the high hats in the bathroom ceiling were to go, but now I'm not so sure."

"Because the plans have been changed so many times," Josie said, standing up. "Most people have to actually be present to mess with our work, but the Van Emberghs are damn good at long-distance interference. Which reminds me, I forgot to check the fax machine at the office on the way here this morning."

"Maybe there aren't any faxes."

"There are always faxes," Josie said. "I'll just hop over there during lunch. I keep thinking that they'll want a change that requires tearing down everything we've done and starting over."

"But that's not a crisis, is it? I mean, they have to pay for the changes they make, right?"

"Yes, but . . ." Josie reminded herself that she was keeping the bonus a secret.

"But it will be easier if they stick to their original plans," Fern finished for her.

"Definitely."

"I can bring the blueprints in here," Fern offered.

"No, I'll come out there. Sitting and sulking isn't doing Tyler any good at all. And it will be easier to show you what we need to do with the mirror than to describe it."

"What mirror?"

"The one that once hung in a palazzo in Italy and is now going to hang over the whirlpool in the master bath upstairs. It needs to be lit from a different angle, which is why we've changed the location of the high hats in the ceiling."

"Are the bulbs going to have deflectors on them?"

"I hadn't thought about it, but that's a good idea. A very good idea, in fact. Let me show you exactly where the mirror's going to hang and you can figure out how to rearrange the cans."

Josie was pleased to discover her crew hard at work. Al was sweating profusely on the roof as she and Betty tried to fit a balky new skylight. "Hey, when you get a chance, I really need you to fill out those employment forms," Josie reminded her.

"Yeah, well I'm pretty busy now . . . have my arms full," Al joked, glancing down at the two-foot-tall skylight cradled in her muscular tattooed arms.

"We can do it at lunchtime. I need to go back to the office to pick up faxes anyway," Josie said, wondering if Al's tattoos moved when she flexed her biceps—or were men the only sex with body art like that? Why, in heaven's name, was she thinking about that now? "Unless—"

"Unless there's some word about Tyler," Betty finished the sentence for Josie. "You'll hear. Don't worry. Tyler is the most self-sufficient kid around—and you know it. Remember when he decided the island should include children in the 'run the island' marathon on Labor Day? He had every kid on the island collecting names on petitions within a week. And remember when the old Boy Scout leader had a heart attack and Tyler personally hounded all the eligible candidates for the job until two men volunteered to take over the troop—"

"And ever since then, they've both been claiming that a troop with Tyler in it was the reason for the old scout leader's heart attack in the first place," Josie reminded them.

"Look, just because Tyler decided to build a tepee—"

"I don't think it was the tepee anyone minded, it was the beef jerky he tried to smoke in it," Josie explained.

"He burned it down?" Kristen asked.

"No. Tyler is very careful and he knew he'd be in serious trouble if he was careless with fire, so he only smoked the jerky when there was an adult around for supervision."

"So what was the problem?" Al asked, resting the skylight against the wall so she could listen.

"Leaving the meat hanging there without a fire going was an open invitation to every flying bug on the island—and many of them were in the tent when the scout leader opened it early the morning after the meeting. The poor man has allergies and was covered with welts for weeks—despite the antihistamines and steroids they pumped into him at the emergency room."

Betty chuckled. "And remember how Tyler organized the boycott of—"

The phone's shrill ring interrupted the story. Everyone in the room froze and Josie, if she had been capable of rational thought, would have realized that her entire crew had been almost as worried about her son as she was. The seconds it took to answer the phone felt like an hour.

"Hello?" She closed her eyes and prayed.

And her prayer was answered. "Sam . . . Yes . . . What did he say? She did? You're sure? Why does she think that? You're sure? Positive? Well, it makes sense. . . . You're right. You're right. It sure does sound like Tyler. Then . . . Well, if you're sure. Okay. And you'll call me if you hear anything else? Okay. Bye." She hung up the phone and turned back to the room only to discover that everyone was staring at her.

"Are you going to tell us what that call was about or—" Betty began.

"Tell us right now!" Fern ordered.

"It was Sam," Josie began.

"Tell us something we don't know." Kristen was so upset that her face was flushed scarlet.

"The man that runs the camp talked with the girl Tyler has a crush on."

"What girl? Who is this?" Betty cried.

Josie explained Sam's mother's theory that Tyler was of an age to go brag to a girl about his plans when he left camp.

"Good thinking," Betty muttered, nodding her approval. "Men are like that."

Josie was surprised to feel a pang in her heart—Tyler involved with a female other than herself? Was she jealous of a fourteen-year-old girl? Was it the stupidest thing in the world to be jealous of a fourteen-year-old gi—

"Josie, what the hell did Sam say?" Betty, who had known her the longest, cried.

"The camp director talked with this girl that apparently everyone at camp knows Tyler has a crush on—"

"And she said?" Betty urged the conversation forward.

"She seems to think Tyler is still in the camp somewhere."

"What?" all four women asked in unison.

"It has to do with what they were studying in Tyler's

wilderness-skills class—something called 'covert approach tactics.' "

"Sounds military," Betty suggested.

"The counselor who gives those classes is a retired army officer, in fact. And apparently Tyler was fascinated with the idea of living undetected right under the enemy's nose. In this case, the enemy is the people at the camp," she added before anyone could ask. "Although Tyler was actually having a good time at camp. At least that's what the director claimed." But what else would the man say? she asked herself.

"But the point is to hide right under their noses—enemy or not," Fern said.

"Exactly," Josie agreed.

"You know that sounds like something that would appeal to Tyler," Betty said.

"It does, doesn't it?"

"And it makes sense," Kristen added. "After all, wilderness skills won't get anyone very far in urban areas and that camp seems to be the closest thing to wilderness Tyler is going to get this summer."

"And you said he didn't have any money, so how could he get away from there?" Al added.

"So what happens now?" Betty asked.

"The official line is that they're going to search the camp, but the director thinks there's another possibility," Josie added reluctantly.

"What?"

"That Tyler is lurking around the girls' camp."

Screams met that suggestion.

"Sam says it's possible, but it doesn't sound like Tyler," she protested.

"The mother is always the last to know," Betty crowed.

"And you know—"

"You said he was fourteen, didn't you? I remember when I was fourteen," Al said.

"So are they going to search the girls' camp, too, or what?"

"They're going to organize some sort of search of both camps," Josie explained, the relief everyone was feeling adding to her own ease. "And then they're going to call Sam back. So I guess there's nothing we can do again but wait."

"Sounds to me like there are no more excuses not to get back to work, then," Kristen said. "There's nothing we can do but wait, and time passes more quickly when you're busy."

"You sound like my mother," Al said.

"I'm no one's mother."

If anyone else noticed the sharpness of Kristen's reply, they didn't say anything, but Josie remembered what she had learned last night about Kristen's son. Why would a mother deny the very existence of a child she had lost? If Tyler died, she knew she would want to remember his life, not pretend he had never lived.

She shook her head so hard that her hair crackled. This was no time to think about tragedies. It was time, as Kristen had said, to get back to work. "Okay. Do you think you know where to put those light fixtures now?" she asked Fern.

"Yeah."

"Then I think we'd better get going on the knee wall in the master bedroom."

"What is it going to be faced with?"

"Beaded wainscoting on the far side. Wallboard on the window side," Josie said, heading back in that direction.

"What is the point of having a knee wall jut out in the middle of the room?" Fern asked.

"Puts the bed closer to the window. The Van Emberghs want a view of the sea."

"They'll be sleeping. What do they need a view for, for heaven's sake?" Al asked.

"Rich people . . . who understands them? Josie, remember the new home we worked on a few miles south of here?" Betty recounted the story to the rest of the group when her boss didn't answer. "A hurricane ripped off the entire wall that faced the sea and the owners insisted on replacing it with glass. Josie warned them that the cost would be enormous and the chances of all that glass surviving another storm were low, but they could have cared less. They wanted to see the sea, they needed to see the sea, their souls longed to see the sea. So we gave them glass from the foundation to the roof. And then their decorator covered the windows with so many swags and drapes and curly things that they could barely peek at the sand."

"As you said, rich people, who understands them?" Fern agreed with Betty's analysis.

"And who the hell wants to?" Al asked no one in particular.

TWENTY-ONE

THERE WAS A porch between the small one-room converted fishing shack that was Island Contracting's office and the street. It was tiny, with room for two Victorian rockers and not much else—except for two large picnic hampers, Josie realized, parking her truck at the curb and jumping out. Not surprisingly, the rocking chairs were occupied. Risa was in one, a fabulous black antique shawl slipping off her shoulders and draping to the floor. Sam's mother was in the other, in a fuchsia running suit with tiny pink satin flowers scattered around the jacket. The two women were talking so avidly that they didn't notice Josie's arrival.

". . . and then I throw in some oatmeal . . ."

Of course, Josie thought, listening to Sam's mother, they're exchanging recipes.

". . . and smear it over my face for half an hour—no less, mind you."

So much for lunch . . . Josie put a smile on her face and greeted her visitors. "Hi, Risa. Hi, Mrs. Greenbaum—"

"Call me Carol, honey," Sam's mother insisted. "And then take some time to appreciate this case of great minds agreeing—we both brought you lunch!"

"Well, I'm starving," Josie admitted. "I was going to stop at the deli and pick up something."

"What did I tell you?" Risa cried. "She works hard and she eats junk!"

"I—"

"Never cooks a meal for herself Sammy tells me."

"He—"

"I know there is nothing fresh in her refrigerator much of the time. And the candy-bar wrappers in her garbage! You would not believe. I think she lives on sugar!"

Josie gave up. "Excuse me, but I need to get into my office," she announced loudly. "I don't have much time for lunch and I have to check the fax machine before I eat," she added, knowing how Risa, at least, would react to that statement.

"See, what do I tell you? She is not eating enough to keep a flea alive!" As she spoke Risa leaped to her feet and pulled her floating clothes out of the way so Josie could pass to her front door unimpeded.

"Do I look undernourished?" Josie muttered, sticking her key in the lock.

"There is no reason for that. The door is no longer locked. Sammy dropped me off here and he was in your office first. He left some papers on your desk," his mother added.

"And I offered him some of my arugula salad, but his mother—"

"I had made him his lunch," Carol explained, a smile

on her face. "Just a simple cold sliced marinated flank steak with rosemary potato salad. And some sliced mangoes for dessert. He can pick out a nice wine at his shop. There was so much food—too much for just the two of us and then I thought of Josie."

"And I, too, think of Josie," Risa explained.

It was nice to be thought of. Josie opened her door and headed straight for her fax machine. The size of the pile of papers that lay on the floor beneath it no longer surprised her. After noting the personnel files Sam had left on her desk, she knelt on the floor to skim through the faxes. She had no qualms about leaving the women on the porch to themselves—she was sure they had a lot to talk about, starting with her eating habits. Risa's concern, she knew, was genuine. Sam's mother was sweet, too, but Josie wasn't all that thrilled to realize Sam had spoken with his mother about her inadequate cooking skills. And now that she thought about it, it was amazing how much Mrs. Richardson—Greenbaum—Carol, Josie corrected herself, knew about Tyler. She stared down at the paper in her hand without really seeing it.

She had always known Sam cared about Tyler. Carol herself had admitted to thinking of him as a possible grandson. Had Sam actually told his mother they were going to get married? Wasn't that just a bit presumptuous of him? Josie felt the blood rush to her cheeks. The diagram in front of her moved out of focus and then back again. . . .

"What the hell?"

"Did you say something, dear?" Carol and Risa had entered the office.

"She talks to herself, too, poor *cara*," Risa explained.

Josie was now too upset to worry about any more intrusions into her life. She shuffled through sheet after sheet of paper. Could this possibly be what she thought it was? Could it be anything else? But where the hell did they expect this to go? What would happen to the wood in the moist environment after the dry heat of Greece—it was dry heat in Greece, wasn't it? Where were the measurements? When was all this going to arrive? How was it going to arrive? What was this note on the last page? Could this possibly say *religious resort*? Were there such things as religious resorts?

"Josie!"

"She gets like this sometimes . . . poor *cara*."

"Does this look like a religious resort to you?" Josie held the paper out to the two women.

"This is smeared so much. Maybe you need a new fax machine," Carol offered, taking the paper Josie proffered.

"It *is* a new fax."

"*Si.* I thought so. I wondered when you got one of these machines." Risa was peering over Carol's shoulder at the document. "What is a religious resort, if anyone knows?"

"Maybe something medical . . . like a spa. The one I go to offers new courses in spiritual things. I, of course, stick to the aerobics," Carol offered. "What are these diagrams? A new floor plan for that house Sam says you are working on?"

"Sort of," Josie admitted.

"Isn't it a little late for you to be getting . . ." Risa paused. "What do you call them—aqua prints or . . . or something?"

"Blueprints." Josie supplied the correct term. "It's pretty late for them, yes. But these aren't blueprints."

"Blueprints are blue," Carol said, nodding solemnly.

"They're . . . never mind." What was it about these women that caused her to forget what she was about to do? "I have to get back to the house."

"She means the house Island Contracting is working on," Risa explained to Carol.

"Maybe you would like to take some lunch with you?" Carol asked.

"We will just put the baskets in the truck," Risa announced. "She will not realize how hungry she is—and maybe the other women are like that also."

"I—"

"And then we'll leave her to get to work," Risa said, walking out the door.

Josie began to speak again, but Sam's mother grabbed her arm and hissed in her ear.

"We must talk!" The words were accompanied by a shower of spit. "I know about the murder and the suspicion falling on your crew—and I have some ideas. There are some very strange things in those application forms."

"Sam showed you my forms?" Josie was outraged. This might be Sam's mother, but those forms were private! "He had no business doing that!"

"He does not know!" Carol hissed. "No one knows. But we must talk. Privately!"

Risa's return interrupted them. "I put both baskets in the back of your truck," she announced. "There is much food there and you might want to share with your friends at your job place."

"Excellent idea!" Carol cried, a mite too enthusiastically, Josie thought. "And I can stop by in a few hours and pick up the baskets."

"I—"

"Josie can just bring home my basket with her tonight," Risa interrupted.

"I—"

"And you know what I was thinking?" Carol continued. "You're going to be busy the rest of the day. Why don't I drop off some dinner for you when I pick up my basket?"

"I don't need anyone to cook for me," Josie began, realizing as she spoke that she was being ungrateful. In fact, she did need someone to cook for her . . . and clean for her, and do her laundry, and find her son. . . .

"I do a lot of cooking for Josie," Risa announced.

Josie thought she heard hurt in Risa's voice. "Risa is a wonderful friend and a fabulous chef—she cooked the first meal Sam and I ate together," she added, knowing the memory would warm her landlady's heart.

"Ah, *si* . . ." The thought seemed to cause Risa to shimmer.

"Sammy has always enjoyed my cooking," his mother stated flatly.

She didn't have the time to listen to this. "I have to get back to work."

"Let her take her blue thing and get back to work," Risa insisted.

"Yes, you do that. I'll see you later—to get the basket."

The women actually backed out of the room. Josie merely shook her head and, after rolling up the faxes, headed off to the work site. Maybe there had been another call from the camp director. Or maybe someone else could figure out the plans for paneling the dining room with wood salvaged from a Greek monastery. There were many possibilities.

But the drive wasn't a long one and she hadn't considered the possibility of a visit from the island's police before she spied the matching patrol cars parked at the curb.

"Damn."

What was worse was the matching patrolmen standing underneath the heart-shaped gingerbread on the porch.

"Double damn."

And where was her crew? Handcuffed and hauled off to jail, Josie assumed—at least they'd better have an excuse that good for the fact that she didn't hear a single sound to indicate work was in progress.

"What's going on?" she asked Mike Rodney as she walked up the path to the house.

"Well, howdy do to you, too," was his inane (Josie thought) response.

The other officer, younger than Mike, was more polite. "Hello, Miss Pigeon."

"Ms. Pigeon."

"Josie's something of a throwback to the good old bra-burning days of the women's lib movement," Mike informed the other officer. They both stared at the spot on her body where a bra might or might not be.

"What are you two here for?" she asked, trying not to sound angry.

"Worried that someone else was murdered, Ms. Pigeon?"

She was worried that she was in danger of being arrested for assaulting a police officer, but she didn't admit her desires. "Why are you here?" was all she said.

"There was a murder, Ms. Pigeon. Remember?"

"And you're here to . . . ?"

"To question your employees," the younger officer said. "And you, too, of course. I hope you don't feel we're ignoring you."

"You've already questioned everyone," Josie said.

"Follow-up questions. We have some follow-up questions."

"So why aren't you inside talking with people?"

"Out of consideration for you. We thought we'd question the boss first. Don't want you to get your feelings hurt."

"Charming," Josie said sarcastically. "Would you like to come inside or do you want to talk out here?" She preferred inside. It wouldn't help Island Contracting's reputation to have a murder suspect on the crew. Although . . . they *could* hire themselves out as the only contracting company with its own private hit man. . . . She started to giggle and then realized how inappropriate it was.

"Anything wrong?"

"I'm just hungry. It's lunchtime, you know," she added more belligerently. "I have food in the truck." Come to think of it, she could use a little food. She always ate when she was nervous. And when she wasn't, if she was going to be honest.

"Do you think she's offering to share her lunch with two hungry cops?" the younger police officer asked.

"I'd be happy to if you'll just get started—and if you can talk and eat. I do have a living to earn," Josie reminded the men. She just hoped that Risa had packed one of her huge, delicious meals. This time it might do more than simply nourish her. This meal just might keep her out of jail.

TWENTY-TWO

RISA HAD PACKED enough lunch to feed a small army. Sam's mother had packed enough lunch for that small army's slightly larger enemy. And these two men seemed to believe that they were entitled to eat every scrap of it, Josie decided, watching potato salad disappear into the large mouth of the man Mike had grudgingly introduced as Officer Koenig.

"So you're claiming you had no plans to meet Sam Richardson here the day the body was discovered." Mike rephrased her answer to his last question.

"I did not plan to meet him. He did not plan to meet me. We did not plan to meet each other. And we did not meet."

"So tell us again about his relationship with this carpenter who looked like you—before she was killed that is."

"I don't know anything about that. You would have to ask Mr. Richardson if you're interested in his romances."

"So you think it was a romance?"

Shit. "I think," she started slowly, determined to watch her words more carefully, "that you think it was a romance. I think, in fact, that you were the person who used the word *romance*. And I know that Sam and I never discussed Amy Llewellyn before she was killed. And before you ask, I haven't spent a lot of time discussing their relationship now that she's dead. Damn it! They hadn't even known each other that long."

"What do you mean by that, Ms. Pigeon?" Officer

Koenig stopped chewing long enough to ask a question. Josie wished he had taken the time to swallow as well. "Did Sam keep his relationship with Miss Llewellyn a secret from you?"

"No, he did not! At least, he had no reason to. We were no longer a couple at that point."

"Why not?"

"I don't think that's any of your business."

"Josie doesn't have very good luck keeping men." Mike Rodney informed his colleague of what he considered to be a fact.

"That," Josie insisted loudly, "is a huge crock of shit! That, in fact, is the type of thing only a complete idiot would say!" She would have continued if Betty hadn't sauntered into the room wearing a bikini top that looked a heck of a lot like a bra—a bra that offered decoration rather than support.

"Hot, isn't it?" she drawled.

The men opened and closed their mouths like fishes out of water. Realizing Betty's titillating exhibition was designed to save her ass, Josie had the good sense to shut her mouth, sit back, and watch the performance—if it didn't make her too ill.

"Whenever it's hot like this, I just sweat and sweat," Betty said, stretching her arms up over her head.

Now this was going just a little too far. "Betty . . ." Josie began in a warning tone of voice.

"Of course, not everyone feels that way," Betty continued quickly. "Some people just want to get away. To take a vacation." She turned her back on the men and stared sternly into Josie's eyes. "To get off the island."

Who the hell was Betty talking about? Everyone Josie could think of was right here. Another distressing thought struck her and she closed her eyes for a moment, praying no one on her crew had decided to take off now. But Betty had returned her attention to the two officers.

"But I love it here on our dear little island. This place has so much to offer, don't you think?"

Officer Koenig attempted a reply but seemed to have lost his ability to speak.

"I know Mike loves to fish," Betty continued. "What about you? Are you a man who would rather fish than do anything else?"

"Now, I don't know that I like fishing that much." Mike seemed to think his manhood needed defending. "I do like to fish, but—"

"You know what *I* like to do?" Betty asked with apparent innocence.

This really was getting to be a bit much. Josie was about to put a stop to it when she realized a large white Lincoln Town Car had pulled up to the curb. That wasn't so unusual; on this part of the island most of the cars came in two varieties: excessively large and expensive, and excessively small and expensive. But Sam's mother—Carol—emerged from this particular car. And there was a worried expression on her face.

Betty, her back to their visitor, continued to strut her stuff for the men as Carol walked briskly up the path to the house. Josie hastened to join the older woman a few feet away and they both watched for a moment.

Then: "Who," Carol asked Josie, "is that woman?"

"Betty Patrick. She's one of my crew," Josie answered. "The police have come to ask me a few questions about the woman who was found dead on this property and Betty just came up to talk with them." She hoped Carol would take the hint and not interrupt Betty's diversionary tactic.

"Has Sam met this young woman?" his mother asked.

"Yes. Of course, they're friends," Josie said.

"She does seem to be very friendly. So how long do you think it will take to get rid of the cops?" she asked, lowering her voice very slightly.

"I don't know. Why?"

"Sammy has disappeared."

"Sam—for God's sake, don't let them know. They already suspect him of murdering Amy Lle—"

"*My* Sammy?"

Josie cringed. No one on the block was going to be able to ignore that shriek—and there wasn't a chance in the world that the police would.

"What's going on over there?" Mike Rodney asked, managing to pry his eyes off Betty's chest. "And who are you?"

"I am—"

"This is Carol Greenbaum. She's a friend of mine," Josie interrupted. She knew if Carol introduced herself as Sam's mother, they were all in for a long interview—one she suspected Sam would prefer to avoid.

"I am—" Carol tried to continue her explanation.

"She's not feeling well," Josie continued. "I think she should go inside and lie down. She's not as young as she used to be, you know." She added injury to this insult with a hefty push to Carol's back.

But the woman was as smart as her son and she could take a hint when it threatened to knock her over. "I don't feel well at all," she lied. "I really would like to go inside and lie down, if you don't mind. I'd hate to faint right here in front of you."

"Maybe we should go," Officer Koenig suggested. "We can come back when Miss—" He stopped, seeming to have forgotten Josie's name.

Well, they couldn't arrest her without knowing her name, could they? Josie thought. "You do know where to find us," she suggested, looking at Betty's back. She suspected Officer Koenig would rather look for Betty than either Carol or herself. "We'll be working on this house for the entire summer, you know."

"We have more questions," Mike said. "But we also have other work to do. Other cases to solve, you know."

Josie nodded, hoping the expression on her face was suitably solemn. She suspected the seriousness of those other cases just might not rival the island's second murder.

"Yeah, we should go talk with that other contracting

company again, too. Renovations and Innovations or whatever. Right?"

Mike nodded as though he didn't appreciate Josie knowing the policemen's plans, but he couldn't do much but agree. "Yeah. Sometime soon. There are other cases, too, you know," he repeated.

"Yeah. Your father wants us to tell that rich woman that her stepson's been shoplifting condoms from the drugstore again, doesn't he?"

Mike scowled. "We have a lot of important things to do," he insisted, stomping off down the driveway.

The other officer paused long enough to say good-bye to Betty and, incidentally, to Carol and Josie as well before tromping after him.

Betty was the first to speak when they were alone. "I know it was sexist as hell and I know what you think about that, but you seemed to be in trouble."

"Please, don't apologize. I don't approve of women using their bodies like that—but I sure am glad you did it for me—and Island Contracting," Josie added quickly.

"I hope I didn't shock you," Betty added to Carol as the women walked up to the house together.

"No. I guess I'm just too worried to think about anything right now. You see, my son is missing."

"With Tyler?" Betty asked excitedly. "Your son and Tyler are friends and they took off together. That means they're probably safe, doesn't it?" she cried to Josie.

"Carol is Sam's mother," Josie explained.

"Sam Richardson? You look much too young," Betty began before reverting to the main point. "What do you mean missing? He's too old to have run away."

"He left a note," Carol said, fumbling in the pocket of her vest. "It doesn't explain anything," she added, passing it to Josie.

Betty read over Josie's shoulder. "It sure doesn't," she agreed.

"He's not missing," Josie protested. "He just went to do something. He could be off ordering some of his precious California vintages—or on a date—or anything from this note."

"It's *very* mysterious," Carol insisted.

"True." Betty nodded. " 'I have something to do. Don't expect me till you see me.' " She nodded again. "Very mysterious."

"What do you think we should do?" Carol addressed the question to Josie.

"Do? Why should we do anything?" *Except work,* she would have liked to add, but didn't.

"Well, calling the police and filing a missing-persons report is out, isn't it?" Betty said.

"Look, we have to get to work," Josie finally said. "Not that I think there's anything at all to worry about, but if Sam hasn't appeared by the time we knock off tonight, I'll get busy and make a few calls."

"I could do that while you work," Carol insisted. "Just tell me their names."

Josie frowned. "There's a small green leather address book by the phone in Sam's bedroom."

"I'll start with *A* and be done with the entire book by the time you get home," Carol said.

"Fine. But I'm going to be working late tonight."

"You do that. Sam's always talking about how much your work means to you."

Josie tried to smile politely. Was there anything Sam hadn't "always talked about" with his mother? "I'd better get going," she announced, turning and heading straight into the house.

After saying a polite good-bye to Carol, Betty followed at a trot. "Hey, what's with you?"

"I'm going to get back to the windows in the bedrooms. All these interruptions are wreaking havoc with our schedule."

"What about Sam? Aren't you worried?"

Josie turned and stared at Betty. "What in heaven's name is there to worry about? Sam had something to do that he didn't want his mother to know about. So he's doing it. When he's done he'll come back and either tell her about it or not. No big deal."

"But . . ."

"But what? What about that note would make any sane person worry?" Josie asked, starting up the stairs.

"You may be right."

"You know I'm right. And when are you going to put on your shirt?"

Betty looked down at her overexposed breasts and giggled. "I forgot. I guess this doesn't look real professional, does it?"

"Depends on the profession," Josie muttered as a loud crash preceded a cloud of plaster dust down the stairs. "And what the hell happened to the drop cloths that were supposed to be hung here?"

"You ordered them taken down yesterday when the tiles were delivered," Betty reminded her. "We've kept the padding on the walls just like you wanted us to."

Josie remembered the woodwork, which was even now on its way here from Greece. She'd deal with that when—and if—it arrived. "Great. Let's get to work."

"You *are* going to tell us why the police were here, aren't you?" Fern asked, the words muffled by the heavy dust mask she wore across her face.

"Just some more questions about the murder and all. They're probably pestering I and R now," Josie muttered, glancing around the debris. She knew she had left her toolbox here somewhere.

"Have they gone through our personnel files yet?" Kristen asked, swinging a heavy sledgehammer.

"No. I decided not to volunteer to give them to the police, but all they have to do is get a court order and the files are theirs."

"I would like to talk with you—privately," Kristen said.

"Maybe we could do it while we work on the box for the whirlpool," Josie suggested. "Everyone will leave us alone in there." She looked around at her crew to make sure the message was understood. Fern nodded. Betty, putting on her shirt, gave the thumbs-up sign. Al was frowning. "Okay?" she added.

"I . . ." Al began. "Look, when you're done with Kristen, can you and I talk?"

"Just get in line," Josie said, heading to the back of the house with Kristen in her wake.

TWENTY-THREE

KRISTEN GOT RIGHT to the point.

"You should fire me for lying on my application form, you know," she announced, picking up a ten-foot pine two-by-four and then putting it back down.

"I *can* fire you for that. I don't have to. It's my choice." Josie began sorting through the piles of lumber, and after a moment Kristen joined her.

"I guess there was no chance of our failed marriage being kept a secret with David living on the island, too. And the police will know about it all when they interview the guys over at I and R."

Josie just kept on working, waiting for Kristen to tell her own story in her own way.

"We were married for a little less than eleven years," she began slowly. "We met at work." She smiled at the memory. "I loved him the first time I saw him. I was the only woman on the crew at the time, but all the guys were easygoing and there wasn't a lot of sexist shit. You know how things can be."

Josie just nodded. She knew. Every woman knew.

"Well, we started dating almost immediately. I was just eighteen at the time. David was twenty. I knew right away that I wanted to marry him. And I did, less than a year after the day we met.

"I got pregnant right away. Which wasn't all that much of a surprise. We weren't taking any precautions and we'd talked about having a large family." She took a deep breath. "Our son was born nine months and three days after the wedding.

"We were so happy then. We didn't have much money, but David was working hard and with the overtime he made we bought a house right before Marty's second birthday."

"Marty's a cute name," Josie contributed when Kristen stopped speaking.

"Martin, really. We named him for David's brother—he died from leukemia in his early teens. I was worried about it being bad luck to name a baby after a dead person—and maybe I was right about that as things turned out."

"So you bought a house?" Josie prompted when Kristen didn't continue.

"Yeah. The traditional fixer-upper. Which we, of course, were well qualified to fix up." She stopped and passed a metal measuring tape to Josie. "Here. Looks like you could use this."

"Thanks. I take it you didn't have any more children?"

"No. I developed a medical problem. I had some miscarriages—finally we just stopped worrying about it. Marty was so special—we felt we were lucky to have him. To tell the truth, I don't think I really missed having other children until I didn't have Marty anymore."

Josie hated to do it, but . . . "Did something happen to him?" she asked, knowing the answer.

"He was killed." Kristen pursed her lips and Josie asked the next question.

"Killed?"

"Yes. I don't want to talk about it." She took another deep breath. "But Marty's death is why I lied on my application form. I didn't want to talk about my marriage because I didn't want to answer questions about it—questions that might have led to talking about Marty."

"I don't want to pry," Josie lied. "It's just that the police might not understand if I tell them I don't know anything about it."

"Yeah. You had to know. I would have told the truth on my application form, but I didn't know you then. I didn't know how discreet you'd be or anything. You're not going to fire me for lying, are you?"

"Of course not."

Kristen sighed loudly. "I almost told you about David and me. But then we ran into each other and I thought he wouldn't say anything."

"He must have his own sadness about Marty's death."

"If he does, he sure had a strange way of showing it."

"But—"

"Believe me," Kristen insisted. "Marty's death made no difference at all in David's life. And that almost destroyed me. That's why we got divorced."

Josie didn't know what to say. She stared down at the piles of wood lying across the subflooring and wished for some wisdom. What she got was an interruption. Al stomped into the room.

"Hey! It's so quiet in here I thought maybe you had left."

"No . . ."

"But I was just going," Kristen said quickly. "Call me if you want to talk more after you two get done."

"I will." She watched Kristen turn and leave.

"I came here to tell you something," Al said immediately, examining the tattoos on her right bicep as though she'd never seen them before.

"Of course . . ."

"I didn't fill out the application forms because I can't write. I can't read real well either. I'm illiterate."

Was that possible in this day and age? Josie wondered silently.

"Learning-disabled is what nice people call it now," Al continued. "But I went to a huge public school in Chicago and what it was called then was stupid. I dropped out when I was sixteen, but I'd been cutting so many classes for so many years that I'd missed most everything since the fourth or fifth grade."

"But—"

"I can write—messily. And I can read real slowly. But I can't spell much better than a third grader—a third grader who can't spell real well."

"You could have told me," Josie said, wondering if there was something about her that intimidated first-time employees. But she also realized the pain Al must feel over this admission. "I wouldn't have minded if you had dictated the answers to the questions on the form."

"I guess. I just didn't want you to think I was stupid."

"I know you're not stupid. Believe me," Josie insisted. "We can just fill out the forms now—before the police start to wonder why yours isn't with the others. If that's okay with you."

"Yeah. Great. I could stop by the office on the way home today."

"Good. The sooner the better."

"Okay. Now what about the top of the knee wall in the master bedroom? Are we going to use a nice sheet of oak to match the floorboards or just a piece of ash or something that can be painted? And the top of the window seat in the hallway—maybe that should match the floor, too."

Josie almost forgot her problems in the midst of the afternoon's work. Sam could take care of himself. The island's police department could bungle the second murder investigation in its history. She had to finish this project on time. And someone had to find Tyler—even if he was only lurking around camp. It was really only her son who mattered. And he seemed to be the only problem she could do nothing about, she realized, slamming a nail into a beam with unnecessary force.

Perhaps, she thought, she should call the camp director herself. Why she had been depending on Sam for all this . . . She stopped hammering and sat back on the heels of her well-worn work boots. The answer was obvious: Sam.

"Sam is looking for Tyler!"

Josie gasped. Had she spoken out loud?

"Sammy is trying to find your son!"

Only his mother still called him Sammy. Josie, smiling, stood up. "I was just thinking the same thing." She smiled at Carol Greenbaum.

"We should have realized. Sammy is just not the kind of man to take off when a child is in trouble—might be in trouble is what I mean. I really don't think your son is in any trouble," she added quickly as Josie paled beneath her freckles. "So now that we can leave that problem up to Sam, I think we should get busy and figure out who killed that young woman before Sam returns."

Before Josie could speak, Carol went on: "Because if we don't, the police are going to assume that my son is a murderer, aren't they?"

Josie thought about that for a moment. Sam would kill her if she got his mother in a tizzy. "You may have a point there."

"Of course I do. They suspected him before and now that he has just taken off . . . Well, I can't think of a better way to spend my time here than finding the real murderer. So what do we have to do?"

"What?"

"You have a lot of experience with these things."

"Some, but—"

"So where do we start?"

Josie looked down at her watch. Apparently she'd smacked the crystal again—it was even harder to read than before. "I have a few things to do this evening—important things," she added.

"Fine, then we'll meet for a late dinner."

"Maybe that would work out."

"I'll call you at the office, shall I?"

"Well . . ." It seemed that Carol was not one to take no for an answer—if she even bothered to listen to the answer. "I may get done and leave."

"Then I'll call you at your apartment. See you." And Carol spun around and almost ran smack into Al walking in the door. She might have found it possible to ignore Josie's protests, but Al's tattoos were something else all together. "Heavens . . . What interesting tattoos." She peered closer. "Did you have them done all at once or are there separate designs that . . . that make up the whole picture, so to speak?"

"To have this all done at one time would kill even a strong person like me. It took years to accomplish this," Al bragged, flexing her muscles.

That explained why a Mickey Mouse ended up sitting on a peace symbol and an almost Gothic Jesus on a cross hung beside Garfield, Josie realized. Al had changed over the years and her tattoo preferences obviously had also.

But Carol was dithering away. "There's a wonderful book on tattoos and their history—it came out a few years ago. I saw an article about it in *The New York Times* and National Public Radio did an interesting feature on the author. Maybe you saw it? Or heard the story?"

"Nah. I don't study tattoos. I just wear 'em," Al stated flatly.

"Yes, of course. I can see that. See you later, my dear," she added to Josie.

"Yes. Later. Are you ready to leave now?" Josie asked Al after Carol had gone.

"Yup. Let's get this over with."

The young women spent a few minutes straightening up the work area and then, grabbing their tools, locked up the house and hurried to the office.

It was well past seven and most of the island's residents and visitors were enjoying their cocktail hour. Josie and Al drove by porches filled with couples drinking gin and tonics as they slapped cooling preparations on their sunburned shoulders, decks where tanned fathers swilled beer as they burned the night's meal over expensive grills and on tiny imported hibachis while their wives sipped wine coolers and tried to keep exhausted children from fighting.

"Do you ever get mad at these people?" Al gestured toward a large deck where a group of women about their own age were lying on brightly cushioned lounges, apparently exhausted from a day spent lying in the sun.

"Mad? Not really. Why would I? They're the people who hire me."

"But why do they deserve all that—all that money and the time to enjoy it while you and I work like slaves for zip?"

Josie didn't have time to defend her pay scale before Al continued.

"And you know what else bugs me? The way they look at us as though we're dirt."

"I don't know about that. But I do know that while some of them are snobs, a lot of these people are just renters. They work hard—as hard as we do—all year long to afford to give their family a vacation at the shore."

"Yeah, well, I think the difference between those women and us is that they married rich men while we have to earn our own living. I don't know about you, but if I could find a rich man, I'd marry him in no time flat."

They arrived at the office before Josie could frame a reply.

Unfortunately, there weren't any men, rich or otherwise, hanging around the office. What was more surprising was that there weren't any messages extruding from the fax machine. After feeding the cat, the two women got down to work.

TWENTY-FOUR

THE EMPLOYMENT FORMS hadn't changed at all since Josie inherited Island Contracting over a year earlier. Not that she had expected they had. They asked the standard questions, and as Sam had discovered the night before, Josie didn't bother to call any of the references. But remembering the night before, she was determined to learn everything she could about Al right now. Then, when Sam reappeared (with Tyler in tow, she prayed silently) he would be impressed with her professionalism. She hoped.

They got to the interesting stuff immediately. "I was named after my grandmother—a true Southern belle if there ever was one," Al said, after announcing that her full name was Alma Althea Magnolia Snapp.

Josie found it difficult not to giggle—until Al started to answer questions about her history and explained that her mother had headed north after being thrown out of the house when her parents learned that she was pregnant—and unmarried. That struck a nerve in Josie. "So you never met your father?" she asked, although, of course, the question was not on the form.

"No, and from the way my mother talked about him, it wasn't much of a loss."

Josie looked down at the next question on the form. Schooling. Well, Al had already told her something about that. "How did you learn your trade?" she asked. "You said you dropped out of school."

"Yeah. And I was going nowhere. Then I got into one

of these government programs—like the Job Corps—and they trained me for a few months. My teacher got me my first job after that."

Josie smiled, remembering how Noel had helped her. "It's nice to find a mentor."

"Yeah, well, I was sleeping with the guy and he just happened to forget to tell me he was married, so he sort of owed me."

Not at all like her relationship with Noel, Josie realized. But she was here to learn, not to reminisce. "And who did you work for and for how long?" She was skipping around on the form, but it was easier to get information this way.

"The company was called Concerned Contracting—they made a big deal about being environmentally correct."

"In Chicago?"

"On the outskirts. They didn't get work in the best neighborhoods and they weren't as environmentally correct as they claimed to be. But they did sell themselves to the middle-aged people who had lived through the sixties and now had enough money to redo their homes. And you know how it is, you learn a lot on your first job. That's where I was when I started getting tattoos. This little baby was my first." She pulled back the collar of her work shirt and displayed a shoulder adorned with a blowsy purplish rose. "The color sucks," Al continued. "It was pink and I hated that, so I went to this guy when I was living in Indianapolis and he said he could turn the pink to red, but whatever he did didn't work and I ended up with the purple passion flower." She shrugged. "What the hell."

It was another question not on the form, but Josie couldn't resist asking. "How many tattoos do you have?"

"Depends on how you count."

"Huh?"

"I've gotten them to commemorate the most important events in my life for the past twelve years. Like the rose is sort of a tribute to the man I first loved. Pete Rose. You know, the baseball player," she added when Josie didn't respond. "Also, I'm a big Cardinals fan. I have a cardinal on my left thigh to prove it. Had it put on the day after the first game I saw them play."

"Oh. So why can't you count how many tattoos you have?"

"Some of them sorta run together. And I've had some alterations. Like this guy I was going to marry? His name was Jeff. And then I found out he wasn't divorced yet and his ex-wife was six months pregnant, and even though he said it wasn't his baby, who needs that type of aggravation, right?"

"Right." What else could she say?

"So I had that tattoo turned into Jefferson Starship—the rock group, you know? They're not my favorite, but I decided I liked them right across my butt more than I liked Jeff. You know?"

Oh boy, did she! "Makes sense."

"Sometimes people . . ." Josie was astounded that Al was blushing. "Well, men actually . . . women don't see me naked . . . they try to count the tattoos and most of them come up with between thirty and thirty-six. It depends on how you count."

Don't think about it, Josie ordered herself silently. "So you've lived in Indianapolis as well as Chicago?"

"I moved to Cincinnati after Chicago. Then spent a few months working for a guy in Detroit. And then I went to Indianapolis for three years. No, I forgot Rockford. . . ."

Josie looked down at the form. It required the names, addresses, and phone numbers of the past three employers. How long would it take to obtain these?

About twenty minutes, as it turned out. Al's life was full of stops, starts, and men who could not be trusted. Josie was beginning to wonder that the woman only sported thirty—or thirty-six—tattoos. If Al had decided to commemorate each man as he came into (or exited from) her life, there wouldn't be a square inch of unadorned skin. And Al didn't seem to have gotten a single job without some sort of male intervention. If her employer wasn't her lover, an important crew member was. Josie finally got the last three names and addresses on the list. And she was relieved more than distressed when Carol entered the office, a large Bloomingdale's bag in either hand and a bag from the local bookshop tucked under one arm.

"Oh, I'm so glad you're here. I found this magazine down at the store when I was checking out the new mystery novels and I thought of you," she said to Al, dumping the Bloomingdale's bags on the desk and passing the book bag to Al.

Al looked down at the bag as though she had no idea what to do with it.

"Open it. It's for you. I love to give people presents. And don't think I forgot you," she added to Josie, opening a Bloomingdale's bag and peering inside. "Now, where is that thing?"

Al peeked in the bag as though expecting something to leap out and bite her. But she was obviously thrilled as she pulled out a thick magazine. "Hey, look at this. An entire magazine about tattoos. Who would've thought."

Not Josie, that was for sure. She glanced over at the pages as Al flipped through them. Most of the words were in the photographs, adorning various body parts. It was definitely a magazine Al would enjoy. She was beginning to relish the thought of her own gift when Carol placed a little paper bag in her outstretched hand.

"There, dear, that's for you."

"Thank you." She pulled the gift from its covering. "What is it?" It looked like a small cylinder of rubber packed in a plastic tube.

"It's a garlic peeler. I just adore mine and I've given them to all my friends," Carol enthused. "You merely pop the clove inside, press it on the counter and roll it around, and voilà! Your garlic is peeled."

"Oh, thank you." Josie hadn't even known garlic needed peeling.

"I gave Sammy one and he just loves it. Of course, I'm

doing the cooking during my visit, but he actually peeled some garlic cloves just to see how it worked. We could eat at your apartment tonight and you could try it out for yourself."

Josie did cook sometimes. She used garlic powder from a jar. "Well, I—"

"I brought dinner," Carol continued. "Most of it's cold and the barbecued brisket just needs to be heated in the microwave. You do have a microwave?"

"Of course . . ." It was full of scorched food that had overflowed the freezer containers, though, and she wasn't sure she wanted Sam's mother to see it. "But—"

"I know how you feel. You've been working hard. Your son is away at camp. You've been doing less housekeeping than usual and you don't want me to see your apartment. Don't even think about it. I understand. I live alone, too, you know."

Actually, Josie's apartment always looked dreadful. But at the moment she had an idea. "But those satanic—" She stopped speaking, realizing that the word had caused Al to jerk the magazine she had been studying intently.

"What did you say?"

"The satin sheets. You were worried about the satin sheets on your bed, weren't you, my dear?" Carol answered Al. "Don't worry about that. I've seen worse in my time. Now let's get going. I know you need your sleep."

Before Al could reply, Carol told her firmly, "It was very nice meeting you. Enjoy your magazine."

Al stood up. "I'd better be going."

"See you tomorrow," Josie said. "And thanks for doing this."

Al smiled. "Yeah, thanks for understanding. And thanks for the magazine," she added to Sam's mother.

"You're very welcome," Carol said as the door closed behind Alma Althea Magnolia Snapp. "What an interesting young woman. I guess you meet a lot of interesting women in your business. You know, more liberated than the rest of us who have always depended upon men."

Josie, remembering the long trail of Al's lovers, only nodded.

"Well, we'd better get going. We have a lot to do tonight. I think we should start with that other contracting company, don't you?"

"I . . . I have to drive to my apartment. I have the company truck," Josie insisted. Everything was happening so fast. She needed some time to think.

"I'll follow you in the Town Car."

"Fine." Josie shoved the forms she had been filling out into an already stuffed desk drawer and trotted after Sam's mother. She really wished she could manage to have a few minutes alone in her apartment before Carol saw it.

But when she arrived at Risa's house, she realized there wasn't going to be any time alone for anyone. The island's police department had the house surrounded—or as surrounded as four police cars and six officers could manage. Risa was standing out front, waving her arms and screaming at the men. Josie pulled over to the opposite curb, parked, and jumped down from her truck.

When Risa saw her, she stopped screaming at the police and started on her. "*Cara*, where have you been? I thought you were dead. I thought you had been murdered. And these men . . . these . . . stupid *polizia* . . ."

"Hey, lady, who are you calling stupid?" An officer Josie didn't recognize leaped to his companions' defense.

"Did I not call and tell you Josie was missing? Did I not ask you all to come here? Did I not?" she demanded.

"So. Here we are."

"And if I knew where she was . . . if I did not believe she was in serious trouble . . . would I then have called you?"

"So . . . ?"

"So why do you question me? I did not know where she was! That is why I called. You should have read the message and begun to search immediately. *Immediatamento!*"

Carol, having apparently found a parking place large enough for her car, joined in the conversation. "Josie was at her office," she explained to anyone who was interested in listening.

"See, she wasn't even missing," Mike Rodney said, glaring at Risa. "She was at her office. You could have called her there and left the police out of it. Jeez!"

"I—"

"How was I to know that? You could have called instead of standing around here and asking me stupid questions." Risa wasn't one to back down easily.

But neither was Josie. "I don't—" she began again, hoping she would get to finish her question before another interruption.

Fat chance.

"We could charge you for this, you know. It's illegal to call the police under false pretenses," Mike continued, moving his face closer to Risa's.

"I don't think that's true," Officer Koenig said quietly. For the first time Josie realized he was holding a large sheet of paper. "And she didn't know there wasn't an emergency. She had reason to think something had happened to Josie."

"I don't understand that," Josie announced loudly. "I don't understand why Risa thought something had happened to me."

"Because of that note." Risa pointed to Officer Koenig. "The one I found taped on your front door."

"Can I see it?"

"It's evidence," Mike answered belligerently.

"There's no case. There's no need to collect evidence. And the note was written to me," Josie insisted. "Besides, I heard how you treated the other note with my name on it. I think I'd rather read this one before you take off."

"Don't you need a search warrant to remove something from her property without permission?" Carol suggested. "Sammy would say—"

"Sammy is who?" Mike asked.

"My lawyer," Carol said proudly. "It's not every mother who has her own son for a lawyer."

"May I have the note someone wrote to me?" Josie asked again.

It was handed over and she read silently.

"It didn't sound like a note you would write. I thought perhaps you had been kidnapped and the kidnapper had made you write it. Although the writing is much neater than yours." Risa stopped and stared at Josie. Then everyone else stared, too.

There was a huge grin on her face.

TWENTY-FIVE

IT WAS TYLER'S handwriting. He'd tried to disguise it by using only capital letters, but it was his handwriting. She was sure of it.

"What's so funny?" Mike asked.

"She's not laughing, she's smiling," Carol corrected him.

"There is no longer any reason for you to be here, is there?" Risa asked, jumping into the discussion.

"You're going to have to check the report I write up, but I could do that at the office and you could come in to sign it in a few days."

"Excellent. I'll do that. Now you can take your cars and all your men and leave." Risa shook her head. "All these policemen. It's not good for the neighborhood."

Officer Koenig looked startled. "Lady, *you* called us."

"Yeah, Risa . . ." Mike Rodney began.

It might have gone on forever if a small child, bored

with the rest of his family's idea of fun, hadn't wandered off and become stuck in the windmill at the Putt, Putter, and Play miniature-golf course downtown. The child, unhurt, was now anxious to return to the game. The owner of the course was anxious that the fifth hole remain intact. Here was a problem the police department could sink their teeth into, it appeared, as men and cars dashed away.

"What's going on? What does the note say? Why were you smiling?" Carol asked as soon as the men were out of hearing range.

"That note is nothing to smile about," Risa, who had read it, insisted. "What is going on, *cara*?"

Josie's grin was becoming broader. "Look at it again," she told Risa, passing the sheet of paper to her.

Risa stared at the words. "Did I read it wrong?"

"Read it out loud. Please," Carol insisted, peering over Josie's shoulder to get a peek.

" 'Josie Pigeon is not here. Josie Pigeon will not be here ever again. Beware. Stay away,' " Risa read slowly. "I was wrong to think this was from someone who . . . who tried . . . ?"

"Who had either killed her or wanted to kill her," Carol finished when the stress of the situation caused Risa to falter in her adopted language.

"Look at the writing," Josie insisted.

"It looks like someone trying to disguise their handwriting by using—what do you call them?—square letters," Risa said.

"Block letters," Carol corrected her. "And it's not a bad disguise. It almost looks like a child wrote this."

"*Si* . . . it looks like Tyler's writing when he was in kindergarten. It *is* Tyler's writing. *Mio bambino* is safe!" Risa threw her arms around Josie. "Thank heavens! Thank the heavens!"

Carol grabbed the note as it flew through the air. "Your son Tyler wrote this? He's here? He made it from a camp in Pennsylvania to this place? That's hundreds of miles."

"*Si! Si!* It is Tyler. That is why Josie is so happy."

"But Sammy went to look for him . . . in Pennsylvania, I think. And why would he write such a strange message anyway?"

"Good question," Josie admitted. "Listen, why don't we go upstairs? Tyler has a key to the apartment. Maybe he left another note there. Maybe he's there himself." The thought turned her into an Olympic sprinter. She was at the front door in record time.

If only she could remember to keep her key ring in the same pocket of her overalls! It took more time to find it and unlock the door than it had taken to get to it. So long, in fact, that Carol and Risa entered her apartment with her.

"My God! You've been robbed!"

"She has not been in your home before, has she, *cara*?" Risa asked. "She does not know that housekeeping is not your . . . your baggage."

"I'm a rotten housekeeper," Josie admitted. "It did look like this when I left here." She looked around. "I think," she added doubtfully.

"You sleep on your couch?" Carol asked, picking up the pillow and cotton blanket tossed across it.

"Sam slept there," Josie answered without thinking. She was looking for a sign that Tyler had been there.

Josie's apartment comprised the entire second floor of Risa's home. Built sometime in the 1930s as a three-bedroom shore cottage for a small family, it was barely adequate for Tyler and herself. Two bedrooms separated by a bathroom and a living area with a small kitchen at one end made up the entire place. There were only two closets, one in each bedroom, and that was the explanation—excuse—she usually offered for her messy home. Today she didn't bother with excuses.

She scratched Urchin's dark brown head as she passed the cat sleeping in a sunny window. If Tyler had been here, he had spent some time with his cat, she was sure of it. If only the animal could talk!

She continued into her son's bedroom. Sometime this summer she planned to go through his closet and drawers and get rid of all his outgrown and worn-out clothing. Then maybe he'd have someplace to put all the things that were spilling off his bookshelves, his desktop, his bed, and his dresser onto the already cluttered floor. On the other hand, the clutter made it impossible for Risa and Carol to see the ragged and torn condition of his wall-to-wall carpeting.

"How messy little Tyler is." Risa's voice came from over her shoulder. "Just like a man."

"Oh." Carol seemed more than a little surprised. "Sammy was always a neat child."

That didn't surprise Josie. Not one bit. But she had more important things on her mind. She rummaged through the pile of stuff on the dresser. Tyler had always struck her as unusually reluctant to give up his past. But he was, at the same time, always growing and moving forward. As a result, his room bore a striking resemblance to an archaeological dig. Under today's pile of sports equipment lay battered Matchbox cars, G.I. Joe action figures beneath them. She suspected the entire structure was supported by millions of Legos. Luckily, this meant she had to go through only the top layers to discover Tyler's recent whereabouts.

She looked and looked but could find no sign of his presence. Risa and Carol, meanwhile, had wandered off. "Come on, Urchin," she added, bending down to pick up the cat. "We should check the refrigerator. Knowing Tyler, he emptied the milk carton and left it on the counter."

Of course, she had to admit that she might have done this herself. But Tyler, she suddenly remembered, was just as likely to put the empty carton back in the refrigerator. Hurrying over to the small kitchen area, she discovered that she was out of milk. And had been for so long that the refuse bin under the sink bore no signs of a carton. She would have searched further if she hadn't glimpsed Carol and Risa out of the corner of her eye.

Once she saw what Risa held in her hands, she could think of nothing else. "What is that thing? And where did it come from?"

"I was just going to ask you the same question," Risa answered.

Carol cleared a space on the coffee table (Josie promised herself she would never, ever leave so many empty dishes around again) and Risa put the object down. The three women stood and stared.

About a foot high, the base of the object seemed to be a piece of an old fence post. Numerous twigs had been nailed to its surface. And on those nails hung what could only be called ornaments—tiny pinecones, seedpods, little shells, beads strung on threads, and origami shapes fashioned from what appeared to be the silver foil from sticks of chewing gum.

"What in heaven's name is it?" Carol finally asked.

"Damned if I know. Some sort of Christmas decoration?" Josie suggested, touching a dangling milkweed pod.

"Christmas?" Risa sounded doubtful.

"It doesn't seem particularly festive," Carol added. "Or colorful."

"It certainly couldn't have any useful purpose," Josie said.

"'Well, that's for sure," Carol agreed.

"Where did you find it?" Josie asked.

"It was sitting in the middle of your bed," Carol answered.

"Was it there when you left home, *cara*?"

"Of course not!"

"But you were with Sammy last night," Carol reminded her.

Risa's eyes widened. "*Cara . . .*"

"Not now, Risa. Believe me, this is not what you think."

"Nothing seems to be what you think these days," Carol said. "At least not what I would think."

"She lives a very up-and-down life, like I told you. She needs a man to take care of her."

Josie took a deep breath. "I need to find Tyler. I need to find out who killed Amy Llewellyn. I need . . ." What she needed was to go to the bathroom.

"What you need, *cara*, is dinner."

"Dinner!" Carol cried. "I have a wonderful meal waiting out in my car. The police and everything made me forget."

"I was thinking of melon—that pale Crenshaw—and prosciutto—from Italy, not that trash the deli sells. And then *funghi* and *tagliatelle*," Risa said. "It will not take a moment."

"I'm starving," Josie stated flatly. As expected, both women rushed out to get food and she was left alone.

What the hell was this thing? It seemed almost cheerful to her. And what the hell was it doing in the middle of her bed? And, most importantly, had Tyler left it? For her? If so, why?

"So where is Sammy?" His mother entered the apartment, winded from climbing the stairs while carrying heavy bags of food.

Josie resisted the temptation to tell her that her son could take care of himself—damn him. But she didn't. "I don't think he had anything to do with this thing—do you?"

The question surprised Carol; she stopped in her tracks to give it her full consideration. "I don't think so. He has—in the past—dated women who called themselves artists and one or two of them might have produced something like this. But he's not seeing them anymore, and anyway, why would he leave this for you—in the middle of your bed?"

"I'm sure he didn't."

"Then let's get this meal eaten. We'll think better with

something in our stomachs. And we still have to think about the murderer, don't we?"

"What murderer? Has someone else been murdered?" Risa appeared in the doorway, a bottle of wine in one hand, a large ceramic dish in the other.

Risa had a short attention span for subjects other than love or food.

"No, we're still talking about the same murderer. No one knows who he is, however."

"Or her. It could be a woman," Carol reminded her.

"A jealous woman," Risa insisted.

"Of what?"

"Of something the dead woman—what was her name? Amy?" Carol continued at Josie's nod. "Of something Amy had that the person who killed her didn't have."

"A man," Risa insisted.

"Well, the only man Amy had right before she died was Sammy," Carol began. "But of course, we all know Josie had nothing to do with the murder. Why don't you take a plate of this shrimp salad and tell me what you know about the victim."

Josie took the plate and dug in. She was still staring at the strange wooden object. "This is wonderful," she said, chewing the mayonnaise-rich mixture. "Does that thing look like it has a face? Right there on the left side."

"I don't know anything," Risa said, setting a platter of melon and prosciutto on the coffee table that Carol was still covering with turquoise plastic containers of food. "Josie knows everything."

"Can you tell us about her while you eat?" Carol asked, putting a large loaf of challah down and, in the process, shoving Risa's offering to the side.

"Nope. I don't know anything." She gulped down a large shrimp and accepted a piece of pâté and popped it in her mouth. "I mean, I know her name, and what she looked like, and where she worked." She swallowed. "But that's all really."

"You should enjoy your food and not bolt it down like that."

"You don't know anything about her?" Carol interrupted Risa. "I thought you and Sammy were investigating this murder?"

"We were. We were looking into the backgrounds of my crew. That's what we did the last time—"

"Sammy told me all about that," his mother interrupted.

"A foolish way for a young woman to spend her time with a good-looking man, don't you think?" Risa asked.

The two older women nodded at each other, apparently having at last found some common ground.

Then Risa frowned. "But this is a different murder. Why not investigate a different murder in a different manner?"

"Sammy," his mother answered. "It is Sammy. He is very methodical. He believes in things like the process of elimination. Only he doesn't call it that."

"Is something wrong? You've stopped eating." Risa was concerned.

"I think Carol's right. We should find out more about Amy Llewellyn. The key to all of this may lie in her life." Josie stopped speaking.

"Are you all right?" Carol asked this time.

"Maybe some melon?" Risa suggested.

But Josie was staring at the object. "It really does have a face," she insisted. "And it's smiling at me!"

TWENTY-SIX

JOSIE HAD GONE to sleep with a full stomach. She woke up determined to find out more about Amy Llewellyn—even if that meant a visit to I and R's office before the working day began. She found some almost clean overalls on the floor in the bathroom. An immaculate T-shirt that her son had given her for Mother's Day (it said THE WORLD'S BEST MOTHER on the front, and BUT WHICH WORLD? on the back) and work boots completed her outfit.

She gave herself a pep talk on the way—she needed one. I and R sometimes gave her what used to be called an inferiority complex. They weren't Island Contracting's only competitors by any means. The island had been experiencing a major boom since the early seventies. Many a contractor had begun building homes for wealthy people and ended up so successful that he could afford to live in one of those homes himself. I and R, in fact, had made its first owner just that wealthy. The present owner had probably done even better. Josie had to admit it (to herself, not the general public), they did fabulous work. And they got the fabulous jobs. Noel had been more interested in helping people than in making lots of money and he hadn't even bothered to compete with I and R, rarely putting in bids for those projects that attracted the other company. But Josie . . .

Well, she had to confess. She'd owned the company for one year only. And when she wasn't worried about failing to make enough money to keep it running, she was becoming ambitious. She wanted Island Contracting to be in the same league as I and R—maybe not as big, certainly not filled with male workers, but as good as them, and in the running for the best jobs, the most prestigious jobs, the big-money ones. Who would have thought she'd end up so middle-class? So conventional? There was no reason to care about I and R . . . she should remember what was important—her son, her friends, her employees, who in a place like Island Contracting, became her friends. . . .

And then she arrived at I and R's office. It was, of course, at the chic end of the island, almost as far from Island Contracting's headquarters and Josie's home as was possible. There was a parking space available. A parking space was always available since I and R's property included a large lot placed conveniently to the right of its austere modern white facade.

Josie pulled into the lot and hopped out of her truck. Potted nasturtiums surrounded her office—that is, when one of the women remembered to water them. Here, a landscaper had been at work—hard at work. The foundation of the building was edged with evergreens artistically arranged in mounds, sprawls, swirls, and lumps. Even their various shades of green were more exotic than the deep, dusty scrub pine that was indigenous to the island. Silvery mounds of artemisia and tall mustard-colored yarrow completed the group. It looked cool and elegant against the shimmering white plaster of the building.

Josie walked up the bluestone path, admiring the effect. She adored the charm of her converted office, but every time she was here, she realized again why potential clients, interested in building modern homes and additions, chose I and R over Island Contracting.

She would have thought about it more if Joe Ellis hadn't chosen that moment to walk out the front door followed by three muscular men in the distinctive red T-shirts of I and R's workers. If she hadn't known better, she might have mistaken the men for the line at Chippendale's. They were, she had always thought, I and R's secret weapon. While Josie had not been above asking Betty to take a potential male client on a tour of Island Contracting's work, she knew they couldn't compete with the I and R crews. Few women wouldn't enjoy the thought of these handsome men sweating and flexing their muscles as they worked around the house. Although, come to think of it, Al had some pretty impressive muscles . . . but this wasn't the time to wonder about that. Joe Ellis had seen her.

"Hi, Josie. I thought you'd be busy up at the house of hearts. What brings you to my office?"

"I need a few minutes of your time, Joe."

"Just let me give these guys some last-minute directions and you can have all the time you want. Why don't you go on in and wait in my office? There's coffee and Danish on the sideboard. Help yourself. I'll only be a few minutes."

"Thanks." Josie walked in through the door the blondest of the men held out for her.

The entryway was paved with Mexican tiles, and following the scent of freshly brewed coffee, she found Joe's office. It was, as she had expected, a room in which captains of industry would feel comfortable. The sideboard was hand-rubbed black cherry. The desk and chairs had certainly come from Thomas Moser. The coffeemaker was Italian. The coffee beans were from Starbucks. The mugs were hand-thrown and the napkins . . . aha, she noticed, thrilled to the core, the napkins were the same cheap ones from the Grand Union that she bought when Tyler was home. (When he was away, she used paper towels.)

Joe's desk was more cluttered than hers, but that was probably because the company was big enough to handle more than one job at a time, not because he was sloppy, she suspected. She poured herself a mug of coffee, chose a cheese Danish from the white bakery box, and sat down in an attractive Windsor chair. It was surprisingly comfortable. Except for the piles of blueprints on Joe's desk, she could have been in the office of most any businessman. Tasteful watercolors hung on the off-white plaster walls. An antique Indian trading rug lay on the floor. Swedish glassmakers had blown their hearts out to create the lamps that adorned the desk and flanked the sideboard. It all looked highly professional; there was no place for stray cats here.

The last thought saved Josie from a case of terminal envy. Her office was cozy; it was, in fact, home to those cats and to herself and her workers. She wouldn't for a minute trade it for this place.

"Sorry that took so long," Joe interrupted her thoughts to apologize.

"It wasn't all that long. And I did help myself to coffee and a pastry. Besides, it's good of you to see me. I know you must be busy these days. I see I and R's signs up all over the island."

"Business is good," Joe said casually. "And it looks like the house of hearts is coming along nicely. I was afraid Amy's death might cause the police to close off the area."

"They cordoned off the pool house, but we weren't going to work there anyway—just storing materials in it. But Amy is the reason I'm here. I was hoping you could tell me about her."

A slow smile crinkled Joe's face. "I gather you don't want to ask Sam that question?"

"I did ask Sam," Josie protested, turning pink. "But he just knew about her . . ." No matter how she put this it was going to sound wrong. "He didn't know anything about her professionally. Her background and all," she ended.

"Oh . . . well, she was an interesting woman," Joe admitted, moving a crystal paperweight from one side of his desk to the other. "Do you want more coffee?"

"I still have some," Josie answered, wondering what

was going on here. Joe had always struck her as remarkably forthright and now he was acting as though he was unwilling to answer her questions. "Is there some reason I shouldn't be asking about her?"

Joe sighed. "Let me make a few phone calls. Then I'll tell you everything I know about Amy Llewellyn."

Actually, there were exactly three phone calls. And Joe was careful, Josie realized, to keep the identity of the person on the other end of the line a secret. To each person he identified himself and then, wasting no words, explained that Josie was sitting right there in his office. He wanted, he continued, to tell her everything about Amy Llewellyn; he thought she deserved to know. When he was done, he got up and poured himself a mug of coffee. Without even taking the time to sip it, he began.

"When you lie, you should be careful not to exaggerate too much."

"Excuse me?" She hadn't, after all, come here for a lecture.

"I didn't mean you, I meant in general. Amy, you see, was something of a compulsive liar."

"I assume you didn't know that when you hired her."

"When I hired her, I thought she was one of the best finish carpenters I'd ever seen and the last two people she worked for agreed."

"You checked her references." Of course he did.

"Of course I did. I thought she was a little strange, of course."

"Why?"

"Well, I've never met a carpenter who wore a long red wig before—unless you . . . ?"

"Mine is real. . . . And you're saying Amy's wasn't."

"Nope. She was blonde, and her hair was short." He looked at Josie and frowned. "I know what you're thinking and it's not true. I didn't have a relationship with Amy Llewellyn and I don't sleep with my employees—not that I usually have the chance since I rarely hire women. I know she wore a wig because it got caught on a nail and came off one day." He took a sip of coffee. "You still look puzzled."

"I was wondering why you hired a woman, to be honest. But that's not important, is it?"

"Actually it is. And before you go getting me sued, I don't not hire women. When I can find a woman who is as competent as a man, I hire her. There just aren't many—I suppose Island Contracting scoops them all up before I even see them," he added quickly. "But for some reason, Amy came to me looking for work."

"When?"

"Early March. I was looking for people for the summer then, of course."

"Do you put ads in the trades?" Josie asked.

"I used to. Now I have enough of a reputation that people look for me. You know."

She'd like to, that was for sure. "So Amy came to you looking for a job. Was she living here at the time? There aren't many visitors to the island at that time of year."

"She said she was just driving up and down the coast looking for summer work."

"And she just happened to stop in at I and R?"

"Yup. At least that's what she said at the time."

"And you didn't believe her?"

"I believed her then. It was only later I came to wonder about that story—among others." He glanced at his watch. Josie noticed that it wasn't a Timex or a Casio.

"It would save us time if you just told me the story," she suggested.

"Fine. Well, this young woman with long flaming red hair came wandering into the office one day early in March and said that she was a trained finish carpenter and was looking for work. I was here alone that day and I offered her an application form to fill out without identifying myself.

"To be honest, I found her intriguing. And her background was certainly a recommendation. She listed the names of two of the most prestigious builders in the

Northwest. And she'd attended an excellent college, one she couldn't have been admitted to if she hadn't had brains. Of course, there were blanks in her past, but she explained that she'd left college to live in a commune, that, in fact, she'd learned her trade there. Building appealed to her more than milking goats is the way she put it."

"It also appealed to her more than gathering eggs."

"What?"

"That's what she told Sam. That her first work had been repairing the roof of the chicken house because she didn't like getting wet while she was collecting eggs. Or something like that."

"Maybe they were eating chicken at the time. Amy had a way of connecting real life with a good story—thus making both a little better than reality, I guess."

Josie frowned. "But it doesn't make any difference if it was a chicken coop or a goat hut or a cow barn, really. The point is the same. She dropped out of college to join a commune and at the commune she learned a trade that she plied until she died. Right?"

"Not really. She left college because she was flunking three subjects and lost her scholarship. She joined a commune whose purpose wasn't merely to go back to the land, but to grow marijuana on it. The chickens weren't raised so much for eggs as for their droppings, which were thought to be wonderful fertilizer for the farm's main cash crop. The commune didn't just drift apart the way they tend to. It was busted by the USDEA and everyone on the property was prosecuted. Amy's particular specialty served her well there, too—she was at the lumberyard in a neighboring county looking for a replacement for an old belt sander she'd been using. When she found out what had happened, she simply never went back. Apparently there were no reprisals."

"And then?"

"And then she worked for a contractor in the area for a few years. Apparently the man was really good because he taught her all the finishing skills she needed to get hired by a good company in Seattle."

"Sam said something about her working for an all-female construction crew out there."

"No. At least there wasn't one that I know of. She probably made that up, too."

"Why would she do that?"

"So Sam would talk about you and the people on your crew. That's probably why she wore the wig, too."

"Joe, I don't understand what you're talking about. Why would Amy Llewellyn care anything at all about Island Contracting?"

"That's why she came here to the island. Because Dave was here. Dave and Kristen."

Josie's mouth fell open. "I don't have the foggiest idea what you're talking about."

TWENTY-SEVEN

"But it has something to do with Amy's murder, doesn't it?" she asked.

"Probably," Joe agreed. "But damned if I can figure it out." He took a deep breath before continuing.

"Of course I checked Amy's references before I hired her."

"Of course," Josie muttered.

"But just to find out the standard stuff. How good a carpenter she was, and like I said, everyone gave her glowing recommendations. Whether she got to work on time, got along with her fellow workers—which can be a problem when there's a lone woman on a crew, but Amy had no problems at all with it. She got along with everyone. In fact, she almost had an instinct for getting along. I suppose a born liar has to be able to read people and then give back what they want."

"And Amy could do that?"

"Amy could probably do it in her sleep. And everyone said she was honest—you know, didn't pick up things lying around houses that didn't belong to her. Of course no one mentioned her penchant for living a fantasy life. And it's more than likely that many of the people who knew her over the years didn't know that she wasn't telling the complete truth, or maybe they didn't care."

"If she was skilled, worked hard, got along with everyone, and didn't steal . . ."

"Exactly. Amy Llewellyn was the perfect employee. If you didn't get involved with her personally."

Josie immediately thought of Sam. How involved had they been?

"I don't think Sam was at all interested in her, Josie," Joe said, apparently reading her mind. "I think Amy went after him. She was using him to get to know people at Island Contracting. She wanted to find out what was going on with Dave's ex-wife."

Josie ran both hands through her hair. "I didn't know anything about any of this."

"It's quite a story. And a sad one. Amy is, I guess, the reason they're divorced . . . as if they hadn't had to go through enough."

"Amy had an affair with David? I thought . . . for some reason, I thought their divorce had to do with the death of their son."

"It did. Amy killed their son."

"What? She . . . Amy Llewellyn was a murderer!" Josie was stunned.

"No. Not really. I shouldn't have said it like that. I guess I've been listening to Dave too much. That's the way he puts it."

"Well, what happened?"

"I don't suppose we'll ever know the true story now. Amy was apparently one of those people who blended in with whatever group she's in. The company where Dave and Kristen worked was made up of family people. Amy became friends with the spouses and the children. She helped out when people were working on their own homes and even made wonderful wooden birdhouses for her coworkers' children at Christmas."

"Sounds lovely," Josie admitted, wondering how such a scenario could have led to a little boy's death.

"Yeah, it does, doesn't it? She went so far as to volunteer to do baby-sitting. It was while she was taking care of Dave's son that a terrible accident took place and the boy died. Dave can tell you more about it."

"He's here?"

"He's coming over. He was the last person I called. He's just finishing up whatever he was doing and then he'll be right over." Joe got up and refilled Josie's mug. He poured some coffee for himself and was about to sit back down behind his desk when the front door slammed. Heavy work boots klunked across the lobby and David entered the office.

"Did you tell her about it?" he asked without taking the time to greet either Joe or Josie.

"Just the bare outline. Have some coffee and you can tell the whole story."

David poured himself a mugful and sat down in the other Windsor chair. Then he looked at Josie. "You must think I'm a pretty shitty guy."

She didn't say anything, not understanding what he meant. Once again she was struck by his good looks. He was certainly one of the best-looking men who had ever asked her out. Then she understood what he meant. "You asked me out to find out what I knew about all this."

"Sorry," he repeated. "I was desperately worried."

"About Kristen," Josie added.

"Yes. I thought . . . well, I guess I'd better tell you what happened before I tell you what I thought.

"Kristen and I met while we were working for the same contractor. I think I fell in love with her the first time I saw her. She was so cute and so serious about her work. I'd never met anyone like her."

The smile on his face reminded Josie of Kristen's when she had spoken of that time in her life.

"Anyway, to make a long story short, we started dating, got married, had a child, and bought a house. I guess there were some problems then. Kristen missed working and she had some health problems—women's things—and was unhappy to discover that she couldn't have any more children. But then she got involved in the community and our son started school and she did some volunteer work and suddenly found that she was busier than ever.

"And then Amy Llewellyn came into our lives and everything changed. . . . Well, not at first, of course. I had stayed with the company that we'd been working for when we met. I was running projects on my own by then, of course, and I was the first person Amy came to when she was looking for work."

"How did that happen?" Josie asked.

"I was working late on a project—a renovation of a fifties home for a family that had exceeded its two-point-three-children-per-couple limit and desperately needed two more bedrooms and a family room—and she just knocked on the front door of the house. I answered it and there she was. She said she was a finish carpenter and was looking for work."

Joe and Josie exchanged looks. "I didn't know that's how she got that job," Joe said slowly. Josie knew he was thinking of the day Amy had appeared in this very office saying the very same thing.

David, not realizing he'd said anything significant (and, in fact, Josie thought, perhaps he hadn't), said yes and continued his tale. "I said I didn't know . . . and we chatted for a while. The addition to that house was going to have an elaborate staircase that connected the family room that was being built on an area dug out of the backyard with a new eating area in the kitchen. The owners were concerned about the appearance of the staircase—it was definitely going to be the dominant feature of the new space—and Amy noticed it right away as we chatted. She made a great suggestion about the stairs—we carried out her idea later and it looked wonderful as well as saving money—and it was apparent that she knew her job. Theoretically at least. So I suggested she follow me back to the office and talk to the people who owned the company."

"It was owned by more than one person?"

"A couple. The Applegates. He ran the crews and all. She did the paperwork. Amy charmed them both immediately. I knew when I went home that night that I was going to be working with a new finish carpenter. Kristen didn't meet her for a few months, but by that time she was kidding about being jealous over the new woman in my life—that's what she called Amy." He looked straight at Josie. "It wasn't true, though. I was never interested in anyone other than Kristen. My family was my whole world back then. Marty was just learning to play ball and I used to come home from work, shower, and toss a ball around in the backyard until Kristen called us in for dinner."

"Sounds like a nice life," Josie said a little wistfully.

"It was. I thought it would go on forever."

"But it didn't," Joe suggested.

"Not once Amy appeared in our lives. First she became my friend at work. Then, when I invited her home for dinner, she became close to Kristen. She seemed to always be around. She played three-person toss with Marty and me in the backyard and cooked with Kristen in the kitchen. She went sledding with us in the winter and attended Christmas Eve mass with the family. It was like that for months. And then she was going on vacation with the family. I don't actually know who suggested it, but everyone seemed to think it was a great idea. Kristen and I had taken Marty camping in the Cascades every year since he was a baby. We were going back to one of our favorite spots that year and looking forward to it."

He paused and looked down at the floor as though the rug was the most interesting thing he'd ever seen. "We drove up together, singing and listening to Marty tell us about the party they had had the last day of third grade. We ate at our favorite restaurant on the way—a hot-dog stand that offered fresh buttermilk—and arrived just as the sun was setting. Kristen wanted to set up the tents, eat the sandwiches we'd brought along, and go to bed, but Marty was dying for a campfire and—I thought—he needed to get some exercise after spending most of the day in the car." He paused, frowning.

"I was the one who encouraged Marty to run around. And I may have asked Amy to play ball with him while Kristen and I set up the campsite. But I wasn't—I was not the person who gave them the ball. I know that's what Kristen has always thought, but I know I packed a softball—two softballs in fact. One was a rubber ball—one of those pink ones that kids like. The other was a Nerf . . . no one ever got killed by being hit in the temple with a Nerf ball. No one."

Josie and Joe again exchanged looks, but neither of them spoke.

"Kristen and I were setting up the tent Marty was going to share with Amy when we heard it." He stopped speaking and seemed to listen to . . . to what? Josie wondered. What was going on in his head that caused such a look of pain to cross his handsome face?

"It was Amy screaming. Kristen started to run toward the sound almost immediately. I followed when I heard Kristen's cries.

"Marty and Amy had been playing ball in a cleared spot that served as a parking lot. When I got there, Kristen was on the ground, holding Marty's head in her arms. Amy was standing above them, just standing there, not moving, like she was in shock or something. Which of course she must have been."

He paused and seemed to pull himself together. "I . . . Kristen and I . . . bundled Marty into the car and drove immediately to the nearest hospital. It was over an hour away. I drove. Kristen sat in the backseat with Marty's head in her lap. Amy sat in the passenger seat up front. I don't think anyone said anything the entire trip. The hospital was a small one in a small town and I think as we arrived either Kristen or Amy suggested that maybe a bigger place would be better equipped to deal with an emergency. But I drove up to the emergency entrance. If he needed moving, it could be done by ambulance. I couldn't go as fast as an ambulance and I had no idea where the next hospital might be found. I was right about that," he muttered, almost to himself.

"So they treated him there?" Joe asked.

"Yeah. There wasn't much that could be done. He was in a coma. . . . He probably hadn't been conscious since he was hit in the head. It was a freak accident. We were all together in the emergency room of this hospital, standing around Marty in his bed, and the doctor said that he was stable, that there was nothing we could do but wait. And then he died." David took a deep breath. "Just like that, Marty died. We knew because a buzzer went off on this TV screen hanging on the wall above his head. Doctors rushed around. And nurses, I guess. But . . . but he was dead. Nothing could be done."

He looked up at Joe and Josie. "You know, I really don't think anyone said anything at all until later. All I remember is the doctors talking, explaining what they were doing as they hooked up the monitors, the nurses telling us where to sit or stand. Someone offered to get us coffee or juice. But it wasn't until Marty was dead that I remember one of us saying anything. And then it was Kristen who spoke."

"What did she say?" Joe asked.

"She accused Amy of murdering Marty. Of course, I

thought it was just hysteria at the time. And Amy . . . I remember Amy crying . . . well, we all were crying at that point . . . and Amy said she was so sorry . . . and we cried. . . . I guess I said that already. The doctors and nurses said we should say good-bye to Marty. I know they were trying to be nice, but he was dead, I didn't even know what they meant at that point. I just turned around and walked out of the room and into the waiting area. Someone gave me a Styrofoam cup of coffee and I waited for Kristen and Amy. But only Kristen joined me. Amy . . . I guess Amy thought we would be better off left alone. I have no idea how she even got back to her home.

"We had the funeral two days later. Everyone from the company came, of course, but not Amy. She'd left town. At least that's what someone told me. She had gone to the Applegates, gotten her last paycheck, and just vanished. Every once in a while over the next few months someone would hear news of her, but I wasn't paying much attention. Kristen and I were having problems. Problems so serious we finally had to get a divorce."

"Maybe you'd better tell Josie about all that," Joe suggested gently. "I think she'll understand."

"If anyone will," Dave said. "You see, Kristen couldn't forgive Amy for killing Marty."

"But I thought you said it was an accident."

"It was. And I was angry, too, for a while—at Amy for coming on vacation with us. At myself for agreeing that Marty and Amy should play while Kristen and I set up the camp. At whoever found that hardball in the car. At Amy for throwing the hardball and hitting Marty." He shrugged. "At God and the fates, too, I guess."

"I understand," Josie said. And she did—that was exactly how she'd feel under the same circumstances.

"But Kristen never seemed to feel most of those things. She blamed Amy from that moment in the emergency room and she . . . she still blames her, I guess."

"So you think she killed Amy Llewellyn," Josie said.

"No. I know she didn't. She was with me when Amy was killed. And I told the police that first thing."

TWENTY-EIGHT

JOSIE REVIEWED THE final moments of her conversation with David on her way to work. Kristen had been with her ex-husband the night of the murder. Unless they had plotted to kill Amy together and then set up an alibi, neither of them could be suspects. So why, she wondered as she drove up to the house, was Kristen being arrested?

"Hey! What's going on here?" Josie yelled, jumping from her truck and running up to Chief Rodney and his son.

They were walking on either side of Kristen. She was handcuffed.

"We are escorting this woman to the county jail, where she will be held on charges of first-degree murder," Mike explained, a smirk on his face.

"That's stupid! I was just with David—her ex-husband. He was with her the night of the murder. . . . Why didn't you talk to him?" Josie cried. Kristen, as well she might, looked miserable and Josie added a reassurance to her carpenter. "Don't worry, these men are nuts. We'll get you out of there as soon as possible."

"We spoke with this young woman's husband right after the murder. He made that same claim to us then. But no one saw them together, so it's not much proof of her innocence, now is it, Miss Pigeon?" Chief Rodney announced.

"Now wait," Josie insisted. "You're arresting an important member of my crew. I think I have a right to know a little more about this." She didn't know much about the law, but she doubted that she had any such right. What she had no doubt about was the reliability of the Rodney family's need to grandstand. That trait was clearly in the ascendant at the moment.

"Maybe we should just take a minute to explain what happened to Josie, Dad."

"Fine, son."

It was no secret that Chief Rodney hated being reminded of his relationship with his son while on the job. And Josie couldn't resist smiling over his angry tone when he addressed his son.

"You might remember, Miss Pigeon, that we spoke with everyone on your crew about Amy Llewellyn's death. And no one admitted to knowing Amy. In fact, there is some reason to believe that this young woman worked hard to cover up her past relationship with the deceased."

"So? Doesn't she deserve a little privacy? There was a tragedy in her family. She lost her son. Can you blame her for not wanting to be reminded of that time? And what does that have to do with this? Her ex-husband has offered her an alibi. That's all that matters, it seems to me."

"She has a point there," Mike surprised them all by saying. "And, you know, her husband said she was with him that night before he even knew she'd need an alibi."

"So maybe he was using *her* for an alibi. Ever think of that?"

"I don't think so. . . ." Mike said slowly, ignoring the growing irritation in his father's voice. "It seems to me—"

"David would never murder anyone." Kristen spoke up. "He's just not that type of person. And he didn't blame Amy for . . . for our son's death. He said no one was to blame . . . that it was an accident."

"And David's neighbor was sure he was in his apartment all night long. He said David lived a very regular life. That you could almost set your clock by the times he went to bed and left the house the next morning. Remember, Dad? He said that when we checked it out. So—"

"So this woman shouldn't be in handcuffs," Josie said dramatically. She felt just like a character on one of those English mystery things on television.

"So . . . why didn't she say she was with her ex-husband when we asked her about that night, tell me that?" The chief of police sounded like a petulant child. If this hadn't all been so serious, Josie would have been thrilled.

"I was afraid if there was a connection between me and Innovations and Renovations, I might lose my job," Kristen said slowly. She gave Josie a guilty look. "I was trying to hide that. I . . . I knew how you felt about the other company, but . . . but I didn't know you well enough to know that it wouldn't matter to you."

Josie looked at Kristen and nodded. "That's why you were at the office so much right after Amy was killed. You did change your application form, didn't you?"

"You noticed. I thought you probably would. It was a stupid thing to do, but I was so worried. All I have now is my work."

"That's okay. I understand," Josie said. And thought that it was possible that Kristen had more than that—she seemed to have the beginnings of a new relationship with her ex-husband. "So are you going to take those handcuffs off and let her go?" she demanded.

"Well, Da—"

"Don't call me Dad, dammit! Dammit to hell!" Chief Rodney continued, doing exactly as Josie asked. "And don't get any smirks on that freckled face of yours, Miss Pigeon. You know who the only suspect in this case is right now, don't you? Your ex-boyfriend, Sam Richardson! And it's pretty strange that he's just disappeared, isn't it?" he demanded, storming off to his police car with his son in his wake.

"Damn right it is!" Mike Rodney tossed the words

over his shoulder as he struggled to keep up with his father.

"So why the hell don't you get off your fat ass and find him?" his father roared, getting into the car marked CHIEF OF POLICE and driving off without another word.

"Wow, that man sure has a temper, doesn't he?"

Josie and Kristen turned around and found that the rest of the crew had joined them.

"They're both sons-of-bitches," Betty explained. "I've lived here all my life, you know, and the stories I could tell you. . . ."

"Maybe you could tell them while we get those replacement windows in," Josie suggested gently.

"No problem at all."

"Could I talk with you for just a minute?" Josie asked Kristen as the entire crew started up to the house.

"Of course. And . . . and I know I should apologize and thank you . . . and . . ." There were tears in the corners of Kristen's eyes.

"I couldn't let them haul you off to jail when your ex-husband had just told me you were with him." Josie put her hand on Kristen's shoulder in what she hoped was a reassuring gesture. "Everything's going to be okay."

"No. That's not true. Nothing's ever going to be okay again. It hasn't been okay since my son died. It never will be again."

Josie began to disagree, but Kristen interrupted her.

"Never. And I'm not going to talk about it. I'll talk about anything else, but not about the accident. Okay?"

What choice did she have? "Okay," Josie agreed.

"And maybe . . ." Kristen seemed less sure of herself now. "Maybe I could help you finish up the framing in the master bath while we talk . . . if you'd like."

"Very much."

The rest of the crew was busy replacing the large windows in the long living room. Josie waited until she and Kristen were upstairs to begin.

"Why didn't you tell me you were getting back together with your ex-husband?" she asked.

"We aren't getting back together. It was just one night."

Josie saw the frown on Kristen's face and didn't pursue the subject. Kristen and David's current relationship was none of her business. But if Kristen didn't kill Amy, and of course Sam hadn't, then wasn't it possible that Fern or Al—

"I'm sure Sam had nothing to do with Amy's death." Kristen's reassurance interrupted her thoughts.

"No. Of course not." Josie stopped for a moment, trying to get her thoughts together. "But I was wondering . . . I mean, you really know more about Amy than anyone else. Could you tell me anything that might explain why she was killed . . . not something about your son's death. Maybe Amy did something to someone else that you know about. Or something else in her past . . ."

"Interesting question." Kristen picked up her tools and began to work as she thought about it.

"Your . . . David described Amy as a person who always tried to fit in with people."

"Boy, that's the truth. And I'm sure most people thought she was just as sweet as anything, but I'll bet there are lots of people who wish she had never been born."

Maybe this conversation wasn't such a good idea, Josie was thinking when Kristen's next words sent her reeling.

"You know, I got the impression that maybe Al knew her."

"Knew Amy?"

"Yeah." Kristen thought a bit. "It's just a general impression, but I think it's true. She said something . . . I can't remember exactly what it was. . . ."

"Who said something?"

"Al did. About knowing Amy, I think."

"When?"

"When did she know Amy?" Kristen asked her own question.

"No . . . well, yes. But that's not what I meant. I wondered when she said something that made you think she knew Amy. And when . . . when did she know Amy . . . ?" Josie frowned. All the caffeine she'd been consuming didn't seem to be helping her concentration. Maybe she needed some more. . . . "Did anyone get any coffee this morning?"

"Both Betty and Fern picked up some at the bakery."

"Fern did?" Josie was momentarily diverted. She had thought Fern was avoiding caffeine these days. She'd said something about it not being good for cancer patients, hadn't she?

"Maybe it was that herbal tea she likes so much," Kristen said, seeming to realize the same thing. She stopped working and looked at the floor. "Fern's been wonderful about having cancer, hasn't she? I mean, you'd almost think she didn't have it."

"Well, I certainly hope I'm half as strong as she's been if it ever happens to me," Josie said sincerely. "Tell me everything you remember about Al and Amy," she insisted.

"It was something she said," Kristen repeated.

Josie realized what was going on. "Look, I know you don't want to accuse anyone of murder—but we've got to get to the bottom of this before the wrong person is arrested. You've just seen how competent the local police are."

"Okay. I know. It's just that I can't remember what it was. I do remember Al made a comment about Amy a day or so after the murder and I thought something like 'oh, so you knew her, too.' I didn't say anything, of course, because I didn't want anyone to know about my past. I know it was selfish of me."

"There's no reason to worry about that anymore." Josie paused and thought for a minute. "Do you remember what provoked Al's comment?" She was hoping to jog Kristen's memory.

"No . . . But I do remember that it had something to do with work," she added suddenly. "I mean, it was something about the job, I think. Maybe something in the past. Not in the Northwest," she added, suddenly sad with the memory.

"Something that happened when they were working together?" Josie mused. "That's very interesting. Amy's only been on the island since March. And Al just arrived a few weeks ago. . . . I suppose it must have been someplace else."

"I'm sorry. I know that's not very helpful."

"Anything at all might help. You never really know where an idea will lead."

"But I don't really remember," Kristen began.

"You remember more than anyone else. It just might be a clue. And if it goes nowhere, at least it eliminates some possibilities. Listen, can you finish framing this in and then build the frame for the pan in the bottom of the shower?"

"Of course. Don't worry about anything. If I get finished, I'll start putting up the beaded wainscoting in the bathroom in the hall. Then the tilers can work around it instead of the other way around."

"Great. I just want to talk with Al for a few minutes. I'll be back soon."

"You won't tell her I said anything about this all, will you?" Kristen asked, a worried expression on her face. "I don't want her to think I've been accusing her of murder. I mean," she added suddenly, "if anyone knows what it feels like to be wrongfully accused of murder, I do."

Josie smiled. "Yeah, I guess you do." Without taking the time for more chat, she left the room and headed downstairs, through the square foyer (which would someday be an elegant introduction to the house, but was now a mass of cracked walls and plaster chunks falling from the ceiling) and into the living room, where the three women were struggling to fit three perfect new windows into three imperfect old openings.

"Anyone need any help here?" she asked, knowing the answer. This was a tough, backbreaking job; no one would even think of refusing such an offer.

"Grab a handful of those shims in the corner and see if you can shove a few in around the left jamb and under the inside sill," Betty answered over her shoulder.

Fern and Al were standing on the porch, holding the window in place while Betty tried to make the inside framing adjust to the new window header.

Josie did as Betty had asked, and the four women sweated and strained for almost an hour until the window was in place, the head and side casings installed, and the outside sill cut, sloped, and nailed in place.

"One down. Two more to go," Fern said, dropping onto the floor.

"I do nothing until I've had a break," Betty announced. "And a nice long drink."

"And something to eat. I'm starving," Al announced, wiping the sweat from her forehead onto a soaking T-shirt. "Who brought doughnuts this morning?"

"I did."

"And I did, too," Fern added after Betty answered.

"But both boxes are empty," Betty noted. "Guess someone has to go to the bakery." She looked at Josie.

"Do you want to go?" Josie asked.

"I'll go if Betty doesn't want to," Fern offered. "I think it's my day and I didn't get enough this morning, I guess."

"Either one of you can go. And the other might go upstairs and help Kristen. If we finish the preliminary work in the master bath this morning, she can join us down here this afternoon. And maybe we can get those last two windows in place." She glanced out the empty hole that was waiting for its glass. "I think the radio said something about a storm coming up the coast. We want to get this place sealed up before wind and rain can damage anything."

"I'll go to the bakery," Betty offered.

"And I'll help Kristen," Fern said.

"And I'll—"

"I'd like to talk to you a minute," Josie interrupted before Al could tell anyone what she was planning to do.

TWENTY-NINE

JOSIE DIDN'T EVEN have time to wonder how she was going to approach the other woman: Al started the conversation right off.

"It was the tattoo that gave me away, wasn't it?" she asked.

"The tat—"

"Oh, I know. You're a really nice person and you probably don't want me to realize that you snooped." Al thumped Josie on the shoulder in what she seemed to think was a companionable manner. Josie suspected she'd have a bruise in the morning. "You don't have to worry. I understand. I would have done the same thing if I'd been in your shoes."

Josie had no idea what Al was talking about—so she let her talk.

"I saw you in that tattoo parlor, you know. I know you're not the type of person to go in for body art, so I guessed that you figured out what was going on."

"Going on?" Josie asked when Al stopped to take a breath. What was this woman talking about?

"How I had my tattoos changed to hide my—well, what some people might call my past."

Caffeine. She definitely needed caffeine! "What about your past—exactly—are we talking about here?"

"You know the woman that was killed here? The woman who looked so much like you?"

"Of course. Amy Llewellyn."

"I worked with her before."

Please go on, Josie pleaded silently. "Really?" she asked out loud.

"Yeah. We had matching tattoos done. But I guess you already know that. That's why you went to the tattoo parlor yesterday, isn't it?"

"It is?" The question was out before Josie could stop it, but Al didn't seem to mind.

"Sure. What did the guy in there say to you?"

"Well, I sort of left before I got anything out of him," Josie muttered, not anxious to reveal the exact nature of her mission.

"Yeah, well, if you'd asked the right questions he'd've told you that you can change tattoos. But I thought everyone knew that. I guess I should tell you everything since you seem to know so much already. It was stupid, of course. I should have known the woman was nuts."

Josie assumed she was talking about Amy. She was beginning to feel sorry for the poor woman—no one seemed to have fond memories of her. Except, she reminded herself, possibly Sam. And with that, she immediately stopped feeling sorry for Amy Llewellyn—especially when she heard Al's next words.

"The bitch stole my boyfriend."

"Really?"

"Yeah, she was that type of broad. Ask Fern to tell you her story."

"Amy Llewellyn stole Fern's boyfriend?" There were getting to be more coincidences than Josie could accept.

"Nah, she tried to steal Kristen's husband—ex-husband now, I think."

"What does Fern have to do with this?"

"She was dating him. Well, Fern dated David Sweeney a few times about a month ago—and he told her that he'd been married to Kristen and that Amy had ruined their marriage. . . . You're shocked, aren't you?"

"Well . . . I . . ." But Al didn't give Josie a chance to explain that she already knew about the relationship.

"Maybe no one told you about it because Fern saw you two together at some Italian place and so we knew the asshole was putting moves on you, too. Men, you can't trust them any farther than you can throw 'em, right?"

Josie's head was splitting. "I guess not." She thought for a second.

"You're confused, right?"

"Very."

"Maybe it'd help if I explained from the beginning, okay?"

"Oh, please do."

"I worked with Amy Llewellyn back in Ohio."

"You worked for the same contractor?"

"Yeah. I hadn't been there long when she arrived looking for work. 'Course she got the job, looking the way she did. Cute and curly and all. The guy who hired me was a sucker for a cute girl."

And for women far more butch apparently, but Josie didn't say anything about that. "The owner is the man you were talking about when you said she stole your boyfriend?"

"Nah. We'd broken up a few months before she arrived. The asshole wouldn't leave his wife like he'd promised me he would, so I told him to stay away from me."

"So you just didn't like her right away?"

"Hah! I was crazy about her. We got along great and became good friends. That's why the tattoos."

"I don't understand."

"Well, we used to go drinking together after work.

There was this bar near the office and a lot of guys went there. And a lot of girls, too, because of Burt."

"Who is—was—Burt?" Josie asked.

"The bartender. One of the best-looking guys in the world. I swear to you. Blond hair. Blue eyes. Huge shoulders . . ." Al sighed. "I really had the hots for him, I can tell you."

"And so did Amy?" Josie tried to return to the subject.

"Yup. We used to sit there at the counter night after night and hope he'd notice one or both of us. But you know how it is with some men—you could strip naked and jump into their lap and they still wouldn't take their eyes off the screen."

"What was on the screen?" Josie was wondering what pornography could be more interesting than a live naked woman—until Al answered her question.

"Baseball. Football. Basketball. Hockey. Even soccer, for heaven's sake. As though we needed another sport in this country. Jeeez."

"What does this have to do with tattoos?"

"Well, one Saturday night Amy and I sat there at the bar a little too long and got a little too drunk and one of us—I don't remember who—thought it just might make an impression on Burt if we each had his name tattooed in an interesting place."

"What interesting place?" Josie couldn't resist asking.

"Mine is right above my left breast, which turned out to be lucky. Amy had hers done on her tush—her butt."

Josie knew what *tush* meant. "So why was it lucky that you had his name put . . . where you put it?"

Al glanced down at her ample chest. "Because there was lots and lots of space to add to it."

"I don't understand."

"Well, when it turned out that the man was gay, I didn't want his name on me forever, did I? So I had the words *and Ernie* added—and a picture of them both. Burt and Ernie, you know."

"From *Sesame Street*. Yeah."

"It's cute. Do you want to see it?"

"No," Josie said quickly. "Thanks, though. Did Amy do the same thing?"

"Nah. There probably wasn't enough space on the tight-assed bitch. She had some sort of design done over it. Something cute and dumb probably." A scowl covered her face. "Cute and dumb was what she liked."

"The boyfriend she stole from you?" Josie guessed.

"Damn right. But I didn't kill her because of that. Men are like fish . . . there are lots of them in the sea, right?"

"I guess so." Although not many of them seemed to be swimming in Josie's direction. "What about Fern?"

"What about her?"

"What did she know about Amy? I mean, I'd rather ask you than bother her," Josie added quickly, and then wondered if that wasn't just about the rudest thing she could have said.

"Yeah. You really hate to bother someone who has cancer, don't you? I understand that completely.

"Fern was dating David—Kristen's ex-husband—but no one had told anyone that Kristen had an ex-husband. No one blames you. You have to keep stuff like that confidential. We know."

Josie began to defend herself before she realized that she didn't have to—and she couldn't. She certainly could not have told what she didn't know.

"Don't worry about it. I'm telling you. We all understand."

"Thanks. So Fern was dating David without knowing that he had been married to Kristen," Josie prompted, although she knew this part of the story.

"Exactly. He told her he was divorced right away, I think. But he didn't tell her Kristen was his ex-wife."

"Then how did she find out?"

"Well, she couldn't understand his reaction when he saw her."

"What do you mean?"

"Fern said that he came to pick her up after work, and

just as she was getting into his truck, Kristen walked out the door of the office and apparently David had some sort of shit fit."

"What did he do exactly?"

"Stepped on the gas so quickly that he almost left Fern's foot back on the curb. I was right there and I saw the whole thing. The man turned pale underneath his tan and just took off."

"You're sure it was Kristen's appearance that caused him to drive off?"

"Oh yeah. He told Fern all about it. And she told me the next morning. They went to an Italian restaurant for dinner—maybe the one he took you to. He ordered a liter of Chianti, drank most of it himself, and then explained that he had acted so strangely because he'd been shocked to see his ex-wife." She chuckled. "At first Fern thought it was me he was talking about. But he said Kristen's name finally. And then he told Fern about how they had been married, but something happened. Fern said he seemed pretty upset and she knew he didn't want to talk about it—you know how sweet Fern is—so she just listened and made sure she was the one who drove home. Because of the wine."

"Good thinking. So did he explain then that their divorce had . . . had something to do with Amy?" She didn't have any idea how to ask the question without mentioning their son's death and she was sure she didn't have any right to tell anyone else about it.

"Yeah. He'd had an affair with Amy and that broke up the marriage. You know how men are."

"True." Josie thought for a moment. "Are you sure Fern told you that Amy and David's affair was the reason David and Kristen got divorced?"

"What else could there be? She said David blamed Amy for the divorce. . . . Men!"

"What do you mean?"

"They always blame the woman. Never themselves for being so damn horny."

"So—"

"Say, do I smell coffee? Are they back from the bakery?" Al interrupted.

"Sounds like it," Josie replied, hearing work boots echoing through the hallway.

"Are we done?"

"Definitely. Thanks a lot for telling me all this." Josie began to walk toward the hallway, following the tantalizing scent of fresh, strong coffee. She hoped Al would follow, then Josie could ask why she had crossed the crime scene tape.

There was, however, no time for further questions. In her starved state, Al practically pushed in front of her boss. They joined the rest of the crew around the bags that Betty dropped on the old table in one corner of the foyer. Hands reached out for crullers and cream-filled doughnuts as though the bodies they were attached to were immune from high-cholesterol counts.

"I need Fern for a few minutes," Josie stated flatly.

Fern glanced at Al, but Al was busy eating. "Fine," Fern said. "They can finish the window without me, but one of us is going to have to help hold the next one in place."

"We'll only be a minute," Josie assured everyone, grabbing the last cream-filled doughnut so fast that powdered sugar flew in the air.

Betty giggled, but Josie noticed that Kristen wasn't smiling.

Neither was Fern as she followed her boss from the room.

"I would never have dated David if I'd known you were interested in him," she began as soon as she and Josie were alone together.

"If you're talking about David Sweeney, I wasn't—am not—interested in him," Josie protested as though good-looking men wandered across her path each and every day. And even if they did, she realized, she wouldn't be interested. Not since Sam had moved to the island.

"Why are you smiling?"

"I didn't realize that I was. . . . That's not important now," she added, determined to get back on track. "I was never upset that you were dating David, but that is what I want to talk about with you—if you don't mind."

"I guess not. That's what you've been talking over with Al, isn't it?"

"A little. She said that you told her David was having an affair with Amy and that's why he and Kristen broke up."

"I never said that," Fern protested. "And David never told me that. How do you know they were having an affair?"

"I don't. It's just that Al seems to think—"

"Oh, Al. To listen to her, all every married man wants is to convince a single woman to go to bed with him—especially if that single woman is Al."

"That sure seems to be true," Josie admitted. "So David didn't tell you an affair with Amy Llewellyn destroyed his marriage?"

"Definitely not. He said Amy had destroyed his marriage but he said something strange. . . . Let me see, how did he put it? He said it was Amy's friendship with them that caused their divorce. Does that make sense to you?"

"Yeah. It does. It's really a very sad story," Josie answered, wondering if it was possible that she'd missed the real connection between that story and Amy Llewellyn's murder.

THIRTY

"SO IT IS entirely possible that this young carpenter with cancer and the name of a plant told the woman with the ugly tattoos on her arms that the dead woman had broken up David and Kristen's marriage and the woman with the tattoos just assumed it was an affair—"

"Because the death of a child is so much more rare than an affair, thank God," Sam's mother finished Risa's summary and wrote furiously on the notepad she had brought with her.

"Yes. And it's true that Al seems to see everything from one point of view—her own—so you're probably right about that having happened. But Fern is the woman with cancer and Al has the tattoos." Josie provided the names to complete Risa's descriptions.

"And they're probably not just on her arms," Carol insisted. "This magazine I was reading said that breasts are among the most commonly tattooed body parts. Isn't that amazing?"

Well, you could have knocked her down with a feather, but Josie decided not to make a comment. Who knew how close Sam and his mother actually were or what they knew about each other's lives? "You know what I think?" she began. And she wasn't surprised when she was interrupted. It had been happening all evening. Carol and Risa were on the case now. And they were determined to "help" Josie find out who had murdered Amy Llewellyn.

"Wait until I get all this written down," Carol insisted. "Then we can sort through everything methodically. My Sammy is a big believer in order and method."

"Your Sammy has vanished," Risa reminded her. "When he should be here to help Josie solve this crime."

"Sammy must have had something more important to do. He knew, of course, that he could leave. He knew I would help."

"*We* will help," Risa said.

Josie wished they would both just keep cooking and leave the detecting to her. Not only were they getting her confused, but she was hungry. "Maybe—" she began.

"I have four suspects," Carol interrupted.

"Who?" Risa asked.

"Kristen Sweeney. David Sweeney. Alma Snapp. And Fern Gast."

"In the first place, Kristen goes by her maiden name, Duffy," Josie said.

"Fine. I'll put that down. Kristen Duffy," Carol said obligingly. "Did I get anyone else's name wrong?"

"No, but Kristen couldn't have done it. David said she was with him all night."

"But do the police know exactly when the murder took place? I know that is very important."

"Yes. They know. Between ten at night and six the next morning—because Amy was seen around ten that night in a bar and discovered early the next morning by Sam—not because of some fancy forensics. The local police are probably incapable of forensics, fancy or otherwise," Josie admitted.

"But I do not like those suspects," Risa interjected. "Why are there not more suspects?"

"Maybe the man who owns Innovations and Renovations," Carol mused, her hand circling the notebook. "I don't remember his name and there *is* the question of motive."

"His name is Joe Ellis and I can't imagine why he would kill Amy and leave her on—oh."

"Exactly my thought." Carol beamed, apparently pleased with Josie's thinking. "He's the person who would leave her at someplace connected with you. He wants to ruin Island Contracting."

"No," Risa protested. "You are new here. You do not know the island. Josie's small company is no competition for the big and important Innovations and Renovations."

"So you don't think we can use that to explain why he would have killed this woman on Island Contracting's property?"

"Job site," Josie corrected. "We don't own it, we work there."

"But still . . ." Carol mused.

"Okay, put him down," Josie said. What difference would it make, after all? "You know, I'm hungry. Maybe we should have some dinner?" She hoped someone would take her hint.

"We've already eaten. Risa made a wonderful pasta with fresh shellfish," Carol muttered, writing as she spoke. "He could have been romantically involved with Amy. We really don't know, do we?"

Risa nodded. "I have an idea. We should go look at the place where the dead woman lived."

Josie remembered the address Sam had given her . . . almost. "She lived over on Twelfth Avenue, right?"

"Sammy said eleven-forty-five Twelfth, I think. If she had a roommate, we could ask to see—" Carol began, excited.

"She lived alone, but we can get in," Risa stated.

"When?"

"How?" Josie asked what she thought was a more appropriate question.

"I am friends with the man who owns the building. He is a nice man. He would have charged her a fair rent for this last summer."

"You mean he knew she was going to die? He knew this was the last summer she'd need to rent a place from him?" Carol said. "What's this man's name?" Her pencil was poised and ready to write him down as a suspect.

"No . . . no. He's going to tear that house down and build another to sell." She gave Josie a guilty glance and Josie realized what was going on.

"And he's not interested in hiring Island Contracting," she said.

"Oh, *cara*, I told him how wonderful you are and how excellent is the work you do, but he . . . he hired Innovations and Renovations. He said they had worked with him before."

"And if he was happy with them and their work, he should hire them again," Josie told her. "That's the way things are in this business."

"But I was so mad at him for not hiring you."

"Of course you were, but that's not important now," Carol said. Josie was beginning to realize that Sam's insistence on sticking to the point was the result of his upbringing as much as anything he had learned in law school. "You must call him and ask if he will let us into Amy's apartment. We might learn a lot there. Sammy once dated an interior decorator—a beautiful young woman who had won all sorts of awards—and she told me you could learn most everything about a person's character from the place where they lived."

Josie realized both women were looking around her apartment. "Please give your friend a call," she told Risa. "Maybe we could see Amy's apartment tonight." She sure hoped it was messier than hers!

Risa's seductive voice over the phone gained them immediate access to Amy's home. It turned out, of course, to be much, much neater than Josie's.

It was impossible for those who made their livings on the island to pay high summer rental rates all year long. Most people solved that problem by living on the mainland and making the three- or four-mile commute across one of the two bridges. But Amy, like Josie, seemed to have found a nice landlord who rented out the top floor of his thirties bungalow at a reasonable rate.

Unlike Josie's home, the space was not divided up, but had been converted into a large studio apartment. It was lovely. Apricot-colored walls were accented by period moldings in shimmering white enamel. The oak floor had been bleached a lovely sandy beige. At one end of the room, a black-and-white Pullman kitchen stood behind a low white Formica counter. A door at the other end of the room led to a deep coral-and-white-tiled bathroom. The furniture was predominantly wicker and pieces picked up, like Josie's, at estate sales on the island. Unlike Josie, someone had been hard at work enameling and staining until everything glowed.

"*Bellissimo,*" Risa breathed.

"Wow. Great apartment," Carol agreed.

"We're here to find out more about Amy," Josie reminded them.

"She had wonderful taste," Risa murmured, walking toward a wall hanging and taking a corner of it in her hands.

"And very neat," Carol commented.

"Maybe a little too neat?" Josie asked, walking into the center of the room and looking around.

"You think she was compulsive or something?" Carol asked seriously.

"I think the island police did their usual inadequate job when it came to searching this place." She picked up a framed photograph by the daybed and stared at it. "How strange."

"What is strange?" Carol peered over her shoulder. "A nice-looking young woman. Maybe just a bit of a hippie, but still nice looking."

"It's Amy Llewellyn. When she was young. What sort of person has a photograph of themselves when they were young by the side of their bed?" Josie wondered out loud.

Risa was looking through the closet and Carol was stooping down to peer into the small refrigerator. Neither of them answered her. Josie, who hated paperwork more than anything, found she had been left to search through the small white-painted desk.

It shouldn't be a difficult task, she realized; everything was sorted and in order. Amy's checkbook had been balanced and, as far as Josie could tell, revealed nothing interesting. Checks to the grocery store, to her landlord, to the local utilities and the phone company predominated. It was balanced each and every month. The rest of that drawer held insurance forms and the like. Everything was in order. Nothing revealed anything sinister or even particularly personal about Amy Llewellyn. There weren't any personal letters, and if there had ever been an address book, the police probably took it when they searched. The rest of the desk revealed interests in exotic foods (recipes clipped from magazines and newspapers, most of them including either cilantro or lemongrass in the list of ingredients) and decorating. There was also a clipping about Island Contracting and its female workers. The local newspaper had run the article early in May. The photograph that accompanied it showed Josie, looking particularly chubby, between Kristen and Betty.

"You've stopped moving, *cara*. Is something wrong?"

"No, but I just found out how Amy knew Kristen was working for Island Contracting." She showed the other two women the clipping.

"So she came here to be with—what's his name? David Sweeney," Carol mused, taking the photo from Josie.

"Do you think so?"

"I suppose it could be coincidence."

"And then this is coincidence also that David and Kristen are here together as well," Risa said as Carol passed the paper to her.

It sounded like a lot of coincidences to Josie. She sat down on the desk chair and tried to think. But Carol and Risa continued to chat.

"This David Sweeney must be a hunk. Two women followed him here."

"Ask Josie," Risa told her. "She dated him."

"You dated David Sweeney?" Carol was surprised.

"Just one date."

"Sammy didn't tell me you were dating."

"I wasn't dating. I had one date. Besides, what business is it of his if I date? He wasn't interested in continuing our relationship. He broke up with me. I didn't break up with him!"

"She is still very upset, my poor *cara*," Risa explained. "She wasn't interested in committing herself to their relationship. Sammy loves her and she doesn't love him," Carol insisted.

"She—" Risa was barely able to speak, but her layers of silk expressed her state of mind by fluttering out in all directions. Someday Josie was going to figure out exactly how she did that. . . .

"Hey, this is me you're talking about!"

"And Sammy. Don't forget Sammy."

"I don't forget him. I never forget him," Josie retorted. She was exhausted, worried, and, dammit, starving. "I just feel that it's every woman's right to decide if she wants to sleep with a man, and if Sammy—Sam couldn't accept my decision, then he had every reason to choose not to continue our relationship."

"Sex? We broke up over sex?"

All three women turned and looked at the man standing in the doorway.

"Sammy, where—"

"You broke this woman's heart, Sam Richardson. You—"

But Josie didn't say anything to Sam. The only person in the world she loved more than Sam was standing right behind him. "Tyler Clay Pigeon. Where the hell have you been?"

THIRTY-ONE

"WHAT'S ALL THIS about sex?"

"Don't you try to distract me, Tyler! You are supposed to be at camp. Whatever made you think you could just leave there and . . . and come home, for heaven's sake. You are in serious trouble!" Now that she was over the relief of finding her son alive and well, Josie discovered that she wanted to kill him herself.

"Mom, you don't understand. I went to camp to do this. No one would even have known I'd gone if you hadn't ended up in the middle of another murder investigation. The only reason I got caught is that I hung around too long to protect you! In a way this is all your fault." Tyler's dark blue eyes radiated charm and sincerity.

But mothers are hard to con. "Do you want to repeat that?"

"I hung around here to protect you. Otherwise I would have been back at camp in less than twenty-four hours and won the bet."

"The bet? What bet? What are you talking about?"

"Boys . . . it always was difficult to get Sammy to tell a story without embellishing it in some way."

"Ah, men . . ." Risa began.

"Wait a second." Josie raised her voice. "Everyone just be quiet and let Tyler explain why he left camp and what he's doing here."

"Excellent idea," Sam agreed.

Tyler stared down at his foot (which was covered, Josie noticed, with a running shoe, which, judging by its cost, should have lasted forever), then up at the ceiling, then around the room.

"Why did you leave camp? What are you doing here?" Josie repeated. It was best to keep conversations with Tyler focused. He was good at going off on an attractive tangent.

"But, Mom, you don't understand. I went to that camp to leave it."

"Tyler . . ."

"Mom, just listen! You won't understand if you don't know the entire story!" Tyler's hair was darker and straighter than his mother's, but when he was excited, it had the same tendency to stick out as it was doing now.

"Fine. Tell me the whole story."

"Okay. See, there's this kid at school whose name is Robbie and he thinks he's such hot sh—such a hotshot. Everyone hates him. All the other kids, that is. But the teachers . . . well, they seem to like him." It was obvious that Tyler considered their judgment poor.

"So what does Robbie have to do with you leaving camp?"

"He went to that camp last summer and all winter long he bragged about how he left camp, hitchhiked home, and then went back without anyone ever knowing he was gone."

"So . . ."

"So he lives in New Jersey—even closer to the camp than we do—and I . . . I just happened to say I could do the same thing—and I'd be able to prove I'd done it. Like there was no proof Robbie did what he said he did. Right?"

"You said this to who?"

"Oh, just a bunch of the guys. We were hanging out one night. You know how it is."

Josie sighed, sounding, to herself, amazingly like her own mother. "And then what happened?"

"Robbie said I'd never do it and his friends started defending him and my friends started defending me, and Mom, before I knew it, I'd told everyone I could do it—if I could get into the camp and get a scholarship," he added quickly. "No way I thought you should pay for all this."

"So you talked me into letting you go to camp. You got a scholarship and you went off. Only to leave three weeks later and come home?"

"Mom, it wasn't that easy! It took planning. Lots and lots of planning."

Josie noticed Carol and Risa exchange looks that said *isn't he a darling?* She raised her eyes to the ceiling, but didn't comment. Right now Tyler's darlingness was difficult for her to see.

"I had to save enough money for bus fare to come

home—after I got the schedules—and figuring them out was sure tough. I had to change buses four times. Public transportation in this country sucks. There's a kid from Denmark in my class and he's been all over Europe by train. And he says—"

"Go on, Tyler," Josie urged. She was relieved that he hadn't been foolish enough to hitchhike, but she could see Risa was ready to launch into some Italian train stories.

"I starved to death for months at school to save my spending money for the buses, and then Robbie—who had no proof at all that he had really been home when he said he was—said I had to have proof or it didn't count." He frowned and Josie had to clench her hands into fists to keep from reaching out to hug him.

"That really got us. We thought of getting a newspaper—but that could've been sent to me. And then I figured the best thing to do would be to have my photo taken on the island—like during the island run, or the big-blue contest, or Sandcastle Sunday."

"What?" Carol had been quiet long enough.

"The island run is a marathon held over Labor Day weekend, the big-blue contest is a blue fishing competition held sometime in the middle of July, and one Sunday is chosen each year when people build sandcastles and they're judged by the lifeguards—it's a fund-raiser for whatever equipment the lifeguards need," Sam explained.

"But I knew I'd never get away with vanishing unless it was over parents' weekend—you wouldn't believe the uproar the camp gets into for parents' weekend. But nothing was happening on the island this weekend! Can you believe that? Next summer we'll have to organize something. There's this kid at school who lives near a wildlife preserve and they—"

"And to think I was feeling guilty about not coming—when it really would have messed up your plans if I had, wouldn't it?"

"That's why I kept sending you letters telling you how horrible camp was. I thought that would discourage you."

"You sent postcards, not letters. And you didn't sound all that miserable. But let's not worry about that now. Finish your story," Josie insisted.

"So I couldn't take a photo that would prove I was here this weekend. There was only one alternative. I had to leave something on the island that could have only been brought here by me."

"Oh, the thing you left on my bed!" Josie cried.

"Yeah, did you like it?" he asked eagerly. "I thought it was sort of artistic. I made the base in conceptual-art class and then everyone who knew about the be—a lot of guys added stuff to it."

"And the one at the police station?" Josie asked, suddenly realizing that the pile of leaves and feathers she'd seen the other night had been left by her son.

"Well, that's where everything got all screwed up. The guys thought maybe you would lie for me and so I said I'd leave another of these things at the police department. The police sure wouldn't lie for me—and everyone agreed with that. But when I was there dropping it off on the front desk, the Rodney rats—"

"What?"

"The Rodney rats. That's what all the kids on the island call them, Mom."

"They are policemen, Tyler. They're supposed to help you."

"Moooom!"

Yeah, even she didn't buy that one. "Okay, just tell me your story—and make sure Mike and his father don't ever hear what you call them."

"Yeah. So I was leaving this thing on the desk when . . . when they came in talking. Well, I couldn't get caught—that was one of the conditions—so I ducked under the desk and waited until they left."

"And they were talking about the murder," Josie guessed.

"They were talking about you and Sam, too—that's what worried me. A whole lot! You know those guys are idiots and they were saying that it couldn't be anyone on your crew. They thought it was someone named Christine."

"Kristen," Josie corrected him.

"Yeah, that's right. That's not the woman with cancer, is it?"

"No, it's not. Do you remember what they said about Kristen?"

Tyler frowned. "Yeah. It didn't make much sense. The police had gotten a report of some kid's death and that made them think Kristen or her husband had done it, but then when they questioned her they were sure they both had alibis."

"You know, I don't get that," Carol interrupted. "Why do they think they're not both lying?"

Tyler seemed to consider this for a minute. "It was interesting. . . ." He looked at her closely. "You're Sam's mother, aren't you?"

"Why, yes, how did you know?"

"He has a photograph of you in his kitchen. It's nice to meet you." He held out his hand.

Despite her pleasure with his manners, Josie told him to get back to his story.

"Yeah." (How the hell, Josie wondered, not for the first time, did adolescents manage to get so much resentment into just one word?) "Well, you see, they talked to Kristen right away—before her husband knew about the murder—and she said that they had been together that night. So the police went to him and asked him about it and he verified it. No big deal if you ask me. They're married, aren't they?" And he glanced at Sam and then at his mother.

Josie did not want him speculating over where she and Sam spent their nights—and there was something else here. "Do you know exactly what they asked him?"

"Not really. I was just listening under the desk, and

besides, I was worried about you, for heaven's sake. I couldn't believe it. They said the woman who was killed looked just like you."

"Only from behind," his mother said.

"Yeah, well, she was killed from behind, you know. I heard that much. And then they said that Sam was a good suspect. And the way they were laughing about that made me sure they'd try to pin the whole thing on Sam. So . . ." He took a deep breath. "I decided I'd better give up the idea of going back to camp and hang around and help out here. I was needed," he ended seriously.

Josie smiled. "That's sweet, honey, but—"

"Please don't call me honey," Tyler protested. "I'm going to be fifteen soon."

"You're going to be fifteen in ten months, Tyler."

"But you're fighting a losing battle, Tyler," Sam added. He looked at his own mother. "Mothers seem to think they can call us whatever they care to no matter how old we are."

"So you've been on the island for a few days," Carol said. "Where have you been sleeping? Who's been feeding you?"

This was no mystery to Josie. "Tyler's lived here all his life. He has lots of friends." She thought for a moment. "You've been sleeping in Jeremy's old clubhouse, I'll bet. And everyone you know has been slipping meals to you."

"I spent one night there, but his cat had kittens there and no one ever cleaned off the mattress afterward, so it stinks. I spent last night in a boat down at the public landing. It was this great yacht. I can't believe anyone just left it there unlocked!"

"Are you still thinking of becoming a lawyer?" Sam asked. "Because if you are, you might want to consider the laws regarding trespassing on personal property."

"Maybe—or maybe a geologist. I took this great course in geo—"

"Tyler!"

"What, Mom?"

"What have you been doing for the past few days?"

"Keeping you safe. Didn't you see the things I left around? They were all variations on American Indian totems. First I purified the murder site and I sent messages to the spirits of the four winds in all the corners. Then I put good-luck charms around our house. I even put special charms at Sam's—just because I thought you might be spending a lot of time there while I was out of town." He grinned.

Well, that explained all the "satanic" symbols. Risa apparently had been right when she suggested they reminded her of jewelry—Native American jewelry apparently. She thought everything over for a moment. "What are you going to lose?" Josie asked her son.

"What do you mean?"

"You mentioned a bet," Sam informed him.

"More than once, in fact," his mother added.

"Oh, well, there's this group of us."

"Go on."

"And there's this group of them—Robbie's friends—and . . . well . . ." He took a deep breath and ran his hands through his hair in a way that reminded three people in the room of his mother. "If I made it home and back without being detected, my group was going to be allowed to do something that's usually done by the older guys. Mom, I'd really rather not talk about it. Maybe I could tell Sam? When we're alone?"

"Tyler . . ."

"Please, Mom." Tyler glanced at Risa and Carol as he pleaded.

"Okay. But Sam . . ."

"Then Sam can tell you. That will be okay."

"Fine. So I have only one question now," Josie said.

"What?"

"How are you going to talk the camp director into calling off the Pennsylvania State Police and then letting you return to camp?"

"Oh, that's no problem. Sam's already done it."

Josie looked at Sam, her eyebrows raised. "Really?"

"I just reminded him that you might sue the camp for negligence—but, of course, if you allowed Tyler to return there, that would be a sign that you trusted them to take care of your only son, thus making it impossible for a lawsuit to be filed."

"So everything's okay," Tyler concluded, and then grinned. "Now let's get back to what you were saying about sex."

Josie affectionately bopped her son on the head. "If I turn gray overnight, at least I'll know who to blame."

THIRTY-TWO

"WHEN DID YOU find Tyler?" Josie asked Sam. They were sitting on the deck over the bay behind Island Contracting's offices. The cat was curled up in Josie's lap. "I'm going to keep this one," she commented idly, stroking the animal's fur.

"Another cat—just what you need."

As if it were any of his business! "You didn't answer my question."

"Around noon today. Once I realized he was on the island, I just checked out all his normal haunts. You and I are a lot alike, you know," Sam continued.

"What do you mean?"

"I thought of that damn clubhouse first, too. In fact, I would have found him earlier if I hadn't hung around there waiting for him to return."

"How'd you know he'd been there?"

"Who else would leave a copy of *Zen and the Art of Motorcycle Maintenance* and the current issue of *Cat Fancy* magazine next to the pillow?"

"Sure sounds like Tyler," she admitted.

"He's some kid," Sam said admiringly. "Imagine trying to call on Indian spirits for your safety. You've done a good job with him, Josie."

"It would have been hard to go wrong with him, he's so determined. Sometimes I think he's raised me," Josie admitted. "He should never have left camp, but it is good to see him."

"You're not the only person to think so. Mom and Risa were having a ball feeding him when I left," Sam commented. "He'll probably go back to camp five pounds heavier."

"You were nice to volunteer to take him back. I really can't afford to take the time just now." She had realized that it was only a matter of time before she lost one of her best workers.

"I'm glad to do it. It will be good to get away for a day. I'm a little sick of the Rodney men leaping out at me from odd corners."

"Idiots. They can't still suspect you?"

"Who else?"

"Couldn't you sue them . . . for bothering you or something?"

"The term you're looking for is harassment. And probably not. At least not until someone else is arrested for the murder."

"Actually," Josie began slowly, "I think I know who did it, but . . ."

"But what?"

She began to smile. "You've given me a great idea, Sam. Do you think you . . . I . . ."

"Just spit it out."

"I want to talk to David Sweeney. I have some questions to ask him."

"About the murder? I don't mind going with you, but why can't you do it yourself?"

"Because I don't want to ask him about the murder. I want to ask him about the police. And if you're thinking of suing the island's police force, we have a good reason to ask a lot of questions."

"I just told you that I don't have a case against the police."

"But David doesn't know that."

"What do you want to ask him about? The murder?"

"No, what I said before—I want to ask about the police." She picked up the cat and started back into the office. "Come on. It's getting late and the sooner this whole thing is settled the better. If I'm right, the police will lead us right to the murderer."

"Well, that will be a first for this island's police force," Sam muttered, following Josie through the office and out to the road.

"My car or your truck?"

"Your car. You drive and I'll explain on the way over."

"Over to where?"

Josie pursed her lips. "We can try I and R's office first. It's late and he's probably not there, but someone might know where he is—or tell us where he lives."

"Good idea."

Six stops later they discovered David Sweeney in the same Italian restaurant he'd taken Josie on their date. If you could call it a date, she thought.

He was at a large table in the back of the room with some friends, and waved when he spotted her coming toward him.

"Hi, Josie. Do you know everyone here?"

She looked around the table. "Looks like I and R's best," she said, smiling and greeting a few people by name. "Have you all met Sam Richardson?"

It took a few minutes, but everyone managed to meet everyone else before Josie asked David if they could have a word or two—privately. "It's about the police department," she explained quickly. "Not the murder."

"Well, only indirectly," Sam said.

"Okay. How about that table by the door?" David asked, leading the way.

"So what do you want to ask me?" he said, after all three of them were settled and had ordered beers.

"Sam is having trouble with the police department," Josie began immediately.

"That's not a surprise. Those idiots probably couldn't find a tube of sunscreen on the beach on a sunny day in August. But I don't see how I can help. They've pretty much left me alone since they realized that Kristen and I are each other's alibi."

"You see, that's the difference. They've left you alone." Josie leaned across the table. "It will help prove Sam's assertion that he's being harassed if he can show that they're acting differently in your case." She didn't know if this was completely true or not, but David probably didn't either. "So, if you could just tell us everything about the questions they asked you right after the murder . . . you know, how they told you about Amy's death. What they said about Kristen. What questions they asked you—" She shut up, realizing David was staring at her.

"Josie is sometimes a little overenthusiastic when she tries to make life difficult for the Rodneys—she and Mike were quite an item on the island at one time, you know." Sam kicked her in the shin as he spoke. She got his message and didn't protest. They did, after all, need to obtain this information. On the other hand . . .

"You dated Mike Rodney?"

"I was young and stupid," she answered, neglecting to tell him that, presently, she was only two years older and probably not all that much wiser. "You were going to tell us about your conversation with Mike and his dad," she reminded him.

"Well, I was eating lunch when they came to I and R's

looking for me. I'm in charge of the addition on that big beach house on Eleventh Street and I was up to my neck in paperwork—you know how it is," he added to Josie.

"Were both Mike and his father there?"

"No, just Mike—the son, right? And another officer. He introduced himself—I think his name began with a *C* or a *K*."

"Koenig?" Josie asked, remembering the man who had been accompanying Mike around the island.

"Sounds right."

"Did they tell you about the murder first thing?" Sam asked.

"Yes, I think so. They said that Amy Llewellyn had been murdered—but I already knew that."

"How?"

David was again staring at Josie. "Well, not because I killed her, if that's what you're thinking. We heard the news early in the morning. Joe was called at home actually, I think. Anyway, he came in to work and told us all about it at the morning meeting."

"Everyone gets together at I and R each morning?" Josie asked. It was something she thought she'd invented.

"Just the project leaders. The crews head straight to the sites."

"And the owner of I and R announced Amy's death before you started the workday?" Sam tried to get the conversation back on track. He knew Josie was apt to become entranced in the minutiae of the competition's daily routine.

"Yup."

"How did everyone react?" Josie asked.

"We were shocked, of course. We'd been working together for the past few months, after all."

"But it must have been different for you," Sam suggested.

"Oh, yeah, I thought about Marty—and Kristen, of course."

"Did you call Kristen and let her know?" Josie asked.

"I tried, but no one answered at her apartment or your office. So I figured she was already at work—so she already knew—I mean, no one at Island Contracting could have missed the police that day."

"So you saw the police?" Sam leaped in.

"Had to drive by the heart house on the way to my job site that morning—and then back to the office before lunch, didn't I?"

"Of course." Josie wanted to bean Sam—he was the one getting off the topic this time. "But you were eating lunch when the police arrived."

"Yeah. I was busy and they were, too—came right to the point. They told me about the murder. Said that they knew of my past connection with Amy and asked me if Kristen had been with me the night before." He shrugged. "And I said yes. That was pretty much it. They seemed happy with my answer—they accepted the fact that I didn't kill Amy."

"Believe me, we're not here because we think you lied to protect yourself," Josie told him truthfully.

"It's what the police said to you that interests us," Sam explained. "Now, I know I sound like a lawyer, but I want to be sure of getting this right. You knew about the murder early in the morning. But you did not—could not—get in touch with your ex-wife."

"Yes."

"Then Mike Rodney and Officer Koenig came to see you at lunchtime that day. They said that they had spoken to your ex-wife, Kristen Duffy, when they questioned everyone at Island Contracting, and she said she had spent the night before with you at your apartment. And you confirmed that."

"Yes, exactly." He stood up. "Is that all?"

Josie and Sam exchanged looks. "Yes," she said sadly. "That's all. Thanks."

She and Sam left the restaurant, his arm around her shoulder, and tears spilling from her eyes. "What do we do now?" she asked, when they were alone together in his car.

"We'd better go to the police."

"I thought . . . I thought maybe we could . . . should talk to Kristen."

"Josie, she—"

"Sam, I know what you're going to say. But she lost her son already . . . and that broke her heart . . . and she may even still be in love with David . . . and . . ."

"None of that matters, Josie. Living through tragedy doesn't excuse murder. Nothing," he added grimly, "excuses murder."

They got back in his car, but Sam didn't turn the key in the ignition and they sat quietly on the street, listening to happy sounds pour from the restaurant's open windows.

"They were the logical suspects," Sam muttered, "but why are you so sure it was Kristen and not David who murdered Amy—just because she seemed to be the one that hadn't gotten over their son's death?"

"No. I think David is more unhappy and angry than he's ever admitted to me. Something Al said made me realize that," she added. "But David has been acting strangely throughout this thing. He asked me out not because he wanted to date me, but because he wanted to know if I suspected Kristen. He's been worried about her all along."

After a moment's silence, she continued. "What interested me the most is that Kristen never, ever, suspected David. And he knew that."

"So you're saying . . ."

"That I knew it was Kristen because David immediately verified her alibi. They both had reason to hate Amy Llewellyn. When she was murdered, David knew that if Kristen didn't suspect him of the deed—was so sure that he had followed his normal pattern of living and was home in bed between eleven and six A.M.—then she was the murderer. If she had suspected him, she would never have used him as an alibi." Josie wiped a tear from her eye. "He was never trying to protect himself. He was just playing the hand to the end. He couldn't save his son, so now he tried to save his ex-wife." She put her head in her hands.

"Are you all right?"

"I will be," she said, sitting up and pushing her hair from her face. "So what do we do now?"

"We go to the police station and tell them what we suspect. We can leave the arrest to them. Then we go back to my house and talk over our problems, straighten things out, and get back together. I love you, Josie. It's time we got on with our lives together."

THIRTY-THREE

"YOU KNOW WHAT I've always wondered?" Fern asked, dipping a piece of crab in garlic butter and popping it in her mouth. "This is absolutely wonderful," she added, chewing.

"Thanks. The recipe was given to me by two crazy, wonderful sisters—that I correspond with, I've never met them," Sam added as Josie gave him a curious look. "Our relationship has been purely platonic."

"What have you always wondered?" Josie asked, grinning at Sam. After a busy summer, dashing from one Elder Hostel program to another, Sam's mother was arriving on the island tonight to spend Labor Day weekend. She'd talk to her and find out just how platonic Sam's relations with these "two crazy, wonderful sisters" actually had been.

"What were doing you at the Van Emberghs' house so

early in the morning the day that Amy Llewellyn was killed?" Fern asked Sam.

"Waiting to see Josie. I knew she would be over early to get started on the new job. I'd even brought a bottle—"

"Of champagne!" Josie exclaimed.

"You found it? You never mentioned it to me?" Sam asked, surprised.

"That's because I didn't find a bottle of champagne. I found a broken champagne bottle. In fact, it confirmed my belief that the spot had been used as a hangout by some teenagers on the island—you know, for illicit drinking and stuff," she added, embarrassed now to admit that she'd also mistaken her son's good-luck totems for satanic-ritual paraphernalia.

"You thought teenagers were getting together there to drink vintage Taittinger's?" Sam sounded incredulous.

"Well . . . you know how little I know about liquor. . . . This is really good," she continued, trying to change the subject. "How many ingredients did you boil the crabs in?"

"Eight—and you steam them, you don't boil them."

"You two aren't going to break up again, are you?" Betty asked. "We were all beginning to enjoy the peace and quiet now that Josie is less . . . well, irritable."

Josie tossed a large scarlet crab at Betty, but she missed and it fell into the bay. "Well, prepare for me to become irritable, as you call it, again. Tyler is coming home tomorrow and Sam and I won't be spending as much time alone together."

"At least not for the two weeks until he leaves for school," Sam added.

"I'm glad I'm going on vacation," Betty said. "Say, don't forget to ask Tyler what that bet was—what he lost when he didn't manage to get back to camp undetected."

Josie and Sam exchanged amused looks. "We already know," she said. "He told Sam about it on the drive back to camp."

"Like mother, like son," was Sam's comment.

"The boy who ran away and returned undetected last year knows the combination to the lock on the room where the bakery deliveries are stored. Tyler's group found out. They were to be given the combination if Tyler succeeded."

"And if he didn't, they promised not to explain why the doughnuts were vanishing between the delivery on Friday afternoon and Saturday breakfast," Sam added. "Always thinking of his stomach—just like his mother."

"Oh, my goodness, I forgot to tell you guys," Josie cried. "Guess what arrived in the office this morning?"

"A contract for a great new job?" Betty suggested.

"A pile of money to be given to us all because we did such wonderful work on the heart house?" Al asked.

"Actually . . ." The real reason Josie had suggested this Friday-night party on the deck was to distribute the bonus that the Van Emberghs, fresh from their European tour, had actually increased because they were so thrilled with Island Contracting's work. And they had promised to hire the company next spring when they planned to remodel the pool house into an entertainment area with a guest apartment above. But Josie's news concerned neither of these momentous events. "Do you remember the note to me that Amy Llewellyn had in her pocket when she was found?"

"Oh yeah. Didn't it get put in someone's lunch or something for safekeeping?"

"In the sandwich bag that Mike Rodney carried his lunch in that day," Josie said. "Yes."

"And it was stored like that in the evidence locker at the station?" Sam asked.

"Not quite. It turns out that the evidence locker is more like a desk drawer and the coffee urn is kept on top of it."

"Don't tell me!" Fern began to giggle. "Someone spilled a cup of coffee into the drawer."

"Actually, someone knocked over the pot and soaked everything in the drawer. But when they were cleaning it out, they found the note. Mike dropped it off at the office today."

"What did it say?"

"It was the strangest thing. I couldn't read all of it—because of the coffee and some smears of grease. But it seemed to be an apology. Amy had told me that someone might be trying to kill me—but it was all a lie. No attempts had been made on her life. She was just protecting herself—hoping to gain some sympathy."

"From David, right?"

"How did you know?" Josie asked Al.

The tattoos moved as she shrugged. "Just a guess. The woman wasn't very good at cutting her losses and moving on. Always harping on and on about her past when I knew her. I figured she was still trying to get David interested in her—and drive Kristen nuts by doing things like looking a little like her boss. Who knows?"

"No one," Josie said a little sadly. "And I guess now no one will."

"I bought a cake from the bakery," Betty said to break the mood. "Anyone ready for it?"

"I am. I'll help you get it," Fern offered, hopping off the rail.

"And I want to check out the litter that was left here this morning. I'm thinking a little cat might be just the thing to keep my aunt company when I leave," Al said, following the other two women into the office.

"She's leaving?" Sam asked Josie.

"Hmm. She met this man somewhere and he works with a contractor in Florida someplace. . . . And you know Al."

"Yeah. I wonder when he'll mention that he's married," Sam said, looking into the crab pot. "There are nine crabs left—they'll be good cold tomorrow or would you like another right now?"

"You sure know the way to a redheaded carpenter's heart." Josie beamed as he put a huge one on the plate she held out.

"Now if I can just get a certain redheaded carpenter to have my name tattooed on her hip," he said quietly, leaning toward her. "Think. At least then you'd be even. One name on each side?"

Josie was turning as red as the crab.

"And then," Sam continued, "the next time you fall in love and refuse to go to bed with a man, you'll have two good reasons to turn him down."

"Well, when I asked at the tattoo parlor, they said it was very expensive and very painful to have tattoos removed. Of course if I'd realized that you had seen my hip the night you and Mike put me to bed, I wouldn't have bothered to check that out—or been forced to make such an awkward confession to you about that particular bit of my misspent youth," she added before taking a deep breath and plunging into commitment. "Besides, I was sort of hoping there wouldn't be a next time."

In affluent, suburban Hancock, Connecticut, murder has become an unexpected next-door neighbor to Susan Henshaw—mother, housewife, and amateur sleuth.

VALERIE WOLZIEN

THE SUSAN HENSHAW MYSTERIES

MURDER AT THE PTA LUNCHEON
THE FORTIETH BIRTHDAY BODY
WE WISH YOU A MERRY MURDER
AN OLD FAITHFUL MURDER
ALL HALLOWS' EVIL
A STAR-SPANGLED MURDER
A GOOD YEAR FOR A CORPSE
'TIS THE SEASON TO BE MURDERED
REMODELED TO DEATH
ELECTED FOR DEATH

THE SUSAN HENSHAW MYSTERIES BY VALERIE WOLZIEN

"Stylish, witty, wicked, and pleasing."
—*Tulsa World*

"Valerie Wolzien is a superlative crime writer."
—Mary Daheim